Jewe

Jewel of Xanadu

ROXANNE CARR

Black Lace novels are sexual fantasies.
In real life, make sure you practise safe sex.

First published in 1995 by
Black Lace
332 Ladbroke Grove
London
W10 5AH

Typeset by CentraCet Limited, Cambridge
Printed and bound by Mackays of Chatham

ISBN 0 352 33037 6

All characters in this publication are fictitious and any resemblance to real persons, living or dead, is purely coincidental.

Jewel of Xanadu

Chapter One

Cirina put the bucket of water on the sand by her feet and pressed her hands against the small of her aching back. Screwing up her eyes against the blinding desert sun, she wiped her forehead with the scarf she wore around her neck.

Looking back the way she had come from the water place, she looked towards the Takla Makan in the distance and sighed. How she longed to cross the desert and see what was on the other side! Since she was a very small child she had wondered what lay across the red-hued sands, listening wide-eyed to the tales of the travellers who used the caravanserai as a resting place en route from one exotic sounding place to another.

Picking the bucket up again, Cirina trudged back to the caravanserai. Whatever lay beyond the desert, surely there had to be more to life than this?

It wasn't fair! Whenever her aunt and cousin were busy entertaining the visitors she ended up doing their chores as well as her own. She couldn't understand why, if it pleased the deity for the women of the house to lie with the travellers, she too was not given that honour. It wasn't as if she was too young now, or too ugly – she had seen the looks some of the men gave her when they arrived at the caravanserai. But her uncle, Lengke, always hurried her away, keeping her out of sight until the place was quiet again.

'I promised my sister, your mother, Cirina, that I would guard and protect you,' Lengke always replied whenever she asked why she could not warm the travellers' beds.

Keta, her aunt, was scathing, constantly nagging at Lengke for, as she saw it, letting Cirina think she was better than the other women. Her pretty cousin, Bortai, often gave her a sly pinch, calling her 'Empress' when Lengke was out of earshot and giggling with her mother about things Cirina had never been given the chance to understand.

She was glad to reach the cool shade of the courtyard. Looking around her, she saw the place was deserted. Her uncle must have gone to round up the goats for the evening, for there was no sign of him. It was polite for the man of the house to make himself scarce after offering his women to his guests, so Cirina guessed he would be gone for some time.

The visitors' horses were tethered by the stable and Cirina went over to pet them. Both were fine animals. She knew that only high-ranking officers in the Emperor's army would be entrusted with such beasts. These were Tartars, by the look of their saddlery – there were many Tartars in the Khan's army.

Cirina glanced up to the unshuttered window as she heard Bortai's high-pitched giggle, followed by a very masculine moan. For some reason the sound made her skin prickle and Cirina moved away, feeling uncomfortable.

They confused her, these strange feelings she had experienced lately. The way the men looked at her, a curious, inner restlessness, the sounds of love-making in the upper rooms when the travellers came – all combined to make her stomach churn and the soft, secret folds of flesh between her thighs to swell and moisten.

Cirina thought she knew all about what went on between men and women. She had seen the animals at the caravanserai mating since she was very small, had even helped when the need arose. It had always seemed like a singularly unexciting process to her, certainly nothing from which she might need to be shielded.

But that didn't explain the breathless giggles, a small voice murmured in her mind as she began to mix flour and water to make the noodles for the evening's soup. Once they were simmering in the mixture of water and sheep's fat over the fire, Cirina began to feel restless again.

She was bored with her own company and the endless heat of the day. The scarf she wore around her neck was grimy with dust and sweat and she longed to exchange it for a fresh one. Surely they would be finished upstairs by now? If she crept up to the tiny room she shared with Bortai, no one would see her from the main sleeping area.

The stone steps were cool beneath her sandalled feet as Cirina ran quickly to the upper floor, untying her scarf as she went. Her steps faltered as she saw that the wooden door to the sleeping area was standing wide. There were two straw pallets inside. On one, Bortai was sitting astride one of the soldiers, her slender buttocks bouncing up and down on his hairy legs. Cirina's eyes widened as the man's rigid pole was revealed, sliding in and out of her cousin's body, shining with the juices seeping from her woman's place.

The man's large, hairy hands were fondling Bortai's pert little breasts, pinching them and making her squeal. From the tone of the cry, though, Cirina was sure that, curiously, it was not one of pain. An unfamiliar, shivery sensation trickled through her body as she watched Bortai ride the man as if he was a horse. Her long black hair hung down her narrow brown back, the silvery coins she used to weight her plaits tinkling almost merrily as she moved her head from side to side. Cirina was transfixed by the sight of the man's cock as it worked its way in and out of the young girl's body.

She was distracted by a low moan from the other pallet where her aunt was crouched on all fours, like an animal. Cirina gasped in shocked fascination as she realised that the soldier servicing Keta was not using her woman's place at all, but was actually thrusting between her buttocks.

Her aunt's head was held to one side, and Cirina could see her face was screwed up with pain. And yet she was smiling, her mouth stretched wide across her yellowing teeth as the man pumped in and out of her sensitive back passage.

Cirina felt the sweat break out across her back and chest and run between her breasts in tiny rivulets. Her breath fluttered like a captured bird in her chest as she watched, wide-eyed, while Keta writhed and panted under the grunting soldier.

Her eyes slid to the man's body, naked from the waist down. His buttocks were flabby, the skin pitted and hairy. But his thighs, supporting his weight as he mated with Keta, were strong and pleasantly shaped, the hair covering them coarse and plentiful.

Suddenly, as Cirina watched, the soldier withdrew from Keta's body and, with a strangled cry, he shot his seed across her aunt's back. Fascinated, Cirina saw the thick, white fluid spurt from the bulbous tip of his cock to land on Keta's fleshy back and she felt her own woman-flesh pulse and grow warm.

At that moment, Bortai's soldier too reached his crisis and Bortai pulled away from him hastily so that his seed shot up in an arc, spattering the girl's chest and hair. To Cirina's surprise, her vain, fastidious cousin merely laughed, darting out her tongue to dab at the man's rapidly deflating cock.

Surely it could not be right to taste the fluid from his body? Cirina was shocked, and yet her body reacted to the sight of her cousin licking the man's cock with a fresh rush of moisture which made the insides of her thighs feel sticky.

Looking back at her aunt, she saw that the woman had turned over. The soldier was suckling her sagging breasts like a babe while his hands worked between the swollen folds of Keta's sex. Suddenly, before Cirina's eyes, something seemed to happen to her aunt.

Her head lolled back on her shoulders and her mouth spread wide. Lifting her hips off the pallet, she seemed to grind herself against the soldier's burrowing fingers, making him let go of her nipple, which shone wetly with his saliva.

'Ai, that's it,' he said, laughing as Keta cried out, a long, high-pitched wail which echoed in Cirina's head as she watched, half appalled, half excited.

Could it be that women climbed the peak of sexual pleasure as did men? Cirina could barely believe it, yet her discovery left her feeling hot and restless.

'Why, cousin – are you coming to join us?'

She jumped as Bortai's sly voice reached her and she realised that the other couple were watching her watching Keta.

'Oh! I . . . I –'

'Come on, cousin – come and see how a real man feels!'

Before she could run, Bortai had leapt forward and grabbed her by the wrist. As she was pulled inside, Cirina lost her balance and fell heavily across the outstretched legs of the soldier lying with Bortai. She could feel his man-flesh, hard again already, pressing into her back. The room smelled of drink and sex, a heady combination which made her dizzy. The man made a grab for her breasts with his hard hands.

'Ahh!' She cried out as he mauled her roughly and he laughed, bringing his thick, wet lips down on hers. She could taste kumiss and vodka on his tongue, feel his hot breath scorch her skin.

Cirina thrashed around wildly, beating her fists against the man's shoulders. She might as well have been caressing him, for all the notice he took of her blows. They bounced off his heavily muscled shoulders ineffectually and she heard the other soldier laugh before he captured her flailing hands.

At last the man stopped kissing her and Cirina gasped for air, catching sight of her cousin's grinning face over the second soldier's shoulder. Did she really hate her so much, that she could let these men paw her so roughly?

Glancing across to the other pallet, Cirina saw her aunt laughing and knew, with a sinking heart, that she could expect no help from that quarter. She yelped as rough fingers began to tear at the fastenings to her shift, exposing her full, naked breasts.

'My, Cirina, how you've grown!' Bortai mocked, reaching to stroke the soft, honey-coloured flesh of Cirina's breast.

As if in unspoken agreement, the two men sat back to allow Bortai between them, though they held Cirina firmly when she would have pulled away. She watched, horrified, as her cousin ran the tip of her fingernail over her skin, scratching gently, closer and closer to the tip.

To Cirina's shame, the soft, rose-brown crest puckered in response to Bortai's mocking touch and the other girl laughed delightedly. Dipping her head, she took the treacherous nub of flesh into her mouth, making Cirina gasp in shock. What was Bortai doing, circling her hot, wet tongue around her nipple like this? She teased it with the very tip of her tongue, flicking it back and forth until Cirina gasped again, fighting the response Bortai had drawn from her outraged body.

Raising her head, Bortai laughed.

'You were right, mother; she is ripe for love.'

'Ripe for the plucking, and no mistake!' One of the soldiers laughed.

Before Cirina realised what they were going to do, each man took one quivering breast into his mouth and she felt herself stretched between them. This was quite different to Bortai's soft caress; the soldiers were rough and careless, their teeth abrading her tender flesh and grazing her nipples. Cirina cried out and began to struggle in earnest, panicking as rough fingers began to fumble beneath her skirts.

Suddenly, the men were pulled away from her and Cirina was left, sprawled across the stinking straw, her breasts exposed and her skirts awry.

'Cover yourself!' her uncle commanded, his voice shaking with fury. Turning his back on Cirina he addressed the others. 'What is the meaning of this?'

Keta's eyes slid away from his and Bortai shrugged her shoulders.

'We were just having a little fun, father,' she replied sullenly.

Lengke looked as if he might explode with rage, his colour was so high, his eyes bulging in their sockets. He eyed the two soldiers swaying drunkenly in the middle of the room, a look of bemusement on their faces, and he swore violently.

'You have had the hospitality of my house. You will leave at first light. Keta, you and Bortai bring fresh straw for our guests. Cirina,' his voice softened slightly as he turned to her, 'tend the supper.'

He helped her to her feet and, with one last frightened look around the room, Cirina bolted for the door.

Once downstairs in the safety of the cooking place, she found that she was trembling. Had she invited such ill-use by watching at the door? After all, she had been excited by what she had seen. And yet she knew, deep down, that it was Bortai who was to blame for the savagery with which she was treated. The soldiers had not hurt her, not really, but they had clearly thought she was theirs for the taking, thanks to her cousin.

As she stirred the greasy soup, Cirina thought how, despite her fear and disgust, her body had responded several times to what was being done to her. The practised touch of Bortai's fingers, the softness of her lips and tongue . . . the urgent thrust of the soldier's man-flesh pressing into her back and the feel of his hard, virile body against hers. By the deity, what was wrong with her?

She glanced up fearfully as her aunt and uncle came into the room. Keta looked sour, her small, black eyes flashing their dislike at Cirina. Lengke was clearly still angry, but Cirina sensed that his fury was not directed towards her and she relaxed a little.

'Why did you go upstairs, Cirina? You know it is forbidden when the travellers come.'

'I am sorry, my uncle,' she whispered, her eyes down-cast, 'I wanted something from my room.'

'For pity's sake, Lengke – she is no longer a child!' Keta burst out irritably. 'You tempt the wrath of the deity by trying to keep her so!'

'Quiet, woman!'

'No, husband, I must speak. Why do you think trade has not been good this past year or more? The deity is displeased because you do not offer the full hospitality of your house to the travellers.'

'Quiet!' Lengke raised his hand as if to strike Keta and she took a step back, clamping her lips together with an effort.

Cirina felt afraid. She had never seen her uncle so angry with his wife that he looked set to beat her in front of others. Though she had no love for her aunt, she regretted that she was the cause of the other woman's humiliation.

'It is I who should be punished, uncle,' she said, her voice horribly small.

'Perhaps,' Lengke replied, without conviction, 'but I will not have any more talk about Cirina joining you and Bortai in your duties, Keta – do you understand me?'

Keta nodded, keeping her gaze downcast and Bortai, who had appeared in time to hear her father's words, bowed her head. Glancing at each of his womenfolk in turn, Lengke swore under his breath and strode from the room, as if he had had enough of them all.

As soon as he had gone, the atmosphere in the room altered subtly and Cirina felt apprehensive again. Glancing nervously at her aunt and cousin, she saw the look that passed between them and shivered in spite of the heat.

'Take care the soup does not burn, girl,' Keta snapped before gathering what was left of her dignity about her and bustling out of the room.

Cirina turned her attention to the pot and stirred the thick mixture diligently, all the while conscious of Bortai watching her from across the room.

'Well, little cousin,' she said after a few strained moments, 'there is heat between those tightly closed legs, is there not?'

She laughed at Cirina's shocked expression and danced forward to brush her fingertips over the younger girl's breasts. Immediately, the nipples hardened beneath the thin fabric of her shift and Cirina felt the heat seep into her cheeks.

'You see? Admit it, Cirina – you *liked* what happened upstairs, didn't you? You enjoyed watching mother and I. Wouldn't you like a man of your own next time? I won't always be willing to share mine, you know!'

Cirina did not reply, keeping her eyes fixed firmly on the soup she was stirring. After a few minutes, Bortai laughed maliciously and left Cirina alone in the kitchen. She let out her breath on a sigh, only just realising that she had been holding it.

Tears pricked her eyelids as she thought about what Bortai had said. She hadn't liked what they had done to her, she hadn't! But it was true – she *did* want a man of her own. Until now she hadn't realised it was that need which was causing the restlessness inside her.

Without realising what she was doing, Cirina pressed the heel of her hand against the join of her legs, inadvertently stimulating the feminine core of her body. Little waves of pleasurable heat rippled through her, unrecognised, unexplored and she closed her eyes for a moment until they subsided before dragging her attention reluctantly back to her chores.

Outside, Lengke was working up a sweat in the stables. He had been so angry when he had found his niece with his wife and daughter and the soldiers that, for a moment, he had thought he would lose all reason. He was lucky the soldiers had been drunk, or one of them might have drawn his sword. Hopefully, when they woke in the morning they would remember only the satisfaction the other women had given them, not the insult perpetrated by their host when he had removed Cirina.

As he worked he mulled over Keta's words. It was true, trade had not been good these past few months. By rights, Cirina should have taken her place alongside Keta and Bortai long before now.

But Cirina was not like his wife and daughter. They were both good women, happy to offer hospitality, but they were coarse and simple. There was something different about Cirina, with her light skin, the colour of honey-mead, and her unusually pale eyes, like the summer sky. Something . . . *refined*, yes, that was the word. He rolled it around on his tongue as if it did not quite fit his mouth. Refined. It was not a word that was normally part of his vocabulary.

Cirina was like her mother, to be sure, but Anya had always been happy to offer hospitality. Even to the travelling monk who had fathered Cirina.

Lengke shook his head to rid himself of the sadness he always felt when he thought of his sister. Blood of his blood, his beautiful Anya.

'Send me a sign, Anya,' he whispered into the hot, still air, 'tell me what to do about Cirina.'

He waited for a moment before shrugging irritably and turning back to his work. What did he think he was doing, asking the dead for advice?

Cirina had changed lately, developed, he supposed. She was ready for a man. As her uncle he should, he knew, break her in himself, but something always made him hold back. It was almost as if, he mused, pausing in his work again, he was afraid that if he lay with Cirina, he would want to do so again and again, that she would get under his skin. The way her mother, Anya, had.

Cursing, Lengke went back to work, pushing the problem of his niece to the back of his mind to ferment for a while longer.

The guard at the head of the caravan called a halt as they approached Kashgar. Here they would be able to exchange their exhausted yaks and pack horses for the hardy Bactrian camels needed to carry them across the desert. As everyone took the opportunity to dismount, or to make for the traders waiting hopefully by the city walls for their custom, Antonio Ballerei took the opportunity to bring his horses alongside Marco Polo's.

'How much further, my friend?' he asked.

Marco turned and grinned at him. 'You are suffering with the heat and the sun, Antonio? Are you not glad to thaw out after our journey through the mountains?'

'Indeed I am!' Antonio agreed, the pain of the bitter

cold still fresh in his memory. 'But this sun is too strong to be a welcome fellow traveller.'

Marco laughed. 'God's teeth, you'd think you'd have grown used to it by now!'

Antonio grimaced, not at all offended by the other man's gentle mockery. In truth, after three years following his kinsman around this Godforsaken territory as official artist for the Venetian Government without getting anywhere near to the legendary Xanadu, he was beginning to yearn for the comforts of his homeland. If he had not been charged with a task so secret that even Marco was unaware of it, he would have completed his drawings and returned to Venice months before.

Maffeo and Niccolo, Marco's uncle and father, drew level and joined in the affectionate banter.

'Antonio, you have the delicate skin of a woman,' Maffeo laughed, watching as Antonio adjusted his head dress. 'What would your father say if he could see you in such garb?'

Antonio laughed good-naturedly. 'He would turn in his grave, Maffeo, as well you know. Enough of this jesting – we need to trade these damned animals for camels and rest ourselves before we start out across the desert.'

Marco nodded. 'Antonio is right. We'll spend the night in the city and leave the caravan in the morning. We'll get food and drink here in Kashgar, and maybe a comely woman or two, eh, Antonio?'

Antonio shook his head in mock sorrow.

'If the great Khan knew the Governor of Langchow to be such a reprobate, I dare not think of the consequences!' he said.

Marco snorted loudly. 'Kublai Khan would recognise a kindred spirit, my friend, as well you know! And besides; I am no longer the Governor. Why else would I have been recalled to Beijing after our trip to Samarkand by our Mongol friend?'

'Why indeed?' Antonio muttered under his breath as the Europeans urged their mounts into the City.

Their departure from the caravan seemed to have gone unnoticed and Antonio wondered once again at the inscrutable nature of the natives. Marco was well known, having the favour of the Khan, and they had encountered few problems on their travels. Yet Antonio always had the feeling that their movements were monitored and that reports were sent back to Beijing. How else would Kublai Khan ensure their loyalty?

The following morning they met up with their fresh camels and supplies and left the city.

'You know the route southeast, Niccolo?' Marco asked his father.

'Of course. It will take us several weeks to reach Khotan, God willing.'

'Hmm. There is a caravanserai no more than fifteen *li* past Khotan as I recall,' Marco remarked thoughtfully. 'It would be a good place to stop and rest before tackling the Takla Makan.'

'Rest, Marco?' Antonio said ironically, noting his friend's drawn face. 'I fancy you had little time for rest last night, my friend.'

Marco laughed.

'You know me too well, Antonio. Ah, but she was a comely maid,' he remarked dreamily.

As they rode out of Khotan several weeks later, Antonio recalled that conversation. He smiled as he thought of Marco's lusty appetites. Even now the lure of the caravanserai and the curious local custom of 'hospitality' was making him spur on the Bactrian, the long legs of the camel covering the *li* with ease.

Personally, he was tired of the native women, though they were comely enough with their pronounced, pink-tinged cheekbones and long black hair. He liked the way they weighted their plaits with coins so that they tinkled with every toss of the head, and the easy, sensual way they accepted him into their beds. But he had to admit, he yearned for the sight of a fair-skinned European woman, less obvious with her charms, yet all the more intriguing for the challenge she would present.

Though he would sport with the others, if there were women enough to go round, his heart would not really be in it. He'd leave the serious whoring to Marco. For himself, he was looking forward to food and a good sleep, with a roof over his head for a change, and maybe some soft, fresh straw on which to lie.

Keta was the first to spot the clouds of dust on the horizon which signalled the arrival of travellers. Her heart quickened in her breast as she counted not one, but four mounted camels, with four more being led with provisions. It had been two weeks since Lengke had sent the Tartars on their way and she was ready for a new diversion.

Since that disgraceful episode with Cirina, Keta had avoided the girl as much as possible, aside from giving her orders. Lengke thought she did not realise that he was saving the girl for himself. Her eyes narrowed as she thought of her husband. Lengke was a fool if he thought she would stand for it! Cirina would bring down blessings on the house, the same as Bortai. She, Keta, would see to that.

As the travellers grew nearer, Lengke joined her in the courtyard.

'Four of them? Can you manage?' he asked her.

Keta glanced at him slyly.

'Have you not noticed something about these travellers, husband?' she asked silkily.

Lengke frowned at her, distrust in his eyes.

'What is in your mind, woman?'

Keta smiled and turned towards the men now entering the courtyard.

'See?' she said triumphantly, 'they are light skinned, like Cirina. It is a sign – the deity wants Cirina to offer her hospitality to these travellers.'

Before Lengke could respond, Keta walked forward to where the men were dismounting, leaving him to absorb her words.

Lengke watched her with a heavy heart. She might be a spiteful woman, but she was wise when it came to the spiritual side of life. After all, had he not asked Anya for a sign, only two weeks before? How foolish he had been to expect an immediate response! Seeing the Europeans walk towards him, he knew there could not be a clearer sign than this.

After he had seen to the travellers' needs and offered them the hospitality of the house, he went in search of Cirina. He found her feeding the chickens, humming under her breath and he stood watching her for a few minutes while she was unaware of his presence.

It pained him to know that now he would never possess her. He should have taken her while he had the chance. As her uncle it was his right to be the first to break her. Now it had been decreed that she should go to a stranger, and his right to her would then be gone.

'Cirina?'

She turned and smiled uncertainly at him and Lengke forced himself to harden his heart against her.

'Cirina, I have received a sign. We have fresh travellers at the caravanserai – Europeans. Tonight you will offer them your hospitality.'

Cirina's thoughts immediately flew to the coarse soldiers who had handled her so roughly and her face registered her dismay.

'But uncle – '

'Silence!' Lengke held up his hand and Cirina bit her lower lip. 'It has been decided. You may use the small room if you prefer. Make yourself ready.'

Cirina bowed her head.

'Yes, uncle,' she whispered dutifully.

Antonio sprawled on his cushion and stretched luxuriously. His belly was full, he was clean after a sluicing with icy water in the yard and there was the prospect of a fresh straw pallet for the night ahead. He could not have been more content. Maffeo and Niccolo were playing with dice and Marco was eagerly awaiting the part of the evening when the women would appear to show them upstairs.

Marco clearly had his eye on the slender little imp who had served their supper, and Antonio could not blame him. He had already declined his friend's kind offer to share her, deciding that, this time, he really would take advantage of the chance to sleep.

The older woman, the mother, had tried to catch his eye, but he was determined that she should be satisfied with the older Polo brothers. He had no desire for her whatsoever.

Picking up his charcoal, he drew Bortai smiling coyly at Marco before she led him out of the room by the hand, and he made a few quick sketches to add to his portfolio of Keta disappearing with Niccolo and Maffeo on either side.

Knowing that it was the custom for the man of the house to stay well away while his womenfolk offered hospitality, Antonio made the most of the rare prospect of solitude, stretching out in front of the fire and helping himself to another cup of goat's milk.

He looked up in surprise as the door opened suddenly and a young girl slipped through.

'Hello,' he said when she lingered in the shadows, 'who are you?'

He heard her clear her throat nervously before she replied in a voice so soft he had to strain his ears to catch her words.

'I am Cirina, Master. I . . . I have come to offer you . . . to offer you my hospitality.'

The last came out in such a rush that the words tumbled over themselves and Antonio smiled.

'That's very good of you . . . Cirina,' he said kindly, 'but there's really no need.'

'Oh! But you must! I mean . . . *I* must! It has been decided!'

'Oh it has, has it?' Antonio said, amused.

Sitting up, he peered into the shadows.

'Well, hadn't you better come closer, let me have a proper look at you? If you're offering me your hospitality, I'd better take a look at what's offered, hadn't I?' he said teasingly.

The girl seemed to hesitate, then slowly she moved into the light cast by the dying embers of the fire. As he got a proper look at her, Antonio sucked in his breath, his desire for rest and solitude forgotten.

'By all that's holy . . . where did you come from?'

She was exquisite. Her long black hair was parted in the middle, falling in a single, thick braid over one shoulder to her waist. Her skin was the colour of the local honey-mead and her eyes, almond shaped, halfway between Asian and European, were a clear, startling blue. As she came closer, Antonio saw that they were fringed with thick, black lashes which cast gentle shadows on her cheeks as she kept her gaze downcast.

The artist in him longed to paint her, the man to reach out and touch her, to see if her skin really felt as silky as it looked. The man won over the artist. Slowly, afraid of startling her, Antonio reached out a hand and stroked his forefinger across the back of her hand as she stood meekly before him.

Her skin was softer than silk and he saw that his touch had caused goosebumps to rise on her flesh. She was so unlike the other women, so . . . innocent, for a moment he felt awed by her.

'Will you sit down and drink some kumiss with me?' he asked her when he had recovered his wits.

She folded her legs under her gracefully and took the cup he offered her. He watched her, entranced as she took a sip of the fermented mare's milk. How could he take advantage of such a creature? The insistent hardness at his groin told him how and he reached forward to take the cup from her. She trembled slightly, keeping her gaze downcast and he placed his forefinger under her chin so that he could tilt her head up, encouraging her to meet his eye.

Her eyes flickered as she was compelled to look at him and he scanned the expression in their clear blue depths. He saw fear in there, and uncertainty. But there was something else, something that made his heart race and his manhood leap in his breeches. Desire; untutored, raw, powerfully arousing.

'I accept your hospitality, Cirina,' he whispered, his lips inches away from hers.

He saw the relief, quickly followed by the leap of anticipation in her eyes and he offered her his hand. Hers felt fragile in his as she placed it in his palm and he felt himself tremble as he hadn't trembled since he was a callow youth.

'This way,' she said quietly, and, rising with her, Antonio allowed her to lead him out of the room.

Chapter Two

Cirina was aware of a feeling of anticipation tinged with terror as she led the European up the winding stone stairs to the tiny room at the top of the caravan-serai. Normally she shared the room with Bortai, but with her cousin occupied by the man they called Marco Polo in the main sleeping chamber on the first floor, she knew that they would have the small room all to themselves.

She was very glad of the privacy. It wasn't every day that a girl took a man to her bed for the first time and the significance of the event was not lost on Cirina.

Glancing over her shoulder she saw that the man picked out for her was watching her closely as she ascended the stairs ahead of him. He smiled at her as he caught her eye and she felt her spirits lift a little. He was a kind man, she was sure, not the type who would be unmindful of her comfort. He would not take her roughly or carelessly, that much she knew by instinct.

He was certainly handsome enough. His long hair was curly and black, reaching past his shoulders. Despite his colouring, his skin was very pale, as if it had never been touched by the fierce sun, and his eyes were the palest blue that Cirina had ever seen. She had noticed that he carried the tools of the artist's trade with him and she was slightly in awe of his profession. As indeed she was in awe of the man himself.

They reached the small, square room that Cirina called her own, and inside it the man seemed to take up all the space, not physically, just by his presence. He was all around her; his scent, his masculinity, as if he had stamped his mark on every inch of space.

'I am Antonio Ballerei,' he announced, bowing slightly in an incongruously chivalrous gesture which made Cirina's heart beat faster in her chest.

Unsure how she should respond, Cirina stood quite still in the middle of the room in the hope that the traveller would sense her inexperience and so seek to guide her.

Antonio gazed at her as she stood by chance in the centre of the shaft of light falling through the single, meagre window. Her hair, black as a raven's wing, shone like a bolt of the finest silk, the single plait she wore lying over one shoulder, reaching to her waist.

Her skin, lent a golden lustre by the dying rays of dusty sunlight, was flawless, and its perfection fascinated him, making him long to touch and taste it. He ran the tip of his tongue over his lips in anticipation. The prospect of the long, hot night ahead was becoming more appealing with every passing second.

Yet something held him back. Recognising the uncertainty reflected in her clear blue eyes, Antonio felt an unfamiliar emotion kick into his chest. A kind of protectiveness which he could not remember feeling ever before. There was something acquiescent. A quiet dignity which stirred him, making him hesitate before approaching her.

'Have you lived here at the caravanserai all your life?' he asked, knowing as he did so that it was probably the most foolish of questions. Where else would she have spent her time?

'Yes, Master,' she confirmed, dropping her eyes to avoid the scrutiny of his. 'All my life.'

'And yet you have not participated in the ancient custom of hospitality before now?'

'No, Master.'

'Do you know why, Cirina?' Being familiar, as he was, with the customs of these people, it seemed odd to him that such a beautiful girl had been kept apart for so long.

'No, sir,' Cirina whispered, aware of a shiver of delight at hearing her name on his tongue. No one had ever pronounced her name quite like that before, emphasising the second vowel so that her name was longer, more voluptuous than it was when spoken on her own tongue.

Antonio moved towards her then, putting out his hand to run the backs of his fingers across the downy, soft skin of her cheek.

'I am most honoured to be the first,' he said solemnly, his voice low and sincere.

Cirina glanced up at him then, as if to reassure herself that he was genuine. His calm, pale blue eyes bore into hers and she felt her heart flutter in her chest as her mouth and throat grew dry.

'I . . . I am glad also,' she said shyly, dropping her eyes away from his so that he could not see her confusion.

For she *was* glad. There was something about this pale-skinned foreigner which attracted her, made her eager to lie with him and find out at last how it really felt to welcome a man into her virgin body.

Antonio looked at her and wondered why she was different from the other native girls who had warmed his bed during his years abroad. Never before had he felt the desire to talk, to find out more about the girl offered to him. This Cirina intrigued him, not least because he could see the excitement behind the apprehension in her clear blue eyes as she gazed at him, and he felt his manhood stir at his groin in response.

'You have the most unusual eyes,' he told her, tracing their outline lightly with his finger.

'My . . . my father was a Nestorian monk, I believe, on his way to the holy city.'

That explained her colouring. Could it be some native superstition that had kept her pure for so long? For Antonio had no doubt that she *was* pure – that guileless, trusting expression could not possibly be faked. She reminded him of a cornered deer, trembling slightly, yet facing the inevitable with a quiet courage which earned the hunter's respect.

He felt a shiver of delicious anticipation as he considered the prospect of deflowering her.

Slowly, so as not to startle her, he trailed his forefinger across her forehead and down her nose, circling her chin and stroking softly across her full, red lips. To his delight, they parted slightly and he rubbed gently at the soft, moist skin just inside her lower lip.

She was a responsive little thing, her eyes half closing, her breath caressing his fingertips as she sighed. Antonio saw that her whole body trembled and he felt an answering tremor run through his own limbs in response. It was going to be an interesting evening.

Cirina was finding it hard to breathe; the touch of the man's fingers on the sensitive skin of her lips made her feel warm all over. She was overcome by the inexplicable, shocking desire to draw the tip of his finger into her mouth and suck on it . . . the image of Bortai, as she had seen her, licking and kissing the soldier's man-flesh, sprang into her mind and at once Cirina understood. A rush of colour surged beneath her skin and she dropped her eyes again, ashamed, yet excited by the strength of her desire. Would this man let her do such things to his body?

She shivered as his fingertips swept across the tender dip of her collarbone and brushed the tips of her breasts. Hidden beneath the shapeless shift, her nipples responded instantly, swelling and hardening to two little peaks of wantonness. Shafts of sensation radiated out from her belly, making her impatient for the feel of his hands on the rest of her body.

'Should . . . should I undress, Master?' she asked, shocked by her own boldness.

Antonio raised his eyebrows. 'That would be most . . . entertaining,' he murmured, moving over to the straw pallet and settling himself comfortably upon it.

She had made the suggestion without thinking, it seemed such a natural thing to do. But now that Antonio was watching and waiting, Cirina felt her nerve waver. What if he found her body displeasing, or her inexperience off-putting?

Then she saw the expectant light in his eyes and a spark of mischief gave her courage. It would be like unwrapping a gift – she would build the anticipation so that by the time the wrapper came off, the contents were sure to delight him!

Holding his eye, she raised her arms and reached round to untie the thong which fastened her hair loosely at the back of her neck. She unplaited the braid and allowed her hair to slip silkily through her fingers, falling forward to brush her cheeks in a soft caress. Encouraged by the way Antonio's eyes darkened, she bit on her lower lip to redden it and lowered her eyelashes the way she had seen Bortai lower hers when she looked at a man she liked.

Running her hands slowly down her sides, Cirina's fingers encountered the hem of her shift and curled around it. She drew it slowly upward, and pulled it over her head, hearing the sharp intake of Antonio's breath as he saw that she was naked beneath it.

'Sweet Jesus,' he murmured, half under his breath, 'by all that's holy – you are beautiful, Cirina.'

Cirina looked down at her small, berry-brown crested breasts and the neat indentation of her waist. She had taken care to groom her pubis with perfumed oil and she could see his eyes were drawn to the neat little triangle of fragrant hair on her mons. She was proud of her body, knew without conceit that she had a pleasing shape, yet she was not sure what to do next.

'Turn around – slowly,' Antonio instructed, coming to her rescue.

His voice was low and compelling and Cirina shivered slightly as she did as he asked, trying to picture what he could see. Her shoulders were narrow, but lightly muscled from lifting and carrying. She knew her waist dipped in sharply before flaring out across her slim hips and down to her legs. Due to her parentage, she was taller than her aunt and cousin by several inches, taller even than Lengke who was short and stocky and strong like most of her people. Thus her legs were long and slender, her feet delicately arched.

Her firm, soft-skinned buttocks clenched involuntarily as she felt his eyes on them and she heard Antonio chuckle softly. Suddenly he was behind her, his hands coming round her waist and moving up to cup her breasts while his mouth swooped on the tender arc of her neck, nipping her skin lightly with his straight white teeth.

Cirina felt a strange, melting sensation at the apex of her thighs and she unconsciously pressed back against him, her own hands coming up to cover his, holding them against the gentle underswell of her breasts where they rested.

This close, she could smell the light, musky fragrance of his skin, could feel the potent swell of masculine arousal pressing into the soft flesh of her buttocks. There was something about being this close to him that was doing strange things to her senses. She was dizzy, as if she had drunk too much kumiss earlier, not just a sip. Her limbs felt heavy and uncoordinated, her stomach churned and her woman-flesh grew heavy. A dull pulse beat within the secret folds of her sex and she felt those tender inner lips swell and become moist in response to his nearness.

Cirina turned willingly in his arms, lifting her face up eagerly for his kiss. His lips were firm on hers, an intriguing contrast to her own soft lips. Welcoming his hard, questing tongue into her mouth, Cirina parried with it, drawing on its sweetness and imagining how it would feel to caress the burgeoning manhood he was keeping hidden from her.

Pressed against his fully clothed body, Cirina felt vulnerable in a way she had never felt before. Far from spoiling her pleasure, though, this unfamiliar sensation served only to increase her arousal, making her mewl with need as Antonio kissed her harder still, running his hands lightly across her back.

As if sensing her need, his touch became more sure, more demanding and Cirina responded to it by pressing herself closer to his hard, male body.

With a muttered oath, Antonio pulled away from her and began to unfasten his shirt. Cirina watched avidly as he divested himself of his clothes, fascinated to see that the skin on the rest of his body was as pale as that on his face. Fine black hairs grew in pleasingly defined patterns all over his chest and on his forearms. Around his navel it grew in whorls which arrowed downward enticingly.

Cirina held her breath as he removed his breeches and his rigid man-flesh sprang into view. By the deity but it was big! How could such a thing enter the secret entrance to her body without damaging her?

Antonio must have heard the gasp she tried to smother, for he glanced quizzically at her before moving towards her again. Cirina would have liked more time to examine that curious part of his anatomy, but she had to content herself with feeling it imprint its shape on the soft flesh of her belly. It felt warm and alive and she longed to hold it in her hand, but she did not dare initiate such a caress.

Antonio was kissing her again now, nibbling gently at her earlobe, his sweet, warm breath fanning her cheek. Cirina closed her eyes and clung to him, glad of his strength as her legs seemed to weaken and give way. He caught her, supporting her body at the shoulders and behind the knees as he swept her up into his arms and strode over to the sleeping pallet with her.

He lay her down gently, towering over her as she gazed up at him wonderingly. So many thoughts and feelings were rioting through her, many conflicting, all new and confusing. As if divining her thoughts, Antonio lay himself down on the straw alongside her, speaking softly.

'Trust me – do not be afraid, *cara mia*,' he said, stroking her hair away from her face and gazing into her eyes with such tenderness that Cirina felt many of her fears melt away.

Scanning her eyes, he saw this and, smiling, he brought his lips down onto hers. There was a new urgency in his kisses now, a driving force which transmitted itself to Cirina, stoking her desire to match his. Her skin became slick with perspiration as Antonio stroked and smoothed it, seeking out each sensitive area, every tender place.

Cirina moaned and brought her arms up around his neck as he worked around her waist in a feather-light caress, making the fine, downy hairs in the small of her back rise up. Her breasts yearned for the touch of his lips and she arched her back in an unspoken plea which Antonio was swift to heed.

'Oh!' she could not contain her cry of surprised

pleasure as Antonio's lips closed over the taut, shiny nub of her nipple. As he sucked and nibbled she felt the sharp flare of desire deep in her belly and her thighs fell softly apart as her woman's place began to throb and weep with pleasure.

Antonio's fingers described small, concentric circles on the sensitive, super-fine skin of her inner thigh as he edged gradually closer to the soft fruit of her sex. As he reached it, Cirina's fingers dug hard into the smooth skin of his shoulders and she let out a long, shuddering sigh.

No one had ever touched her there before and she was overwhelmed by how good it felt. Her labia opened and closed around his fingers, drawing them closer to the hot well of arousal which seeped fresh moisture every time her womb contracted with delight.

Was this why Bortai and Keta enjoyed lying with the travellers so much? Cirina understood now why it was so addictive. Yet she could not imagine the rough Tartar soldiers who had pawed at her possessing such finesse, such exquisite sensitivity as the pale-skinned foreigner who was now watching her face, enjoying her reaction to his love-making.

He teased and coaxed her slippery flesh, running his fingertips between the petal-soft folds of skin before circling the hard, pulsing bead of flesh at the apex of her labia. Cirina had never dreamed that such a tiny jewel was hidden between her thighs, had never imagined that a man's touch could bring her such heady pleasure. She tensed slightly as he explored further, slipping inside her body and encountering the barrier of her maidenhead. She sensed his excitement as he confirmed its presence and realised at once that he considered it a rare delight to be the first.

Smiling a little at this curious trait well known in Europeans, Cirina forced herself to relax her untried muscles, battling against her instinctive desire to close herself to him. Would it hurt when he breached the barrier of her girlhood? Cirina feared that it could not be otherwise and she promised herself that she would be brave.

To her surprise, Antonio did not attempt to widen her passageway with his fingers, rather he brought them back up to that newly discovered pleasure-place. As he rubbed them rhythmically back and forth over the sensitive pad of flesh, Cirina realised that she grew more moist, the juices seeping out of her and running along her bottom cleft. Surely this lubrication from her own body would make his passage easier?

'That's it, *cara,*' he was murmuring in her ear, 'open wider . . . do not be afraid.'

Cirina did as she was asked, clinging to him as the deep, warm sensations flooded through her. She felt as if she had entered a spiral which was climbing, climbing, ever higher, reaching out for a pinnacle which she had never reached before, not even in her wildest imaginings.

Her sex was so wet now, soaking Antonio's fingers and easing his path across her eager flesh. She could smell the sweet, slightly musky scent of her feminine secretions, heavy in the air, mingling with the wholly masculine odours of Antonio's body. She felt hot all over, as if she had a fever, and her head tossed from side to side on the pallet, knocking against his naked shoulder.

Suddenly a jagged spear of sensation travelled up her spine, so acute that her eyes opened wide with shock and a long, low cry escaped through her lips. She was aware of Antonio watching her closely, approving her reaction, pressing harder onto that wanton nub of flesh before tapping it with his fingerpad.

Cirina thought that she would faint. Her body rocked back and forth and her legs opened wide, out of her control as she thrust her hips up, against Antonio's fingers. She felt his tongue flick against her straining nipples, was aware of the cool kiss of the air against her wet skin as he moved his attention further down, pressing his lips against her navel before dipping into it with his tongue. Then she was aware of nothing at all except the all-involving convulsion of her body.

Letting out a long, high pitched cry, she curled herself into a ball, bringing her knees up to her chest and squeezing her thighs together as the sensation became almost too intense to bear. Her breath came in little, panting sobs as, at last, she gained some respite and she uncurled herself.

Gradually, Cirina became aware of Antonio's voice murmuring in her ear in his own tongue, his tone soothing. He had shifted his position so that his body was covering hers, his knees between her calves. The head of his man-flesh nudged gently at the hot, wet centre of her and his hands, gentle, but insistent, drew her knees up so that her legs were wrapped around his waist.

Slowly, so slowly that she felt she could not bear the suspense, he began to push into her, stopping as he reached the barrier of her maidenhead. Opening her eyes, Cirina saw that he was watching her face. His features were softened with desire, yet there was concern for her in the pale blue of his eyes.

She could not bear this waiting, this anticipation of pain before the further ecstasy she was certain would follow. Wanting him to be sure that she wished him to continue, Cirina placed the palms of her hands on the small of his back and exerted a gentle pressure.

Antonio smiled at her, then thrust into her waiting body with one firm, smooth movement. There was an instant of pain and Cirina opened her mouth to cry out, only to find her cry captured in Antonio's mouth. He kissed her, so hard that she began to forget the pain he was inflicting as he began to move back and forth inside her body.

Allowing her time to get used to the discomfort, he

kissed and caressed her, murmuring soothing words in her ear and gentling her, licking away the salty tears which spilled from her eyes.

At first Cirina was aware of little else but discomfort, but gradually as he patiently coaxed her untutored body, she was aware of other sensations creeping beneath the pain. Slowly, gradually, the pain subsided, to be replaced by a new kind of pleasure.

Sensing the moment when it changed, Antonio began to move his hips faster, pumping in and out of her now welcoming sheath as he raced towards his own climax. Cirina clung to him, raking her nails across his back as his movements became more urgent, less controlled.

She cried out in dismay as he suddenly pulled out of her, gasping as she felt the first hot rush of ejaculate spill over her belly and thighs, understanding at once why he had left her.

Antonio's face was taut, his eyes glazed as the last of his seed left his body and spilled onto hers. Cirina felt a pang of ancient, purely feminine triumph. For the first time she recognised her power as a woman and she was enraptured by the discovery.

Antonio cleaned her body with a handful of straw, and she saw that his hand was trembling.

'Are you all right, Cirina *cara*?' he asked her huskily as he folded her into his arms.

'Oh yes,' she whispered, turning her face into his shoulder to hide her smile.

She lay very still beside him for some time, absorbing the heat of his skin, familiarising herself with the shape and scent of his body as it pressed against hers. She could feel his heart beating steadily against her cheek and she watched the rhythmic rise and fall of his chest as he breathed deeply and evenly.

After a while, Cirina realised that he had fallen asleep. She was disappointed at first, thinking that it had all been over far too quickly. At the beginning she had been too afraid to really relax and enjoy what was happening to her. Now that she knew what to expect, she wanted to go back to the start and do it all over again.

Moving carefully so as not to disturb him, Cirina moved out of the circle of Antonio's arms so that she could see him better.

There was a full moon shining in the inky black sky outside and some of its milky, pale light came through the unshuttered window and fell across his skin. Knowing that he was asleep, Cirina felt able to really look at him and she ran her eyes freely over his sleeping form, admiring the breadth of his shoulders and the tautness of his belly before resting on the sleeping monster which lay curled slightly on his thigh.

How soft it looked, how vulnerable in this state! Cirina scrutinised him curiously, wondering at how it could alter so dramatically in such a short time. Could this small, tender appendage really be the same one that she had feared would tear her when it entered her body?

She had never seen a man this close before and she made the most of the opportunity to study him. Glancing at his face, she reassured herself that he was still sleeping. His long, black lashes lay unmoving against his cheekbones and his face bore the relaxed, untroubled expression that only sleep can bring.

Tentatively, for fear that she might wake him, Cirina ran her hands over the hard, clean lines of his chest, feeling the silky-coarse black hair which grew on it tickle her palms. She caressed his body, moulding the muscles in his arms with her hands and sweeping her palms across the flat, hard contour of his belly. As she touched him there, his man-flesh stirred. Intrigued, Cirina repeated the action, watching in wonder as his male appendage swelled slightly before her eyes.

Emboldened, Cirina touched her fingertips against the soft, wrinkled flesh, drawing her hand back as if it had been burned when she felt the hard core of it within the loose skin. Antonio slept on, oblivious to her curious exploration and Cirina closed her hand over his penis and squeezed gently.

Immediately, the sleeping flesh began to waken and stir, as if it were truly a separate being apart from the man who still slept on. Running her hand up and down the lengthening shaft, Cirina watched, fascinated, as the loose skin moved independently of the firmer core, pulling over the bulbous end, only to reveal it fully when she pulled her hand back again.

She liked the bulb at its end. The skin there was as soft as that of a newborn babe and Cirina ran her thumbpad backward and forward over it, revelling in its texture. It was pinker in colour than the rest of the shaft which had swollen now so that it filled her hand.

There was a deep crease dissecting the head on one side and, as she watched, a clear drop of moisture appeared at the end, like a teardrop. After another glance at Antonio's face to check that he was still sleeping, Cirina lowered her head and dabbed at the salty fluid with her tongue. Immediately, the teardrop was replaced with another, then another, until she was fully occupied with licking and sucking the soft-skinned tip which gradually suffused with blood and turned a deep, dull pink.

Cirina was enjoying herself. She liked the taste of the fluid seeping from his body, loved the feel of the now fully erect shaft lying heavily in her hand. Gradually, she took more of it into her mouth. Caressing and stroking what remained of the length with her hand, she drew the responsive column into her mouth and toyed with it.

Her hair fell across her face, enclosing her in a fragrant curtain where only she and the male pleasure-flesh she was sucking were all that mattered. Breathing in deeply the heavy, musky scent of him, she cupped the hairy sacs which held his store of seed and ran her thumb back and forth over the taut, hot skin.

It seemed to shiver in her hand and she left the rigid shaft to kiss and lick the flesh beneath. Gently, knowing instinctively that this area of his anatomy would be extra sensitive, Cirina sucked the twin balls into her mouth and rolled them on her tongue.

Her reward was a sudden clenching of his buttock muscles as he came close to spending. Cirina was gripped by the urgent desire to taste the fluid which would come out of his body and she hastily went back to holding his shaft in her mouth. It didn't take much to tip him over the edge and there it was, a hot, viscous spurt which hit the back of her throat, half choking her.

Reluctantly, Cirina drew away, swallowing frantically at the ejaculate which felt as if it had lodged in her throat. The rest of the creamy white fluid flew in a graceful arc to land on his own naked chest and belly.

Running her eyes up his body, Cirina was horrified, if unsurprised, to see that he was awake, and looking straight at her. At which point had he become aware of what she was doing to him? Cirina blushed darkly, her eyes dropping to her hands which folded meekly in her lap.

'Oh no, *cara mia,*' Antonio said softly, 'you can't fool me now with that demure expression! You are a little wildcat, and no mistake!'

He laughed, not unkindly, but with delight and approval and Cirina ventured a small answering grin. Antonio seemed to regain his strength at once for he swung her round by the waist and pushed her back on to the prickly straw, bringing his body down to pin hers to the bed.

'Two can play at that game, Cirina,' he said playfully, pinning her wrists effortlessly above her head with one large hand and dipping his head to take one nipple between his teeth.

Cirina gasped as he stretched the tender flesh before letting go, creating a tiny dart of pleasure-pain which made Cirina's heart miss a beat. To her delight, he seemed eager to play with her, despite his own recent climax. She could feel the semen drying stickily on his skin as he pressed against her, but Antonio seemed oblivious to it as he licked and nipped a path down the centre of her body towards her nub of pleasure.

'How would you like to wake to find me burrowing between your delectable thighs?' he asked her, not waiting for an answer before he parted her labia with his tongue.

Cirina froze with shock. Could it really be that he derived pleasure from kissing her there? Evidently he did, for he continued to tease her swelling flesh with his tongue, darting it right into the well of her arousal and smearing her own fluids along her most intimate flesh.

She moaned as he found the hub of her pleasure once again and drew it into a small cone between his lips. The intense surge of delight this caused took her by surprise and she felt the glorious, sweet warmth sweep through her body.

Antonio worked away at her sex with every appearance of enjoyment, as if she tasted of the finest honey-mead. Reaching down, Cirina tangled her fingers in his unexpectedly soft hair and held his head against her as the first pulsings began.

She was not afraid this time, rather she welcomed the heady sensations sweeping through her body and the urge to curl herself into a ball did not overcome her.

This time, though, Antonio did not wait for her to savour every last tremor; he drove into her even as the last of her orgasm ebbed away. Cirina's body welcomed him, her legs going round his waist, gripping him to her as her fingernails dug into the smooth skin of his shoulders.

This time she knew what to do, gave into her instinct

to meet him stroke for stroke, and before long his body burned like a furnace, the heat of his skin seeping into hers so that she felt she was on fire.

Lifting her hips to clash against his, Cirina felt abandoned in a way she had never dreamed could be possible. Nothing mattered to her but the moment as she raced with Antonio towards the inevitable conclusion of their coming together.

She knew the moment when he lost control. His head went back, his lips stretched wide across his teeth and he let out a cry which sounded very close to anguish. Cirina clenched her muscles around him and milked the seed from his body. Though she did not understand his words, she was aware that he was revelling in his submission to her, giving up his seed as though it was the most precious gift he could offer her.

Cirina was almost disappointed when he pulled out of her to spill his fluids over her breasts and belly, though she knew such an emotion was irrational. This time it was she who soothed and calmed him, drawing him down into her arms and cradling his head on her breast.

Antonio kissed her softening nipples, not with passion, but with tenderness and he nuzzled the damp, fragrant flesh of her underarm before making himself comfortable beside her. The moon bathed them in its pale light, outshining the stars which watched over the desert.

It was very quiet, the air still and cold after the heat of the day, and Cirina pulled over the furs lying at the side of the bed to cover them both. Listening to Antonio's deep, regular breathing, she relived the past few hours with a sense of wonder. Never had she dreamt that it could be like this between a man and a woman.

Or was it this particular man who had made the experience so good for her? No, she chided herself, pulling the furs higher round her shoulders as she shivered, it was foolish to think that way. Antonio would be leaving in the morning – she would never see him again.

She consoled herself with the thought that she would never forget him. Perhaps the Europeans were right to value a woman's first introduction to love as they did. Perhaps Antonio would remember her and this night they had spent together as she would.

On this thought, Cirina finally fell asleep.

Chapter Three

The following morning Cirina woke to find Antonio's lips roaming her naked breasts and belly, his hands stroking gently over the soft skin of her thighs. She smiled and turned her body towards him, reaching unashamedly for the tumescent shaft which was making its presence felt alongside her.

'Good morrow, *cara*,' Antonio murmured, drawing her rapidly hardening nipple into his mouth and rolling it on his tongue. 'Did you sleep well?' he asked her after a few minutes.

Cirina giggled and wrapped her arms around him, breathing in the sleepy, early morning smell of him. Antonio responded by slipping his first two fingers between her sleeping sex-lips, coaxing a response from them as, with his other hand, he gently pushed her thighs apart.

As soon as she was ready for him, he slipped inside her, lying there, for a moment, watching her face in the pinkish light of dawn. She looked even more lovely this morning, if that were possible, gazing up at him serenely, completely unabashed by what had happened between them the previous evening.

Antonio could not remember the last time he had been this glad to wake up to find the same woman beside him as he had bedded the night before. Indeed, it was rare for him to continue to desire a woman once his initial thirst for her body had been slaked.

Surprised by this insight into his own sexual psyche, he looked at Cirina with new eyes as he began to move inside her. She must be very special to have invoked such an atypical response from him. The simple fact of her beauty would not have been enough; Antonio had always had a penchant for beautiful women and a knack for persuading whichever one he wanted into his bed.

Perhaps it was her innocence, or maybe her sheer, uncomplicated pleasure in the act of love? He smiled at her, a wondering, loving smile, before closing his eyes and losing himself in the liquid ecstasy of her body.

Cirina saw the smile and felt her heart turn over in her chest. She had been sure that this was no normal encounter, that men and women coming together for just one night to slake their lust did not usually feel this depth of emotion, and Antonio's smile confirmed her suspicions.

As Antonio closed his eyes, she squeezed experimentally with the muscles which enclosed his man-flesh, her eyes widening as she realised how much her action increased her own pleasure. To her delight, she found that she could draw him in more deeply, could hold onto him for a split second as he withdrew, so that she set up a kind of chain reaction all along the cleated walls of her passage.

Experimenting, she was hardly aware of the sensations she was causing by her actions, and her orgasm took her by surprise, coming as it did from deep inside her. As she gasped aloud her release, she wrapped her ankles round Antonio's waist and held him tightly to her. The vibrations from her climax seemed to bring him on and she could tell he had to struggle with his conscience before he pulled out of her to spill his seed.

As she met his gaze, Cirina saw a new respect dawning in his pale blue eyes and she blushed.

'You learn fast, little one,' Antonio murmured as he sprawled, unconcernedly naked, on the straw beside her. Trailing an idle finger between her breasts he paused thoughtfully.

'What is it?' Cirina ventured softly.

Antonio smiled, as if embarrassed by his thoughts.

'I was wondering if I might ever get to pass by this way again,' he admitted truthfully.

Cirina felt a pang at the thought of never seeing him again and she allowed her feelings to show on her face.

'I do hope you will,' she replied fervently.

Antonio chuckled and bent to kiss her lightly on the tip of her nose.

'If ever I did, you would have forgotten me long before – there will be many more travellers to warm your bed from now on.'

Even as he spoke, he was aware that the idea of this beautiful creature offering her 'hospitality' to all and sundry was an anathema to him. Somehow by being her first lover, he felt she was marked as his. By all that was holy, it was a foolish notion, but he could not seem to rid himself of it. Cirina's eyes mirrored his own distress.

'Perhaps that is true,' she whispered fervently, 'but I will never forget you, Antonio, never!'

'I wish I could take you away with me,' he blurted impulsively.

'Could you? Oh yes, Antonio, please say I can come with you!'

Antonio dragged his eyes away from her guiltily. What on earth had made him utter such an immature proclamation? Now Cirina was looking at him with wide, hopeful eyes and he would have to hurt her.

'I cannot, *cara mia*,' he said gently. 'I am sorry.'

Tears glistened on her lashes and he saw that she was trying desperately hard to blink them back. He cursed himself for a mangy dog for complicating things between them. Before he had given voice to such madness, she had not expected anything from him at all. Now by letting loose his unwise tongue, he had set her up for disappointment.

'But I will come back one day.'

It was offered as a kindly, if inadequate consolation but Cirina seized upon it eagerly.

'You will? Do you promise?'

Antonio looked down into her wide, deep blue eyes and felt as if he were drowning. How could he not tell her what she wanted to hear, even though he knew in his heart it would be a promise he could not ever hope to keep.

'I promise,' he whispered, feeling like the lowest beggar as her face lit up trustingly.

Her arms came up, about his shoulders and she kissed him fervently. Holding her slender form in his arms, Antonio felt suddenly, inexplicably sad, and he buried his face in her long, fragrant hair to hide his expression from her.

Soon after it was time for the travellers to make ready for the long journey ahead and Antonio was forced to rise. Cirina brought him water which had been collected earlier by one of the serving girls from the nomad tribes who came when the caravanserai was busy. She watched as he washed and dressed in fresh hose.

Her heart was heavy as she followed him down the stairs and served him breakfast. Trying to ignore the curious, amused glances afforded her by her aunt and cousin, Cirina did everything she could to serve Antonio. She wanted him to remember every detail of his trip here so that he would want to come back for her when his business in Beijing was concluded. He would not forget her, she was determined that he should not!

There were so many questions she wanted to ask him; about his homeland and his life there, about his business with the Khan and, most importantly, how long it might be before he returned for her. But there was no time to ask him any of those questions for they were not able to be alone together at all amidst the preparations for his departure from the caravanserai.

In no time, it seemed, Antonio was loading the camel which would carry his belongings across the Takla Makan and preparing the one that he would ride. Cirina looked on admiringly as he wrapped a cloth scarf around his head so that, from the back at least, he could be mistaken for one of her kinsmen. Though no man of her people had that long-legged stride, nor towered a full head taller than Cirina, she thought proudly.

For one awful moment, she feared he would follow suit when the Polos mounted their camels, without having said a proper goodbye to her. Her heart soared as he strode over to her and kissed her, hard, on the mouth, pressing her body against the length of his as if trying to memorise the feel of it.

Cirina watched him mount the camel, and the camel rose up onto its feet. Impulsively, she dashed forward and lay her cheek against his leg as he towered above her. Antonio reached down and rested his hand lightly on the top of her head, then he turned his mount and left her, standing in the courtyard, watching until they were swallowed up by the desert.

'God's teeth man, are you still mooning over that unusual looking little piece at the caravanserai?'

Antonio jumped as Marco appeared at his elbow and saw the sketch of Cirina on which he was working. He knew from past experience that there was little point in trying to hide what he was doing, so he suffered his friend's silent scrutiny of the picture.

It was accomplished enough, showing Cirina in profile, her long hair piled up on top of her head in the manner of a Venetian lady. But Antonio was as dissatisfied with this as he was with all the other drawings he had executed since he had left her. Somehow, although he knew he had captured her likeness, he could not seem to capture that special essence which made his encounter with her so vivid.

Marco stayed his hand as he would have vented his frustration on the drawing.

'Nay, Antonio, 'tis a fine piece of work.'

'It shows a face, not the woman within,' Antonio snapped irritably.

'It is a beautiful face nonetheless,' his friend pointed out reasonably.

Antonio made an impatient gesture with his hand. 'There are thousands of beautiful women. None have that extra quality Cirina has which my charcoal refuses to describe!'

Marco looked at him sympathetically. 'You have fallen very heavily, my friend. I would advise you to put the wench from your mind and look forward, to Beijing. There's many a willing serving girl there who will help you forget, eh?'

He clapped Antonio on the back and Antonio managed a sickly smile.

'You are right,' he conceded with false heartiness. 'Life is too short to spend it hankering after the unattainable.'

'Well said, my friend. Onward, then, to Beijing!'

Antonio watched as Marco strode over to the camels and began the early morning tasks which would make them ready for the day's journey. Though he knew Marco was right, Antonio also knew that his own words were false. He did not want *any* woman – he wanted Cirina. None other would serve to quench the slow burn of longing in his loins which had stayed with him from the moment he left her.

Looking back the way they had come, he saw nothing

but the burnt orange sand and recalled the hardships of the crossing so far. Cirina was far away, beyond that treacherous desert which they had now almost crossed. She would spend her life at the caravanserai, tending to the animals and the occasional traveller and before long the all too short time they had had together would blur in the mists of time and she would forget him. Just as he would her, once he had returned to Venice, he told himself without conviction.

When, at last, they reached Beijing, all were heartily relieved to bathe and obtain fresh clothing before seeking audience with the Khan. While the others threw themselves into the diversions offered at the palace, Antonio grew steadily more restless, desiring only to complete his business in the province before returning to Venice.

'Relax, Antonio – it could be days yet before Kublai will decide to summon us. You may just as well make the most of the holiday.'

Smiling as if in agreement, Antonio took himself off for a walk in the grounds. He had never felt less like a holiday. Since his encounter with Cirina he had felt restless and out of sorts; he was fast approaching the time when he knew he would have to admit defeat where his mission was concerned and return home without that for which he had come.

Pausing to gaze into the waters fed by a series of fountains in the grounds, Antonio reviewed his quest so far. Thirty years before, when his father had served Emperor Baldwin of Constantinople, the Emperor had been overthrown by Michael of Nicaea. Antonio's father had been with Baldwin when he was rescued by the Venetian fleet and so had his confidence.

Exiled in Venice, Baldwin had lamented the loss of the Imperial crown which had been left behind in Constantinople. This crown was decorated with a priceless ruby, which had mysteriously disappeared, and its loss had become symbolic for the exiled Byzantium peoples.

Antonio's father had spent the rest of his life trying to recover this ruby. The quest had become an obsession which dominated his life, leaving his wife and son in the shadows. Eventually it made him ill and he died young, his failure a heavy burden to take to the grave.

Upon his death, the search was abandoned. Not until the rumour had reached them that the ruby had been seen in the possession of Kublai Khan did the Venetian Government entrust Antonio with the task of recovering it.

He sighed as he thought of the years he had wasted travelling with his kinsman, Marco Polo, hoping that, through him, he would gain access to the fabled city of Xanadu. For this is where Antonio felt the ruby would be found, if at all. So far though, he had watched and waited in vain, for, apart from their most recent trip to Samarkand, Marco had spent most of the three years since Antonio had joined him in Langchow.

Antonio's official role, as artist-recorder, had been an interesting one, but he had longed to honour his father's memory by retrieving the Byzantine ruby. Not until he had met Cirina had anything come close to distracting him from his main aim.

'Signor Ballerei! Signor Ballerei!'

Antonio stood up, his hand automatically going to the hilt of his sword before he saw the chief eunuch striding towards him. The man must have been seven feet tall, his skin the colour of darkest ebony. He stopped as he reached Antonio and gave a brief nod of acknowledgement which Antonio supposed passed in his native lands as a bow.

'Signor – your presence is required in the great hall.'

Antonio strode after the eunuch wondering why he had been sent to find him instead of one of the Khan's guards. He soon stopped wondering about it – there seemed to be no rhyme or reason to the Emperor's edicts, as far as he could tell.

Arriving in the presence of the Khan, Antonio bowed low, noticing from the corner of his eye that the Polos had already been seen and were standing to his left.

'Rise, rise!'

He straightened at the Khan's impatient command and waited. This was the closest he had ever been to the legendary Kublai Khan and he studied him covertly. He might well have been a great warrior in his younger days, but the man Antonio saw before him was far from the almost mythical Western expectation of how the grandson of Gengis should look.

Obese and ailing, he was in his late seventies and it was rumoured that he now spent less time here at the glittering Beijing court than he did in Xanadu. The day to day administration of the great empire now fell more and more to the legions of relatives and lesser aids, making the political situation in the country dangerously volatile.

This, however, was the least of Antonio's worries as he waited for the Khan to speak. A beautiful woman stood by the Emperor's throne, her eyes boring into him as he waited. This must be Chabi, rumoured to be the Khan's favourite wife.

As his gaze met hers, Antonio found himself caught by the unusual emerald of her piercing eyes and he shivered inexplicably. The woman smiled, almost as if she had seen his reaction to her, then she leaned forward slowly and whispered in Kublai's ear. He nodded slightly, his rheumy eyes focusing on Antonio.

'My friend, Marco Polo, tells me you are an artist, Antonio Ballerei,' he said, his breath wheezing in his chest.

'That is correct, your Highness,' Antonio confirmed, bowing low once again.

Kublai made a glottal sound in his throat. He clicked his fingers and a servant sprang forward, holding Antonio's portfolio of drawings. Antonio's fingers itched to snatch his property away as the Khan thumbed through them perfunctorily before signalling for the servant to take them away again.

'You will capture the likeness of my favoured falcons when we reach Shang-tu.'

With a languid wave of the Khan's fat fingers, Antonio found himself dismissed. His mind raced as he backed away from the Khan's presence. Shang-tu – Xanadu! At last he was to go to Xanadu!

As the horsemen bore down on the caravanserai from the east, Cirina shielded her eyes against the sun, her heart leaping in her chest as she thought, at first, that it might be Antonio, returning for her at last. Her hopes were dashed as she realised there were several travellers, none of whom were on camels, which meant that they were either soldiers, or bandits, or both.

Running into the stables, she called for her uncle. Feeling the hot sting of disappointed tears behind her eyelids, she lingered in the cool shadows of the stables as the rest of the household ran to see who was coming. She could not face their knowing glances, not yet.

Though her aunt and cousin mocked her mercilessly, Cirina still clung to the belief that Antonio would keep his promise to return for her. Night after night on her lonely pallet, she would dream of him. After Bortai's snores signalled that the other girl was sound asleep, Cirina would touch herself on that special, secret place he had helped her to discover. By reliving the things they had done together behind her closed eyelids, she had discovered that she could bring herself to that peak of pleasure, even though she was alone.

Nothing she did, though, could replace the feel of Antonio's strong body covering hers, nothing could come close to the ecstasy of feeling his man-flesh moving inside her. And now here were more travellers to whom her hospitality would be offered. Cirina did not think she would be able to bear making love with another man when it was Antonio for whom she was yearning.

'Cirina! What are you doing skulking in here, girl? Enough of your skiving – fetch fresh water, and don't dawdle about it.'

Keta's harsh voice sliced through the still air of the stables, jolting Cirina out of her reverie. She ran to do her aunt's bidding, knowing that to be too slow would probably earn her a cuff fit to set her ears ringing.

When she arrived back with the water, she saw that there were some half dozen soldiers preparing to rest at the caravanserai. As she entered the room, the low buzz of conversation stopped and Cirina found herself under the scrutiny of all eyes.

'You girl – come here.'

It was a short, stocky man who had spoken, his skin swarthy beneath the round, spike-tipped helmet he still wore. Glancing at Lengke she saw him nod imperceptibly, so Cirina stepped forward, trying to hide her reluctance.

The man's uniform proclaimed him to be a captain in the Emperor's guard. He eyed Cirina critically as she moved to the centre of the room and she was aware that an expectant hush had fallen.

'This girl,' the man said, directing his question to Lengke, 'she is yours?'

'My niece, captain,' Lengke replied with exaggerated obsequiousness.

'Virgin?'

'No, Master – though she has only recently been broken.'

'Good, good.'

Cirina, feeling like a horse who has been brought to market, shivered slightly as the man's hard, black eyes raked her body. She felt as if he could see right through her thin clothing, as if he was assessing her body, though, curiously, his gaze was quite without passion.

The captain turned to one of his men and beckoned him forward.

'I would wager she will score at least the twenty carats the Empress has decreed, would you not agree, Mongor?'

The other man, taller than the first and handsome, for a Tartar, ran his eyes up and down Cirina's body.

'Her hair and eyebrows are of the finest quality. Her lips – yes, two carats, by my judgement. Her eyes are unusual – that might mean a higher score, or a lesser one, depending upon the lady, Chabi's whim. Fifteen carats, I would say.'

'I agree. Most interesting.' The captain stroked his drooping moustache thoughtfully.

Cirina felt cold as the men discussed her, not understanding the way they graded her beauty, as if such a thing was quantifiable. The fine hairs at the back of her neck prickled as the captain spoke again.

'I would see more of her – remove your clothing.'

Cirina's jaw dropped. Surely she had misheard? The low murmur of anticipation which rippled through the watching soldiers told her that she had heard aright. The captain quickly grew impatient with her hesitation.

'By order of the Khan, I say – strip!'

Cirina's fingers felt paralysed as they fumbled with the fastenings to her shift. Her mind flew back to that other time when she had undressed joyously for Antonio. This was quite, quite different. She could feel the soldiers' hot, lustful eyes on her as she pulled the shift over her head and stood in her undershift, looking expectantly towards the captain.

'Everything,' he said, confirming her worst fears.

From the corner of her eye, Cirina could see Bortai smirking openly, while her aunt looked on as if bored. Lengke's expression was inscrutable, but she could see that there was to be no intervention by him this time.

The room felt unbearably stuffy, so hot that not a

breath of air disturbed the highly charged atmosphere. With a sense of fatality, Cirina slipped the thin straps of her undershift off her shoulders and allowed it to fall to the floor.

Cirina kept her eyes fixed firmly at a point on the far side of the room as she felt all eyes turn on her naked body. The soldiers' reaction she could understand – they were all looking at her with simple lust shining in their flat brown eyes. Her cousin and aunt scrutinized her slyly, as if comparing her womanly charms to their own.

The captain, however, and Mongor, merely studied her dispassionately, as if she was indeed merely a beast to be bought. She tensed as they approached her, flinching away from Mongor's large hands as they lifted one breast. Ignoring her reluctance, he tested its weight and its pliability, nodding approvingly at the captain. To Cirina's surprise, his hands were quite gentle and, although she hated the humiliation he was inflicting on her with every fibre of her body, some of the fear left her.

Suddenly Mongor flicked his thumb over the crest of her nipple and to Cirina's shame it hardened almost immediately. The captain watched as his deputy dipped his head and licked the puckered areola, just once, as if tasting her skin.

Cirina was finding it hard to breathe. The heat of the room was suffocating her, the people watching seemed to be closing in, their eyes avid on her exposed body. There was worse to come.

'Turn around,' the captain commanded and, unsuspecting, Cirina did as she was told. 'Bend from the waist – don't waste my time, girl!'

Cirina's cheeks flamed as she presented her bottom for the men's perusal. She gasped as Mongor prised her buttocks apart to reveal the puckered rose of her anus and she clenched her muscles tightly in shame.

She saw the captain's booted feet walk around to the

front of her and she tensed even more. Nothing, though, prepared her for what he did next. Without warning, he took his riding whip and flicked it sharply against her dangling breasts, making them judder and causing Cirina to gasp with shock and pain.

'Her teats are firm,' he said to Mongor, not pausing to acknowledge Cirina's reaction. 'Stand erect.'

Cirina did so, aware of the stinging sensation in her breasts as she faced the assembled soldiers. Tears stung her eyes and she blinked them back furiously, determined not to give the men the satisfaction of seeing her cry. Mongor noticed and smiled kindly at her.

'Almost over now,' he murmured, for her ears only, and Cirina was grateful for the few words of kindness.

Standing behind her, Mongor reached around her waist and stretched the taut skin of her belly upward, so that her pubis was tipped up. Cirina closed her eyes momentarily in horror as he parted her tender woman's flesh to reveal the inner lips to the watching men.

'Good, good,' the captain approved.

He stepped forward and, without removing his leather glove, he slipped his forefinger into her body. Drawing it out again, Cirina saw the fluids glistening on his glove and felt ashamed that her body had betrayed her. How could it be that while her mind was repulsed by this whole charade, her body had secretly reacted to it?

The captain brought his finger to his mouth and licked it, smacking his lips in approval as he tasted the fruit of her body. Cirina thought she would faint with shame and she leaned heavily against Mongor who had now released her mons from display.

'She is fresh – a worthy contestant. You have heard of the Khan's beauty contests, Lengke?' he asked conversationally, turning away from Cirina as if she held no further interest for him.

She listened to the conversation taking place between the captain and her uncle as she dressed in the clothes which Mongor passed to her. Her relief that her ordeal was over was quickly tempered by her growing dismay.

'It is every officer's duty to look out for suitable women for the Khan. It is a great honour to be chosen – there is a stringent grading system to be observed. You will be amply rewarded for the loan of your niece, my friend.'

Lengke's eyes slid regretfully to Cirina, and she realised that her fate was sealed. Keta and Bortai were looking at her with ill-concealed jealousy and the soldiers, though they clearly lusted after her, turned away respectfully as they realised she was marked down for the Khan.

Her heart sank as she watched Lengke accept the bag of gold offered to him. With a muffled sob, she turned and ran from the room.

Lengke found her sobbing in the stables.

'Do not distress yourself, Cirina – it is a great honour to be chosen for the Khan.'

'How could you, uncle?' she blurted, her voice thick with tears. 'Is this how you look after your sister's child – you sell her for a bag of gold.'

Lengke's skin reddened, though whether with anger or shame Cirina could not tell.

'Anya would have been proud of you, Cirina. Come now – it need not be forever. You will learn much at the Khan's palace and you will be able to travel, just as you have always wanted.'

This last inducement had the desired effect of stemming Cirina's tears and she wiped her face on a handful of clean straw.

'But what of Antonio? How will he ever find me if I leave here?'

Lengke sighed and sat down beside her. 'Antonio will not pass this way again, my child.'

'But he promised!'

Reaching over to her, Lengke wiped the last of her tears away with his thumbpad.

'Men make many promises when in the arms of a beautiful woman, Cirina. He meant well, I am sure, but he will not return.'

Her uncle's words only confirmed what Cirina had suspected in her own heart and she leaned her head against his shoulder.

'I shall miss you, uncle,' she whispered.

Lengke was not generally given to gestures of affection and he patted Cirina's shoulder awkwardly in response.

'Go and rest now, you have a long journey ahead. Go to the Khan and bring down blessings on this, the home of your kin.'

'Yes, my uncle,' Cirina whispered meekly.

Cirina was dozing on her camel as they finally approached Shang-tu. The sight of the valley, after so long in the desert, was enough to spur the travel-weary soldiers on and their rediscovered high spirits roused her.

After several weeks travelling across the Takla Makan and then the Gobi desert, Cirina was beginning to think that her desire to see what was beyond the desert was a foolish one. As far as she had seen so far, there *was* no beyond, only *li* upon *li* of endless, scorching sand shimmering beneath the merciless sun.

Now she found herself gazing with disbelief, on green fields served by the water streaming from the mountains which bordered the valley on the far side, just visible in the distance. And there in the middle of this vision of plenty, was Shang-tu itself, like a mirage in the desert.

Cirina could well understand the soldiers' excitement for she felt her own heart quicken as she looked down on their destination. It was the first time she had felt any kind of kindred emotion with them, and she grinned, sharing in the moment.

Because of her special status as gift to the Khan, Cirina had been allowed to ride unmolested for most of the journey. Only when a soldier lifted her from her camel did a hand slip beneath her cloak to caress her breast, or a hot mouth brush the delicate skin of her neck.

Their lust for her since her very public humiliation at the hands of Mongor and the captain did not recede with time. Always, she was aware of being watched, of feeding their fantasies merely by her presence and she always felt that danger was not far away.

Mongor seemed to have become her self-appointed protector and there were several occasions when she had been glad of the taciturn Tartar's friendship; as now, when he drew alongside her and explained that it would be another day's travel before they reached the distant city.

That night as she lay restless beneath the canopy of stars, Cirina allowed herself to ponder her fate for the first time. What was in store for her at Kublai Khan's famous 'pleasure palace'? She had only Lengke's assurance that she would be treated well and what did he know, confined as he was to the land around the caravanserai?

Staring up into the sky, she prayed to the deity to watch over her. Gradually, she became aware that someone more earthly was watching her. Her skin prickled as she slowly turned her head, only to encounter the glitter of Mongor's inscrutable eyes, staring at her from some distance.

Even in the dark, she could feel the intensity of his gaze and Cirina was troubled by it. How could she be sure whether Mongor was her friend, or merely her gaoler? Resolutely, she closed her eyes against him and tried to rest for what was left of the night.

It was late afternoon by the time they approached the city. Slowly, they rode towards the palace. The magnificent building was surrounded by an enormous wall, impossible, it was said, to scale from either inside or out.

There was only one entrance to the palace grounds and that was through a pair of enormous gates which required a contingent of eight men to operate them. The small party had to wait outside the gates while the captain rode through to report to the palace guard. He seemed to be gone for hours as they waited beneath the merciless sun for his return. At last the great gates began to creak apart and they were waved through.

As they rode through the gates, Cirina caught her breath. Here was a garden the like of which she had never dreamed existed. Ornamental trees were planted as if native to the country, interspersed with innumerable fountains which provided a background symphony of gurgling water, ever present.

As they made their way through the gardens to the palace, Cirina caught a glimpse of the huge summerhouse where, it was reputed, the Khan indulged his voracious appetite for the pleasures of the flesh. Cirina shivered as she reflected that, very soon, she would be but another item on the menu.

But now she gasped with wonder as a white mare galloped across their path. Wild animals and birds roamed free, imported to the pleasure palace to provide sport for the Khan and his entourage. They passed the pampered falcons and the predatory leopards chained to a wall. At the base of the great stone steps, they stopped and Mongor lifted Cirina from the horse she had been given to ride when they reached the city.

With a gentle push in the small of her back, he indicated that she should climb up to the huge wooden door which was opened by unseen hands the moment she set foot on the lower step.

Cirina's mouth and throat suddenly felt dry. Whereas before she had distrusted Mongor, now she was afraid to go on without him. At least he had afforded her some degree of protection. Whatever lay beyond that vast door, Cirina knew she would have to face it alone and she was afraid.

Slowly, her legs feeling as if they had been weighted, she ascended the steps. Though she could not see beyond the patch of darkness in the doorway, she was quite sure that her approach was being watched by unseen eyes.

As she reached the top of the steps, Cirina stopped and looked back over her shoulder. Mongor was still watching her and he waved his hand to show that she should go on. Reluctantly she stepped through the door, into the cool shade of the building.

At once the huge door was closed behind her, shutting out the daylight. Blind for a moment having stepped in from the bright sun, Cirina had heard the door close with an awful finality and she knew that there would now be no turning back.

Chapter Four

Antonio lay back in the perfumed water of the bath and closed his eyes. His long legs floated idly to the surface and he brought them down again. The water was warm, lapping over his tired body in little waves caused by a serving girl who was operating a fan-like contraption at the far side of the bath. Another girl poured clean water over his head and shoulders and began to soap his hair whilst another submerged herself in the water and began to bathe him, starting with his feet.

Above him the bath-house was covered with a huge, blue silk-lined dome shot with golden thread which gave the illusion of a bright summer's day and glorious sunshine. Exotic birds flew freely about, their twittering providing a pleasing accompaniment to the soft voices of the serving girls.

Opening his eyes, he looked at them and smiled. As far as he understood, these three women had been assigned to him on his arrival two weeks before at the pleasure palace. He had not seen any of the Polos for more than a few minutes at a time since then; each appeared to be well occupied with his own three serving women, trained to attend to their temporary masters' every need.

For Antonio the days had slipped into a pleasant, if uneventful routine. This morning had begun like all the others. He was woken mid-morning by one of the girls – Ailie, he thought, smiling at her as she massaged his scalp – crawling beneath his bed covers and taking his sleeping cock into her soft, wet mouth.

Ah, but it was a blissful way to wake! Coming round to find a beautiful woman working diligently to draw the seed from his body had to be one of the finest awakenings. Afterwards he had been led to a secluded area of the courtyard outside where his body had been doused with icy-cold water.

The first time he had been subjected to this, he had gasped with shock. But immediately afterwards his entire body was rubbed briskly with a coarse towel which made the blood sing through his veins, warming him and chasing away the last vestiges of langour from his limbs. He had soon come to appreciate the invigorating effect.

It took two of the women to attend to his morning ablutions. Meanwhile the third would lay out fresh clothes for the day. Court dress if the day was to be taken with leisurely pursuits, hunting dress if hunting was on the agenda, as it had been today. Recalling the thrill of hunting with the highly trained falcons kept by the Khan made him smile.

The girl, Beijei, who had been carefully cleansing his body, caught the tail end of that smile and gave him a glance which, had he not already had full and varied use of her delectable body, Antonio would have described as coquettish.

She began to slow her movements down, taking her time, tickling his chest gently with the cleaning cloth and bringing her naked body closer so that she was straddling him. Her tender flesh leaves kissed the hair-roughened surface of his thighs, opening generously over his skin. Beneath the water, Antonio could feel the heavier moisture of her feminine dew moving slickly against his leg and he felt his cock stir in response.

Tali left the far side of the bath and swam towards them in a graceful breaststroke. All three girls giggled as she put her arms around Beijei from behind and Ailie slid her body sensuously between Antonio's back and the side of the bath.

Antonio could feel her small, soft breasts pressing into him as he leaned gently against her, feeling her warm breath fan his neck as she bent to kiss his shoulder. His body felt weightless, totally relaxed as the three women began to make love to him. All that was required of him was to lie acquiescent in their arms and to enjoy what was being done to him. With a ragged sigh, Antonio closed his eyes and gave himself up to sensation.

From behind the tropical plants growing at the far side of the pool, Chabi reclined on an oyster, silk-covered chaise and watched, unseen, as the women played with the pale Venetian's long, lean body.

He interested her, this one. The others held no particular fascination for her – Marco Polo and his elderly kin were common enough men in their desires. Such men yearned only for plentiful sex, they were rarely open to the kind of experimentation Chabi liked to employ.

This man, though, the one they called Antonio, she sensed that he was different. For a start he was fastidious in his tastes – she had had to choose his attendants with the utmost care. Beijei, Ailie and Tali were each known for their sweet, compliant natures. All natural courtesans, they had all been personally trained by Chabi herself.

Not for Antonio the quick, boisterous gratification with any woman who offered it – this man liked to feel he was the one doing the choosing, the one in control.

Which, of course, was what made him so interesting to Chabi – she fed off other's delusions of control and she would enjoy watching this one give up his. As he would, eventually.

She leaned forward, waving away with an impatient gesture the youth fanning her as she strove to get a better view. The girls were towing the European's body towards the floating platform in the middle of the bath. Good – they were obeying her instructions to the letter. With a smile of satisfaction, Chabi sat back in her seat and held out her hand for a cup of refreshing lemon juice which had been freshly squeezed and sweetened for her that morning.

Her eyes widened appreciatively as Antonio hauled himself up onto the float and his body was revealed to her expert eye. He was tall with a sparse frame, wiry and quite strong. Compared to her countrymen his skin was very pale, a vivid contrast to the blackness of his hair.

Chabi approved of his hair – it was long and thick, curling in unruly hanks across his broad, smooth-skinned shoulders. She imagined that the sparse covering of black hair she could see on his body would be fine, silky to the touch.

It was his cock that interested her most, though. Rising up from the dark nest of pubic hair at his groin, it quivered like an angry baton, the uncircumcised tip bulging from the protective foreskin. His balls looked ripe, fit to burst as the first girl pushed him gently onto his back and lowered her head.

Chabi licked her lips as the girl stretched her mouth over the swollen cock-head. She could see everything from her vantage point, could see how the girl's cheeks bulged and the man's scrotum tightened still more in response to the stimulus.

What fools they were, these travellers who entered the secret city in search of pleasure! Slowly, slowly, over the weeks, Chabi had watched the restlessness of this man ease as he had been drawn ever deeper into the sensual web Chabi had cast for him.

Soon his will would no longer be his own, nothing would matter to him but the continual seeking of sensation, the ultimate gratification of the flesh. Chabi smiled to herself. That would be when she would summon him – when all his normal, everyday desires were slaked and he began to yearn for the deeper, darker pleasures of which she, Chabi, was mistress.

Antonio groaned softly as three accomplished mouths worked at pleasuring his body. His cock, his mouth and his nipples were all being attended to as he lay, spread-eagled, on the float, trailing his fingertips in the warm water.

Beijei drew away from him slightly so that she could watch his face, as if gauging his reaction to the stimulation he was receiving. Smiling slightly, she turned her back to him and straddled his upturned face.

Antonio breathed deeply of her musky, intrinsically female scent as her sex hovered over his face. He could see the darker flesh of her inner labia poking enticingly through the outer lips and he darted out his tongue to taste her. Sweet, heavy honey coated his tongue and he moaned softly, hungry for more. Obligingly, Beijei reached beneath her body and opened herself to him.

He could see the moisture clinging to her sensitive flesh, had a perfect view of the deep, dark chasm of her woman's place. Taking a deep breath, he filled his lungs with the scent of her as she lowered herself with tantalising slowness onto his face.

Antonio's cock leapt in Ailie's mouth at the first touch on Beijei's sex-flesh against his face. Making his tongue rigid, like a miniature penis, he thrust it deep into her body, making her mewl with delight as she wriggled her hips, drawing him further inside her.

Vaguely, he was aware that Tali had slipped her small hands beneath his buttocks and was rubbing oil into his flesh, every now and then letting her fingers run suggestively along his bottom cleft to brush against his anus. Lapping at Beijei's sex, he found the hard nub of her pleasure centre and flicked his tongue back and forth over it almost roughly, extracting a fresh trickle of love juice which ran down his throat.

Tali was, by now, working the slippery oil into the tight little entrance to his anal orifice. Instinctively, Antonio tried to clench his muscles against the unwanted intrusion, but found he could not. As Beijei's vulva began to pulse against his lips and tongue, Antonio felt Tali's slender finger push past the token resistance put up by his anal sphincter, delving into his body right up to the third knuckle.

He came at once, spurting his seed deep into Ailie's greedy throat, on and on until he thought it would never stop. Bright lights seemed to flicker behind his closed eyelids and he was barely aware of Beijei and Ailie slipping quietly into the water and swimming away.

When he opened his eyes, there was only Tali on the float with him. She smiled at him and slowly turned her middle finger which, he was half horrified, half excited to realise, was still buried deep in his forbidden orifice.

Chabi smiled delightedly. So, the Venetian was uncomfortable with the idea of anal sex was he? What a wonderful inhibition for her to play with!

Signalling to the manservant standing attentively at the end of her couch, Chabi parted her perfumed thighs and pointed to her own swollen sex-flesh with one long-nailed finger. Well trained, the servant dropped to his knees and immediately went to work, licking and sucking at her delicate flesh while Chabi watched the scene unfolding on the float in the bath.

Tali had managed to stop Antonio from pulling away,

as was his instinct, and she held him captive purely by the strength of his forbidden desire. Expertly, she found the secret, special place in his passage and began to stimulate it with her finger while with her other hand she stroked his still semi-hard cock.

Antonio groaned, a delicious sound, so eloquent. Chabi hugged his shame, his complete subjugation to her and gripped her manservant's head with her thighs. He immediately stepped up the speed of his ministrations so that she could feel the waves of heat begin to roll over her, making beads of perspiration stand up on her skin.

As she watched, secretly, Tali brought Antonio's cock to full erection again. With a strangled, almost pained cry, he climaxed again, more weakly this time, his semen spurting up in an arc and splashing into the water around the float.

At that moment, Chabi pushed out the pad of flesh which was pulsing between her thighs and ground her hips against the servant's obedient face.

'Ahh!' she whispered, her climax made more poignant by the knowledge of what she had planned for the European who was now lying face down on the float, breathing heavily.

When she had done, Chabi tapped the servant sharply on the shoulder with a small flywhip she always carried with her and he moved away. Adjusting her clothing, she watched as Tali began to kiss and caress the man, as a lover might. Though he groaned in half-hearted protest, he took her into his arms and, after a few minutes, Chabi saw that his shaft was beginning to stiffen once more.

She arched her delicately plucked eyebrows. The man had stamina then – better and better! Losing interest now that the couple before her were enjoying each other's bodies in the conventional manner, she sipped her lemon drink and toyed with the shaven pubis of the slave girl sitting quietly at her feet.

The girl was dry, so Chabi picked up a grape and crushed it against the delicate flesh of the girl's labia. Her fingers, slippery now with the sticky juice of the grape, moved lazily over the open sex-flesh, casually bringing the girl to a reluctant orgasm.

Soon after, she heard Antonio give a long, shuddering moan and saw that he had climaxed for the third time in an hour. At that moment, the door to the baths opened and a second entourage entered the pool which was cut off from the area where Antonio lay with Tali by an artfully cultivated plant screen.

Chabi smiled when she saw that it was the new girl who had been brought from the Western provinces. Shifting her position, she arranged herself so that she could comfortably watch, preparing herself for another diversion.

Cirina heard the unmistakable groan from behind the screen as she entered the bathing place and felt hot colour suffuse her cheeks. The two serving girls accompanying her giggled behind their hands, indicating by gesture and example that Cirina should follow them into the water.

Reluctantly, Cirina shrugged off the luxurious silk wrap she had been given, and stepped into the water gingerly. It was warm, perfumed with jasmine and she began to relax a little.

When she had been escorted through the palace to the women's quarters, she had been told to strip before being subjected to a humiliating examination by an old hag who poked and prodded her all over. The toothless harridan had looked in her ears and tugged at her teeth before scrabbling roughly through her long hair in search of lice. She had almost seemed disappointed not to find any, nor did she find anything untoward in the hair which grew on Cirina's mons.

She lifted each of Cirina's breasts in turn and squeezed

as if she were testing the ripeness of fruit in the market. Then she had indicated by gestures and grunts that Cirina should lie down on a fur-covered stone slab and spread her legs wide. No one had listened to her objections when her woman's place and her anus were penetrated by the woman's fingers, but afterwards, when, presumably, she had been pronounced fit and clean, these two doe-eyed beauties, so alike that they had to be twins, had come to attend to her. Since then she had been treated with nothing but gentleness and courtesy.

Now she immersed herself willingly in the warm, perfumed water, letting it enclose her in its silky embrace. Yet still she could not quite rid herself of the feeling that she was being watched by unseen eyes and she ran her gaze searchingly around the pool. Though she could see nothing, the feeling persisted, tantalising her. With a sigh, she decided there was nothing she could do about it, so she gave herself over to the attendants' care.

Chabi nodded in satisfaction as the new girl's naked body was revealed. Lovely indeed – the soldiers had chosen well. She made a note to reward them. Settling herself more comfortably, lying full length on her stomach, she sipped at her freshly re-filled cup and watched.

Cirina was being bathed by her attendants, a novel experience for her. Back home at the caravanserai she had been obliged to clean herself by sluicing her naked body with cold water; she had never experienced the luxury of a bath before.

As soon as she had relaxed, the two young women came to stand either side of her in the perfumed water. Cirina opened her eyes and smiled uncertainly at them. The girls' twin expressions reassured her slightly, but there was a mischievous glint in their eyes which Cirina did not quite trust.

She felt two pairs of arms, soft and slippery with the water, but surprisingly strong, slip beneath her. They raised her up gently so that her toes broke the surface and she realised that she was floating. Once she had become used to this, one of the girls moved away and fetched a large pad of silk which she soaked in the water.

Cirina gasped at the first touch of the wet silk against her flesh. It slid along her arm like a warm, living thing, barely touching the skin, yet making the whole area vibrate with awareness. The shock was soon chased away by delight as the girl polished her skin with the silk pad, stroking rhythmically along the sides of her body.

She tensed momentarily as the girl began to circle her breasts, aware that her nipples, responsive as always, had puckered into two prominent, berry-red cones which crested the water. Embarrassment was quickly replaced by pleasure, though, as the silk pad was moved further down her body, to her legs.

Barely aware that she was doing it, Cirina leaned her head against the soft, strong arm of the girl who was supporting her in the water. She could smell the gentle scent of the other girl's skin, could feel the steady beat of her pulse as it travelled along her arm. She wanted to turn her head and taste the smooth, brown skin, but something held her back, some deeply buried memory of taboo and she frowned slightly.

She had not recognised at first that the pleasure she was experiencing whilst being bathed by the two girls was of a sexual nature. Now though, she was intrigued and not a little embarrassed to realise that her limbs had grown languid and there was a heavy, secret moisture gathering between her thighs, which had nothing to do with the perfumed water.

The girl soaping her smiled knowingly as she caught

Cirina's eye. Holding her gaze, she brought the silken pad, heavy now that it had absorbed so much water, closer and closer to the centre of her desire. The other girl shifted her position slightly so that she was now standing behind Cirina, supporting her shoulders so that her head did not go under the water. Her head was resting on the other girls large, cushiony breasts and Cirina felt an overwhelming contentment as she lay back against her.

The water made her body feel buoyant, her legs floated on the surface, shimmering with the oily perfume which scented the bath. As if in a trance, she allowed her legs to part as the girl rubbed gently at her inner thighs.

Cirina sighed as the soft cloth brushed, as if by accident, against the soft folds of flesh between her thighs. She knew that the lips of her sex were swollen, puffed with pleasure, their need unmistakable to the searching gaze of the pretty girl who stood between her splayed legs. She teased her for a few moments more, then slowly, excruciatingly slowly, she passed the silk pad across Cirina's exposed woman's place, back and forth in small, butterfly-light motions which made Cirina moan softly.

She felt warm, cocooned in the fragrant water and cradled by the voluptuous girl who supported her. Above her, exotic birds flew across the huge, domed ceiling and a profusion of bright, beautiful flowers leaked their heady scent into the air. Cirina barely knew where reality began and ended, at that moment all she wanted was to gain satisfaction.

Lifting her hips slightly she signalled her need to the girl. She answered the unspoken plea almost immediately, splaying her free hand beneath Cirina's buttocks and lifting her hips higher, above the water line. Although the air was warm, Cirina shivered as it kissed her wet skin.

Unravelling the silk pad, the girl dangled the length

of fabric above them so that just the end danced across Cirina's exposed flesh. Tickling and teasing, it drove her to distraction, its kiss too light to satisfy her, yet too stimulating to ignore.

After a few moments' sport, the girl took pity on her and spread one end of the wet silk across Cirina's gently rounded belly. It felt cool and heavy against her skin, and she shivered again. Catching her eye, the girl smiled before slowly pulling the end of the silk down into the water, between Cirina's legs.

The wet silk rasped deliciously against the sensitive sex-flesh, sending little prickles of delight up and down her spine. The second girl reached over her shoulder with one hand and caressed a breast, rolling the nipple between her finger and thumb, drawing it out.

Meanwhile the silk was drawn back up, between her legs, then down again, back and forth, back and forth, creating a gentle friction which made her breath come in short, sharp bursts as the sensations began to build.

The girl said something to her in a language she did not understand and she shook her head, distracted. Suddenly, the girl touched her through the wet silk, tracing the outline of her labia and the tiny, responsive bead of flesh which began to pulse between her fingertips.

'Oh!' Cirina gasped involuntarily. 'Oh yes! Please, please . . .'

Her hips bucked as the girl applied more pressure and her orgasm burst from her. She opened her mouth to cry out, only to find her cry captured in the soft mouth of the girl who was supporting her. There was no time to think, to analyse, Cirina merely rode the waves of sensation, kissing the sweet, feminine mouth avidly as she scissored her legs against the all consuming pulsings in her woman's place.

Soft arms came about her waist and lowered her gently so that she was standing in the water, and she clung to the two women, half suspended between them, almost sobbing with emotion.

Chabi smiled with delight. Ah, what fun she would have with her new sex toys! Antonio and this girl – Kublai would be enchanted. Chabi never missed an opportunity to curry the Emperor's favour, and she had made a career out of knowing what pleased him most, which is why she had lasted far longer as favourite than any of his other wives.

Stifling a laugh, she stood up and stretched. With one of the mercurial changes of mood for which she was famous, she grew tired of her voyeurism.

The young woman was being lifted from the water now and the girls were swaddling her in thick, warm towels. They would take her to the place of preparation and dress her in readiness for her presentation to the Khan at the entertainments that evening.

Chabi yawned. She herself would need to rest if she was to be at her best for the evening. She was hungry and eager to find a strong young man to service her before she rested.

Earlier, a travel weary young soldier had caught her eye and she had had him taken to her quarters. She had left strict instructions that he was to be fed and given water, but that he was not allowed to clean himself, or change from his dusty uniform.

Something stirred between Chabi's legs as she thought of the young, virile, sweat-streaked body waiting for her and her step quickened.

Meanwhile, Cirina was allowed to rest for a while after her bath. Lying on her silk-covered sleeping pallet, she gazed up at the plain ceiling and thought about the caravanserai. Was there anyone there who would be missing her? Her uncle, perhaps, but she could not imagine Bortai or Keta mourning her departure. They thought they knew so much about the pleasures of the flesh – what would they think of her now?

Cirina's mind slid towards what had happened at the bathing place. Never had she dreamed that women might find pleasure in each other's bodies. It opened up so many exciting possibilities, possibilities she felt sure had never even occurred to her aunt and cousin.

The idea made Cirina feel a little superior for once, after years of feeling that she was the only one who knew nothing. She felt a little shiver of anticipation as she thought of the night ahead. The girls had explained to her, by means of gesticulation and mime, that she was to be presented to the Emperor and his wife. What interest could a simple country girl like her hold for such sophisticated people?

So many unanswerable questions whirled and eddied in her head that they made it ache. Closing her eyes, Cirina resolutely made herself think of nothing. She had a feeling she would need her wits about her this evening, and to that end, she willed herself to allow sleep to claim her.

The sun was dropping behind the mountains when the girls came to wake her. Disorientated, Cirina thought at first that she was back at the caravanserai and she frowned. Then her attendants giggled behind their hands and beckoned her forward and she smiled and followed them.

She was bathed again, in a more practical metal tub this time, then she was urged to lie, still naked, face down on a fur-covered couch. The fur tickled her breasts and belly, curling up between her tightly closed thighs to tantalise her sleeping woman's place. Cirina turned her head and rested her cheek against the soft pelt, waiting to see what would happen next.

She could hear the girls chattering softly behind her, but she had long since stopped trying to work out what they were saying. Their voices were light and musical, pleasing to the ear, and Cirina let their chatter wash over her like a soothing breeze on her heated skin.

Small, soft hands began to move against the backs of her calves, one pair to each leg. The heady, heavy scent of musk filled the air as a warm, rich oil was massaged carefully into her skin.

Cirina had never had a massage before – there was no time for such vanities at the caravanserai. At first she held herself stiff, unsure of what was expected of her, but gradually as the girls worked their way slowly up the backs of her legs, she began to relax and enjoy it.

Her face reddened a little as they worked on her buttocks, opening and closing the cleft between them as if taking a frequent, illicit peek at the puckered entrance to her body which was hidden there. To her surprise, she felt her woman's place moisten and swell and she shifted slightly on the couch so that the warm fur rubbed against her sensitive flesh.

The girls worked in tandem, kneading and smoothing her skin as they worked up her back to her shoulders and down her arms. Each finger was manipulated in turn before they ran cool, clever fingers up, under her hair to massage her neck and scalp.

At first Cirina was reluctant to turn over. They had seen her naked before, of course, but then she had had the illusory cover of the water to spare her blushes. Somehow, to display herself totally naked before them made her feel odd.

The girls giggled before rolling her effortlessly between them and positioning her just as they wanted her. Cirina's skin burned as she felt their eyes rove her body approvingly, remembering the feel of their hands on her skin at the bathing place.

Again, they started at her feet, rubbing the oil carefully round her toenails and between her toes before beginning to move up her legs. As they reached mid-thigh,

Cirina's legs parted slightly of their own volition. How she longed for the touch of those skilful, oily fingers *there* . . .

One of the girls smiled at her and shook her head. They began to talk to each other in their strange, sing-song tongue and Cirina understood that their instructions tonight did not include giving her pleasure. Biting back her disappointment, she closed her eyes and concentrated on enjoying the touch of their hands at her waist and belly, their strokes long and voluptuous as they lingered over her breasts before finally sweeping up her neck.

Cirina felt as if she could not move, such a delicious languor had invaded her limbs. She groaned good-naturedly as she was urged to move across the room to a chair. It was designed to allow her to lean her head back into a bowl full of warm water with flower petals floating on the surface.

While one girl began to wash her hair in the floral-scented water, the other shaped her nails into neat little ovals. When she was finished, she began to paint them with a shiny, pale pink liquid, first her fingernails, then her toes.

Cirina submitted stoically to the long process of combing out her hair, watching as several bolts of the finest silk she had ever seen were brought and laid before her. There was crimson, brighter than any she had ever imagined, purple and the palest green. Sugary pink lay alongside the boldest yellow which dazzled her and made her smile. Understanding that it was for her to choose which should be used for her costume, finally, she chose a deep lilac, shot through with gold and silver thread which made it shimmer in the candlelight.

Once her hair was free from tangles, it was plaited and primped and threaded with gold beads and tiny, sweet smelling violets. As she sat patiently for her hair to be dressed, Cirina mused how strange it was to be sitting naked in an Emperor's palace, waiting to be dressed for his pleasure. What would Antonio think of her now?

The thought had come from nowhere, as if from a mischievous spirit whispering in her ear. Cirina frowned, aware of a dart of pain which reminded her of her loneliness since he had left. Strange how since her arrival at this strange place she had not spared him a thought. He whom she had thought never to forget, who until now had filled her mind through every waking hour.

She looked up in surprise as one of the girls touched her fingertips lightly against Cirina's puckered brow. Catching her eye, the girl shook her head and Cirina smiled. Clearly, it was not acceptable for her to entertain anything other than pleasant thoughts, or at least to keep all others from view. Obligingly, she smiled and forced her face into its usual serene lines and the girl smiled her approval.

At last her hair was ready and Cirina was urged to stand. A brush made of eagle feathers was brought and dipped into a tub of golden powder. Quickly, with brisk, workmanlike strokes, Cirina was covered from head to toe in a fine film of golden powder.

The fabric she had chosen was brought and unrolled. To her dismay, she realised that she was not to be given an undershift, that the beautiful, lavender-blue material was merely to be draped around her body, fastened in strategic places by wooden pins.

It was diaphanous, light as the morning mist across the desert and Cirina gasped as it whispered against her skin. As the two girls passed the fabric across each shoulder and over each breast in turn, it soon became apparent that the material was designed to enhance rather than conceal her body. Cirina could see the golden glow of her skin through the fabric and she realised that, when she walked through the palace to be presented to the Khan, she would be as good as naked.

At last, the girls stood back and regarded their work

critically. They conferred for a few moments, then one ran to fetch a pair of golden slippers with high, exquisitely carved heels. Cirina, who had never had occasion to wear anything other than her rope sandals, gasped in disbelief.

'I could not walk in such shoes!' she protested.

Ignoring her, the girls urged her to lift first one foot, then the other and she found herself towering over them, teetering on the unfamiliar high heels.

It was obvious that her attendants were pleased with their handiwork for their bright faces were wreathed in smiles. Cirina smiled with them, happy that they were happy, but becoming more apprehensive by the minute. The weight of the gold beads pulled at her hair and her calf muscles protested at the extra strain imposed by the impossibly high-heeled shoes.

One of the girls stepped forward and kissed her lightly on the cheek.

'Beau-ti-ful,' she pronounced carefully, and Cirina smiled, her eyebrows winging upwards in surprise.

There was a knock on the door, breaking into the intimacy surrounding the three women and one of the girls ran on silent feet to open it. Cirina heard deep, male voices and the second girl took her hand and urged her forward.

She moved uncertainly in the new shoes, quickly learning to adapt her stride to stop herself from toppling over. The effect, she was sure, was to make her steps tiny, mincing, making her hips roll beneath the diaphanous fabric.

Her eyes widened as she reached the door and recognised Mongor leading the small contingent of palace guards who had come to escort her. He gave no sign of recognition, though, merely waiting for her to take her place in the centre of the diamond formed by himself and the other three soldiers. Cirina could feel his eyes on her though as she began to walk, his gaze following the movement of her buttocks, and her skin burned with an emotion she could not quite identify.

They walked through endless corridors, each more elaborately furnished than the last. Finally, they turned into one whose walls were lined with golden silk and Cirina guessed that they were nearing the great hall where the Khan was holding court.

As they neared the great doors at the end, her step faltered. She could hear voices, familiar, European voices approaching along a corridor which would soon converge with this. Marco Polo emerged first, in boisterous high spirits as always, unafraid and jovial. He paused and bowed slightly as Cirina's procession passed and she craned her neck to see his companions.

Pale blue eyes clashed with hers and she recognised that the leap of shock which passed across them matched that in her own.

'Antonio?'

Her lips formed the word, but some instinct greater than her confusion and joy made her stay silent. Conscious of Mongor's curious eyes on her, she turned her head and, hardly breaking her stride, continued on to the great hall.

Chapter Five

Antonio's mind was racing as he followed Marco into the great hall. How in the name of God could it be that Cirina was here? Then his sluggish brain recollected the state of her costume and the escort assigned to her and he felt the bile rise in his stomach. There was only one reason why a woman should be so arrayed in Kublai Khan's pleasure palace.

Helplessly, he watched as the press of palace courtiers parted to make way for the small procession. A hush fell over the room as Cirina was revealed by the soldiers' withdrawal. Antonio was not surprised by the reaction; she looked even more beautiful than he remembered her. Even in the plain, rough clothes she had worn at her uncle's caravanserai, Cirina had shown a remarkable beauty. Dressed in the exquisite silk available at Kublai's pleasure palace, with her skin brushed with gold, she looked regal, almost other-worldly, like a pagan goddess.

Antonio closed his eyes and recalled how her long black hair, falling in a straight, unadorned curtain, had caressed his naked skin. He shivered. The way it had been dressed here, with its clever combination of precious beads and fresh flowers was inspired. It spoke of sensuality, coupled, conversely, with innocence – they had captured the very essence of Cirina in the way that they had chosen to dress her.

For the first time, Antonio became aware of Kublai Khan sitting on the great, jewelled throne, and the lady, Chabi, standing at his side as always. The old man was leaning forward, rearranging his enormous girth across his lap as his bright, beady, black eyes sought to focus on the vision of loveliness approaching the dais. As Cirina stopped at the foot of the steps, Antonio saw that she had inadvertently stepped into a pool of light cast by the thousands of flickering candles lighting up the room. He sucked in his breath as her nakedness was glimpsed beneath the semi-transparent fabric of her gown, every line and sinew of her lovely body clearly defined.

Everyone else seemed to realise this at the same moment, for there was a communal intake of breath and the room fell silent. Antonio watched Cirina raise her head and square her shoulders slightly, and his heart went out to her. His lovely Cirina. How could she bear it?

Cirina raised her eyes boldly to meet those of the Khan and schooled her features not to betray the dismay she felt at her first sight of him. She had not expected him to be so . . . so old! And he was big, so very big with rolls of flesh beneath his chin which reminded her of the solid fat of the sheep's tails which they cooked and ate on special occasions at home.

He was looking at her, his eyes tiny in the folds of flesh covering his face and she shivered as the bright gaze touched her skin. So this was to be her master; she was to be a slave to this man's desires?

Cirina's eyes skittered sideways and encountered the cold, emerald gaze of the woman at the Khan's side. She was tall and slender, and her black hair piled high on top of her head in elaborate coils which appeared to defy gravity. She had a sweet, heart-shaped face which somehow managed to contradict its own hint of sweetness with a hard edge and a firm, out-thrust jaw.

Cirina felt a jolt of something like recognition as the woman's gaze bore into her. Yet that was impossible – she was quite sure she had never set eyes on her before. As if acknowledging Cirina's confusion, the woman's red-stained, bow-shaped lips curved slightly into a small smile. Cirina recognised the cruelty of the smile and shivered.

'So – you are the jewel found in the desert!'

Cirina's attention snapped back to the Emperor as she heard his voice wheeze into life and she lowered her eyes quickly, hiding her revulsion.

'Come – come closer.'

He waved a pudgy hand at her and Cirina began to walk hesitantly up the steps. Conscious of all eyes on her, aware that Antonio was somewhere in the throng, she teetered precariously in the golden slippers. When she reached the throne, she stood uncertainly, hands folded at her waist, eyes downcast, aware that both the Khan and the beautiful lady were watching her closely.

She leaned forward as the Khan signalled that she should do so, gasping as he pulled the fabric away from one breast. The action was all the more shocking because it was unexpected. His hot, fleshy fingers pinched at the soft nipple and the wanton nub instantly betrayed her, hardening beneath his unwanted touch. Cirina felt the heat rise in her cheeks and kept her eyes downcast to conceal her shame.

From the corner of her eye, she saw the woman lean over the throne and whisper something in the Emperor's ear. Kublai Khan laughed, a swift, bark of laughter which quickly turned into a cough. He nodded his head, his eyes watering. As he nodded, his several chins wobbled until Cirina felt his head would disappear into his neck.

'Good.' He clicked his fingers and Mongor stepped forward. 'Into the alcove for now.'

Mongor touched her arm and Cirina realised that the Khan had lost interest in her. Covering her breast, she followed Mongor down the steps and across the room to a wall which, she saw with a trickle of unease, had a recess carved in the centre. Glancing questioningly at Mongor, Cirina took his outstretched hand and climbed up, onto the wooden platform fitted into the recess.

'What is this, Mongor?' she whispered as he stepped up beside her.

With his back to the rest of the courtiers, who had resumed a hubbub of conversation around them, the big Tartar pressed his forefinger to his lips.

'All you have to do is stand very, very still,' he whispered as he reached around her body.

Cirina's eyes widened in horror as she realised he was fastening a leather strap around each wrist.

'Do not be alarmed – the straps are not meant to be a restraint – see?' He pulled the fastening open with a flick of his wrist to demonstrate how easy it would be for her to release herself should she so desire. 'The straps will support you when you grow tired. No one will harm you.'

Comforted a little by his words, Cirina stood meekly while he similarly anchored her ankles to the wall.

'Does that mean I am free to step down if I want to?' she asked, her voice small.

Mongor regarded her quizzically, his head tipped slightly to one side.

'*Do* you want to?' he asked her.

Cirina considered for a moment what would happen if she stepped down from the alcove and walked from the room, unchallenged. She would be alone in a strange city with no means of returning to her home. And she would never know what was in store for her here.

Remembering her delight in discovering how another woman could pleasure her, Cirina smiled. Instinctively, she knew that there was much, much more for her to discover. What other delights might she find here at the Khan's pleasure palace? If she left now she would never know.

'No,' she whispered and Mongor's eyebrows rose.

Standing down from the platform, he bowed briefly to her, then marched smartly away.

Cirina regarded the room from her vantage point and wondered what on earth would happen next. Several people came to admire her, commenting in various languages on her hair and her skin, but none touched her, and none spoke directly to her. It was as if she was no more real than a work of art displayed for their pleasure and her cheeks burned with the humiliation of being treated as less than human.

Gradually, though, as fewer curious eyes appraised her and she was left to herself, Cirina grew more used to her bonds and she began to relax a little. Looking round the room, she admired the play of candlelight against the luxurious fabrics covering the cold stone of the walls. Jewel-rich colours – sapphire, emerald and ruby – gave the large, square room the aura of a boudoir. The heavy smell of burning incense added to the atmosphere which was already thick with an undeniable sensuality.

In one corner a harpist played a continuous, muted refrain providing a background for the low murmur of voices, punctured periodically by a peal of laughter or a shout of merriment. The mead and the vodka flowed seemingly without end, a plethora of slaves provided for the sole purpose of scurrying here and there to fill every upheld cup.

Nowhere could she see Antonio, though her eyes strained to catch a glimpse of him. At the moment she had seen him in the corridor, Cirina felt as though time stood still. A thousand questions had raced through her mind, never to be uttered as she was hurried through for her audience with the Khan.

That episode had distracted her for a short time, for she had been the cynosure of all eyes and had been nervous of the outcome of the audience. Now though, bound and left in the recess, Cirina's thoughts returned to Antonio and she speculated on the reason for his presence. What business could have brought him here to the pleasure dome at Shang-tu? Had he planned to return for her when he left this place?

Cirina hoped with all her heart that this was the case, but she had seen the flare of shock in his pale, blue eyes which signalled his discomfort at finding her again, and she knew, deep down, that Lengke had been right – Antonio's promises had been false.

She blinked hard as she felt tears of self-pity well in her eyes and tried to make her mind go blank. Her calves were protesting ever more painfully at the high heels and her back and neck began to ache with the strain of keeping herself upright. By concentrating on each little part of her body, one by one, she forced herself to relax, to let go of her taut muscles and to lean against the silk lining of the wall.

After a few moments, she sensed someone was watching her. Turning her head, she saw that the lady who had been standing by the Khan's chair was walking towards her, flanked on either side by dark-skinned men bigger than any men Cirina had ever seen before. Both had bald, shiny heads and massive shoulders, shown off by decorative gold thread wound around the upper part of the body, which was otherwise naked. Cirina's eyes widened as she took in the scimitar held at the belt of one which bounced against his tautly muscled thigh, reflecting from the pale blue silk of his breeches.

The lady looked tiny as she walked between them, yet

there was something about her, a certain vibrancy, which drew all eyes to her. Cirina's heart began to race and she felt a thin film of sweat push through her pores. She was frightened of this woman, and she could not understand why.

As the small group reached her, the woman smiled at her slightly, showing small, pearly-white teeth. One of the men dropped to his hands and knees and the other took the lady's hand. Cirina watched uneasily as she stepped up onto the first man's broad back. Her spiked heels pressed into his smooth, black skin, making two small, vicious looking dents.

Now she was level with Cirina and Cirina could smell the rich, musky scent of her perfume. It seemed to curl around her senses, making her feel dizzy.

'Here, little one – I have brought you something to drink.'

The woman's voice was musical, quite high and sweet. For the first time Cirina noticed the bowl cupped in her hands and she regarded the clear liquid inside suspiciously.

'Who – who are you?' she ventured timidly.

The woman smiled, a small, hard smile which did not quite reach her eyes.

'I am the lady Chabi. You and I will get to know each other very well, I think. Drink.'

Cirina touched her lips to the bowl reluctantly. The liquid was very sweet, and thick like runny honey. Chabi held the bowl up until Cirina had finished every drop. She smiled.

'Good girl.'

To Cirina's surprise, the woman leaned forward and pressed her soft, red-stained lips against the corner of Cirina's mouth. Too shocked to react, she held herself rigid as Chabi drew her tongue gently along the join of her lips, coaxing them apart.

Some part of Cirina's mind registered that the sensation of the other woman's lips on hers was pleasant, far more pleasant than she had ever dreamed was possible. She closed her eyes, allowing her head to fall back slightly as Chabi deepened the kiss, probing more urgently with her tongue, demanding access to her mouth.

Cirina's lips parted on a small sigh of surrender which quickly turned into a frightened yelp of pain as Chabi bit hard on the soft, sensitive flesh of her inner lip.

She could taste blood welling on her lip and she probed it tentatively with her own tongue, wincing. Her eyes flew open and she encountered the amused, hard green gaze of the other woman. At once she understood the fear she had felt when she had first encountered the woman. Chabi had the power to hurt her.

She was smiling now, trailing her long, red-painted fingernails down the side of Cirina's face.

'We will encounter each other again soon, little one,' she purred throatily.

Cirina was unable to respond, merely watching as the lady Chabi was lowered slowly to the ground. She did not understand what had just happened between them, but she was left with the feeling that it was Chabi, not the Khan, who would be her master.

Antonio gazed at Cirina from across the room and took a deep draught of his drink. He had seen the emerald-eyed woman approach her and had wondered at the exchange, but his view of Cirina had been obscured by the woman's body.

Now, displayed artfully against the deep blue silk of the alcove, she looked almost other-worldly, ephemeral in the dim light. The shadows danced across the tender oval of her face, flickering on her skin.

For an instant he was reminded of a statue in St Paul's in Venice of the Madonna; the serenity of her expression both shocked and awed him. Shaking his head to clear it of such blasphemy, he finished his drink and signalled for another to be brought.

Ah, but finding her here had shaken him! When the Khan had touched her breast, he had automatically reached for the hilt of his dagger. Marco had stayed his hand, throwing him a warning glance.

'Do not be a fool!' he had whispered fiercely, and Antonio's eyes had dropped away, hiding the impotent fury which he knew was shining in their depths.

Even now, Antonio was aware of Marco flashing him the occasional, concerned glance from over the head of the woman with whom he was talking. Antonio cursed himself silently. How imprudent his action had been. Had Marco not stopped him he would have allowed emotion to override good sense and in his efforts to reach Cirina would have put both her and himself in mortal peril.

His eyes slid back towards her now and he realised with a jolt that she was looking in his direction. Could she see him across this sea of people? What was she thinking, standing there still as a saint? Would she be wondering why he was here?

Of course she would! he told himself impatiently. Of all the places for them to meet again, this had to be the most unlikely.

Caution had kept him in the shadows thus far – to reveal their prior knowledge of each other might be dangerous to both Cirina's situation and his own. Far better to watch and wait and hope that eventually there would be an opportunity for them to talk.

He must go to her, say *something* to reassure her. He took a step towards her, but was brought to a halt by the sound of a large gong being struck.

Turning towards the Khan's dais, Antonio saw the old man struggling to his feet, helped by an attendant on either side. Antonio swiftly hid the disgusted curl of his lip as he contemplated the once great man, reduced to a mass of oily blubber.

All fell silent as he held up his hands. Hard to remember now that those fat little hands were once so feared, so soaked in blood.

'The entertainment will begin!'

As the people surged to form a circle around the centre of the floor, Antonio gave up all hope of approaching Cirina unnoticed. He watched, seething with frustration as a wooden dais was carried in by half a dozen soldiers and placed in the centre of the floor. Four Chinese handmaidens ran to lay pelts of fur across the hard wood of the makeshift stage before disappearing, giggling, the way they had come.

An expectant hush had descended on the company. Unobtrusively, servants went around the room dousing the candles in their iron sconces, leaving only those around Cirina's alcove still burning. Even from this distance, Antonio could sense her apprehension, could imagine the taut lines of her body as she wondered what was about to happen.

Four torches were lit and fastened to the square, fur-covered dais, drawing all eyes to it. A roll of drums heralded the arrival of the 'entertainment'. Antonio's eyes widened as he saw a young man, bound by the wrists, led through the door by means of a leather collar and rope.

His initial reaction was relief – for a moment he had thought that Cirina was to have some part in this barbaric public ritual. His second reaction was to be reluctantly intrigued by what was taking place before him.

The captive was tall, towering over the mainly Mongol and Chinese audience, though his hair and skin were as dark, his features as Slavic, as most. Antonio guessed him to be from the lands to the North of the mountains and he wondered how he came to be here.

There was a proud tilt to the man's well-shaped head which belied his inherently subservient position. He seemed not to notice the avid stares of the crowd as he walked towards the dais, his dark eyes fixed at a point directly ahead of him, his expression vaguely beatific.

As he mounted the steps of the dais behind his captor, Antonio saw that the man was naked. His skin glowed bronze in the torch-light, oiled, no doubt, specifically for this spectacle. Without realising what he was doing, Antonio shifted his position slightly so that he had a clearer view of the captive.

He was a fine looking young man with glossy black hair which flowed across his broad shoulders and onto his glistening chest. His body hair had been depilated leaving his obvious strength with an edge of vulnerability which made him strangely appealing.

Antonio's eyes moved downwards, widening with shock and a brief, unwanted flare of excitement as he saw the cock-harness fastened at his waist. It was made of thin strips of black leather, criss-crossed over the tumescent white flesh, binding it so that it lay against his finely ridged belly, a mere symbol of potency, doomed to be unfulfilled.

As Antonio watched, the young man sank to his knees and bowed his head in supplication to the Khan. The man with him towered over his prostrated figure, drawing Antonio's eye.

Naked save for a pair of dark-coloured, hide breeches, the man's face was hidden behind a black leather mask. Even from where he was watching, Antonio could see the glitter of his eyes through the slits which served as eye holes and he shivered. There seemed to be something sinister about those overbright eyes.

More sinister still was the belt he wore around his waist. For hanging from it was a selection of instruments the like of which Antonio had never seen before, except perhaps in a stable. He recognised a flywhip, but he could only guess at the usage of the other items. One thick-handled instrument had some half-dozen thin pieces of rope hanging from it, each with a cruel knot tied in the end.

At first, Antonio thought that this was to be a public punishment, but as the man rose up onto his hands and knees, an unfamiliar *frisson* alerted him to his mistake. The expression on the man's face was not what one would expect of a man who was about to be whipped for some horrendous misdemeanour. Rather, he looked almost eager, his eyes alight with anticipation as he raised his head to look at the masked man.

Antonio felt an uncomfortable constriction in his chest as the atmosphere in the room became thick with tension. To his horror, he realised that his own cock had stiffened in response to the man's helplessness. Or was it in response to the dominant pose struck by the masked whip master?

At once he was assailed by the unwanted fantasy that it was *he* who was kneeling, waiting for this public scourging, that they were *his* bare buttocks upraised in indecent hope, *his* erection constrained by the tight leather bondage. By the saints, he must be possessed of a madness to be aroused by such a scene!

He wanted to turn away, to run from the room before it began, but his feet seemed rooted to the spot, his eyes fastened to the scene which was unfolding before him. The whip master had walked around the waiting man several times before selecting a thin, whippy cane from the collection at his waist.

Everyone in the room seemed to hold their breath as the masked man raised his arm. The supplicant tensed every sinew, every muscle as he waited for the cane to descend and Antonio felt himself waiting with bated breath. The room was so quiet the sound of the cane whistling through the air seemed to vibrate in the stillness. It cracked across the upturned buttocks to a communal intake of breath.

The man's head reared up, his face contorted with the effort of remaining silent, then, incredibly, he smiled. Antonio witnessed the wordless communication between the man and his tormentor, and a thrill ran through his veins.

Again, the masked man raised the cane and it whistled through the air before making contact with the other man's rapidly reddening buttocks. A low murmur of appreciation rippled through the enthralled crowd as the third stroke landed.

Antonio could not drag his eyes away. Half of him was repulsed, the other powerfully aroused by what he was witnessing. He knew that some men enjoyed other men as well as women, of course, but he had never counted himself amongst their number. Yet he could not deny the heaviness now at his groin.

It seemed that the caning was now over, for the masked man was making a great show of scooping a handful of a jelly-like substance from a stone bowl held up by one of the handmaidens. He spread the thick lubricant over the man's flaming buttocks, massaging it into the skin and dragging his arse-cheeks apart.

By all that was holy, surely he wasn't going to use the man as he would a woman? Antonio was aware that he was sweating as he watched the whip master working the jelly deep into the other man's shadowed anus. He positioned him, knees apart, rear end high, before standing and relieving himself of his leather breeches. He preened as the audience gasped at the first sight of his engorged penis. It was huge, bouncing against his hairy belly as he moved from side to side, showing it off.

Walking round to the front of the man waiting before him, he nudged at his cheek with his enormous member. Immediately, the man's mouth stretched wide and he enclosed it. Antonio imagined taking that distended appendage into his own mouth and drawing on it . . . his breath quickened.

After a few moments, the whip master pulled out and went round to the back of the man. He barked what sounded like an order and the man reached behind himself and pulled his arse-cheeks apart with both hands.

Antonio had a clear view of the darker flesh of the man's crease and the puckered, secret place, stretched wide now and glistening with the lubricating jelly. How must he feel, waiting for the violation of his body by such unnatural means? Antonio tried to dredge up some vestige of disgust, of denial, but could find only envy in his heart. May the saints help him, but he wanted more than anything to be in that man's place!

He watched, mesmerised, as the big cock head nudged at the opening, feeling his own anal sphincter burn in sympathy. The man let out a long, low moan as the whip master's cock eased its way inside him and the crowd murmured approvingly.

Once he was inserted to his satisfaction, the masked man reached round to release the other man's cock from its uncomfortable restraint. It sprang free, long and slender and very hard, juddering a little as the whip master's hips pumped against him.

Antonio's hand slipped discreetly across the front of his breeches so that he could re-adjust his own erection, which was quite painfully constricted. He imagined how liberating it would be to allow it to hang there while another man used his back passage.

At that moment, the man let out a cry, a mixture of joy and anguish, as his seed was spilt across the fur-covered dais. Spurt after spurt pumped from him before Antonio's incredulous gaze, and he felt that he too was near to climaxing. It was then that the small hairs on the back of his neck began to prickle and he became aware that someone was watching, not the 'entertainment', but him watching it.

At first he thought it must be Cirina and his eyes crept guiltily towards her, aware that for the past few minutes he had not spared her so much as a thought. Gradually, though, he realised that it was not Cirina whose eyes were boring into him like two spikes of ice.

Slowly, he turned his head. It was a mistake, for his gaze immediately clashed with the lady, Chabi's. She smiled slightly at him, her bright green eyes knowing. In that instant he felt that she had read his mind, that she knew every shameful thought running through it.

Antonio struggled to hold onto his calm demeanour and he inclined his head slightly in acknowledgement. Chabi continued to stare at him, as if wanting him to know that she could divine his every thought. Antonio shivered, sure, without really knowing why, that it would be dangerous to let this woman know his innermost desires.

Too late! he scoffed at himself, unable to look away. Already he felt, ridiculously, he knew, that this woman held some kind of power over him and he resolved to be doubly careful to not allow his emotions to get out of hand.

When, at last, Chabi broke eye contact, Antonio breathed out, unaware, until then, that he had been holding his breath. He trained his eyes on anything then, trying his utmost to avoid both the dais where the 'entertainment' was now being concluded, and Chabi's gimlet eye.

His eyes fell on the jewelled throne and at once all the conflicting emotions of the past hour fled from his mind. For there, set in the centre of the throne's back, lay the Byzantine ruby itself.

Chapter Six

Cirina woke the next morning to the sound of bird-song. Stretching languidly, she wound the silk sheet around her naked body and went to the open window. A pair of small birds with vivid blue colouring, quite unlike any she had ever seen before, were hopping from bough to bough of the tree growing beneath the window. Their bright yellow beaks were opened wide and the most glorious song vibrated from their tiny throats.

Cirina smiled, her heart lifting at the sound. When she had finally been released from the alcove after hours of display the night before, she had felt exhausted and dispirited. Witnessing the ritual sexual humiliation of the man had troubled her, though she could not deny that she had also been intrigued to learn of this new facet of human sexuality. He had actually appeared to enjoy his ordeal at the hands of the over-endowed whip master.

Cirina had watched wonderingly as the man raised his head and smiled at his tormentor after each stroke of the cane. At one point, she had found herself straining towards him, overcome by the inexplicable desire to run to him, to kiss his face, to catch his tears on her tongue . . .

She wondered what Antonio had made of it, if, indeed, he had been in the great hall at all. Cirina's face clouded a little as she thought of him. He had made no attempt to speak to her, or even to see her after that initial chance meeting and she feared to know the reason for his reluctance.

Leaning over the balcony, she breathed the cool, sweet air, drawing it deeply into her lungs and holding it there for a moment before breathing out. How different to the excesses of the previous night was the simple pleasure of feeling the early morning sun kiss her upturned face, soothing her troubled thoughts as she listened to the sweet birdsong!

'Cirina!'

Her eyes snapped open as she heard her own name whispered on the gentle breeze. Scanning the shadowy ground below the tree, she saw a movement, then Antonio revealed himself to her and her heart leapt. It was as if her thinking about him had conjured him up, for there he was, large as life, and as dashing as ever in his snowy white shirt and dark red silk breeches.

'Antonio?'

'Cirina – are you all right, *cara*?'

'Yes – yes, I am all right. What are you doing here?'

'I am here with Marco. And you? How did you come to leave your uncle's caravanserai?'

Cirina lowered her eyes for a moment, then raised them to stare defiantly at him.

'I was chosen for the Khan's beauty contest. It is a great honour,' she continued defensively. 'My coming here will bring down many blessings on my home.'

'I'm sure it will, *cara*,' Antonio said gently.

'Besides,' Cirina continued slyly, 'is it not good fortune that we should both be here? We have found each other again. Are you not glad it is so?'

He was too far away for her to see his expressio
clearly, but Cirina fancied that Antonio looke
uncomfortable.

'Of course I am glad, *mi amore*. But it might b
dangerous for us to meet openly. How may I see you?'

Cirina thought fast. She could hear footsteps on th
stairs outside her quarters and knew that in a fe
moments her attendants would arrive. Instinct told he
that a tryst with a European guest of the Khan woul
not be looked upon kindly and she felt her stomach roil.

'Tonight – after I have retired. If it is safe, I will tie m
red scarf in the boughs of the tree.' The door creaked o
the far side of the room as the knob was turned. 'I mu
go!'

'Until tonight!'

Antonio's urgent cry echoed in Cirina's ears as sh
turned away from the window to greet her attendants.

Antonio took himself off for a walk in the grounds. H
mind was sorely troubled by the twin concerns of Ciri
and the ruby.

Surely, it was fate which brought him here to Xanad
He had located the ruby at last, at the point in his searc
when he had felt most inclined to give it up. And he ha
been reunited with the girl who had been uppermost
his thoughts since the moment he met her.

It was almost as if he had been sent a sign – a sign th
showed him that he must keep his rash promise
Cirina. It surely could not be mere coincidence whi
brought them here at the same time?

But Cirina, it seemed, was safe for now, and he ha
the night to look forward to when he would be able
speak to her properly. The retrieval of the Byzanti
ruby was an altogether trickier problem.

Of all the places for it to have been set, the Empero
throne had to be the most challenging! His luck cou
not have been worse. Catching sight of it at long last h

ekindled his waning passion for its recovery, but the neans by which he should accomplish such a task were eyond him at the present. He would have to mull it ver, keep a watch on the palace guard and the comings nd goings in the great hall in the hope that a plan might egin to form in his subconscious mind.

Pausing to rest beside a fountain, he dipped his fingers nto the cool, clear water and wiped them over his face. h, but that felt good! The heat of this place was too nuch for him, leaving him feeling enervated for much f the time. Or perhaps that was due to the constant ttentions of his serving women? Antonio smiled wryly o himself as he thought of their busy hands and mouths. t had almost been a relief to escape them this morning, ll three were so diligent in their self-appointed duties!

He felt a pang of guilt as he thought of Cirina. How vould she feel about his attendants? Then he shrugged. Iis romantic heart might assume that, because Cirina ad surrendered her virginity to him she would give nd expect to receive sexual fidelity, but he was worldly-ise enough to know that there was a vast cultural ivide between them. In this country it seemed that a oman's purity was not prized as it was in his native enice, nor a man's chivalry. He felt a sudden, unex-ected rush of homesickness.

It was cool by the fountain, shaded as it was by the preading branches of a flowering tree which Antonio ould not name. Glancing around him, he saw that he as alone and gave in to the urge to strip to the waist nd cool his sweating torso with the cool water.

The silvery droplets evaporated in the heat almost as on as they touched his skin. Leaning over the stone m, he submerged his entire head in the clean water, aking it from side to side so that his hair flowed like a lken ribbon over his scalp. He stayed underwater for long as his lungs could bear it. Finally, he rose and, flicking the hair out of his eyes, he sent water sprayin everywhere, dappling the surface of the fountain pool.

When at last the water quietened, Antonio slowl became aware of a second reflection joining his in th pool. A small face, dark hair and amused, cat-like eye He turned slowly, carefully arranging his features into mask of polite enquiry.

'Lady Chabi?'

She inclined her head slightly and looked up at hi from beneath lashes which were, Antonio saw, as thic and black as charcoal.

'My lord. Signor Ballerei, is it not?'

'At your service, madam.'

Antonio bowed from the waist, conscious of his sem nakedness. So inappropriate in the presence of a lad particularly one of such high standing as this. Remen bering how she had caught his eye the night before ma him feel doubly uncomfortable, though he fought keep his expression neutral.

Chabi placed her small hands on the cool, rough sto much as Antonio had before she arrived, and gaz across the pool to the flower garden beyond.

'The garden is beautiful, do you not think?' she sai There was a wistful inflection in her voice which h Antonio intrigued.

'Exquisite, my lady,' he concurred, his eyes resting the pleasing contours of her smooth, golden-toned chee

Chabi turned and caught his eye.

'You like it here, at our pleasure palace?'

'Indeed, madam, I am most grateful for the Khar hospitality.'

Chabi inclined her head slightly at his adherence diplomatic form, but he was sure he could detect a hi of mischief in the startling emerald-green of her eyes.

'You Europeans – you have your own name for th place, I understand?'

'That is correct, madam. We call it *Xanadu*.'

Chabi nodded thoughtfully, her eyes never leaving his.

'Xan-a-du,' she repeated, carefully enunciating the unfamiliar word. 'What does this mean?'

Antonio was a little taken aback.

'I . . . It doesn't mean anything as such, my lady. I think it conjures up a vision of paradise.'

Chabi smiled, clearly delighted with his answer.

'Paradise – ah, Signor, how right! We have many jewels with which to entice you, no?'

Antonio's eyes widened, though he moved hastily to conceal his shock. How could she know about the ruby?'

'Your girls are not to your liking?' she teased him gently and he realised at last that she was referring to his attendants.

'On the contrary, madam, I am being very well looked after.'

His relief made him incautious and Chabi smiled. Antonio suppressed a gasp as he saw the way the smile lit up her unusual eyes, making them glow, like a cat's in the dark. He was entranced, forgetting, for a moment, his previous distrust of her.

'I am glad you are comfortable, Signor. You must visit me one day and you can tell me all about your native land. Venice, I understand?'

'That is correct, madam. I should be honoured to visit with you.'

Antonio bowed again from the waist, his mind racing as he thought of the implications of such a visit. Perhaps he could find some excuse for Marco to accompany him. It would not be seemly for him to spend time alone with the Emperor's favourite wife, not if he valued his life!

As he drew himself upright again, his eyes locked with Chabi's and he again had the strangest notion that she could divine his thoughts. There was something about the way she was smiling at him, something so *knowing*.

Antonio caught his breath as she began to move towards him. Holding his eye, she drew level with him, not stopping until they were standing toe to toe. Antonio held himself very, very still, afraid to so much as breathe deeply lest his body should brush against hers. He could feel the warmth of her skin through the gauzy costume which covered her, could feel the hairs on his chest and forearms stand up and quiver as if seeking contact.

Her perfume filled his nostrils. Heavy, musky, slightly sweet, it made his head swim. This close, he could see the fine texture of her flawless complexion, could see the tiny lines criss-crossing her lips and the minute signs o age around her eyes.

His entire body tensed, anticipating danger, yet he fel unable to move or speak. Wordlessly, he watched as sh raised one hand and touched his cheek. With the tip o her sharpened fingernail, she gently scored a line fron the corner of his eye to his chin.

'Such a fine face, my handsome Venetian. So noble, s *proud*!' She laughed, a light, tinkling sound that mad the hairs on the back of his neck stand on end. 'I lik you, Antonio! I like you very much.'

The fleshy pad of her forefinger passed lightly acros his slightly parted lips. Antonio felt a shiver pas through him, part pleasure, part apprehension. Th reaction seemed to please Chabi, for she smiled agair splaying her palm against his naked chest, covering th place where his heart beat an erratic tattoo.

'Ah, you are a man of fiery passions, I think,' sh whispered throatily, 'a man who enjoys the pleasures c the flesh?'

'Madam, I –'

'Hush!' She interrupted his attempt to stand on hi dignity by placing her palm over his mouth. He coul taste his own sweat on her skin, mingling with he unique perfume and he swallowed.

'We do not live by any rules of society here, other tha

hose decreed by Kublai Khan himself. When we are
ungry, we eat, when we are thirsty, we drink. When
ve see a person we would like to know better . . .' she
emoved her hand and replaced it with her lips.

Antonio stared into her bright green eyes, mesmerised
y their intensity as she probed his tightly clenched teeth
vith her tongue, tasting and teasing until he gave way
vith a groan, drawn from deep inside his body. Her
lender tongue flickered against the sides of his mouth
nd circled his before withdrawing. As she drew away,
he tilted back her head, allowing her eyes to half close
s if she was reluctant to bring the kiss to an end.

He did not know what to do. For the first time in his
fe he felt completely at a loss and he did not like this
vidence that he could be so susceptible to a woman's
ure. He liked to be in control where his sexual behaviour
vas concerned and the feeling of abdication of control
vhich this strange woman seemed to be able to invoke
vith a single kiss bothered him.

'In my country,' he said tensely, 'certain proprieties
ave to be observed before such feelings are acted upon.'

Astonishment and displeasure flashed across the beau-
iful face in front of him, then, to his confusion, Chabi
hrew back her head and laughed. He did not like the
ound. He felt that she was making fun of him. He made
o remonstrate with her, but Chabi was already gather-
ng up her diaphanous skirts and was moving away with
sensuous rustle of fabric, leaving a trace of her perfume
anging in the air to remind him of her presence.

irina was alone in the room where her attendants had
rought her. Aware that she was waiting for something
or someone – she felt uneasy, restless as she paced the
oom.

Her attendants had bathed and dressed her once again
n the gauzy folds of fabric which draped, but did not
uite conceal, her body. Pink, this time, with a silver

border which wound its way around her breasts, down to her hips from where it fell in soft folds to her ankles. Her midriff was bare, and her navel had been filled with a curious glittery powder which seemed to have se hard. Though not unduly uncomfortable, Cirina wa conscious always of the hard button of glittering stuf which protruded slightly and the fullness there seeme to be echoed in the fullness in the secret place betwee her legs.

Her labia and mons had been dusted with the fin gold powder. The twins had shown her the end result i the jewelled mirror kept in her room, inviting her t admire the way the powder clung to her dark, silk pubic curls, drawing the eye to the gold-coloured fles leaves just visible between her closed thighs.

Such attention to that part of her served to focus he mind on it, which made her supremely conscious of th fact that she had been thus groomed and adorne Similarly, a great deal of time had been spent coiling he hair and fastening it on top of her head. The dressing c her hair had caused the girls much frustration since i was so straight and soft it resisted all their attempts t fashion it to their design. Finally, with the help c countless wooden clips, they had forced it into a respec able arrangement which Cirina was constantly afraid sh would disturb.

Suddenly, the door opened. Spinning on her heel Cirina eyed the man who had entered nervously. H was tall and broad with golden, wildly curling ha which fell onto his plain, cream, linen blouson. The shi was open at the neck to reveal the sparse, golden fur c his chest and a glimpse of sun-kissed, freckled skin. H smiled, opening his mouth to reveal impossibly whit even teeth, and Cirina swallowed.

'H – hello?'

'You must be Cirina.'

The golden-haired man strode towards her, pausing mid-stride as Cirina took a step back.

'I am Robert – your attendant for the day. Do not be alarmed. I have sent for food and wine. I am here purely for your pleasure.'

'My – my pleasure?' Cirina whispered, eyeing him warily.

He had a strange way of speaking which was unfamiliar to her, a flat, clipped tone which, along with his colouring, marked him out as a foreigner. Cirina cocked her head on one side, appraising him. What did it mean, this declaration of intent? Surely not . . .? A sudden spark of mischief chased away Cirina's apprehension and she smiled at him.

'Really? And how do you propose to *pleasure* me, sir?'

Robert stepped forward and regarded her intently. Cirina saw that his eyes were a deep, fathomless blue, like the sky over the desert. This close, she could feel the heat emanating from his light-skinned body, could smell the slightly lemony tang of his skin. To her surprise, her body reacted instantly to his nearness, her nipples hardening, her woman's place growing heavy and moist, as if he had touched her. She swayed slightly towards him.

'In any way that you choose, Cirina,' he murmured huskily.

There was something intoxicating about having a total stranger walk into your room and offer himself to you, Cirina mused dreamily, especially when that stranger was as handsome and appealing as this Robert. She had come here expecting to be the one offering to give pleasure, not to have it offered to her. Impulsively, she crossed the few inches dividing them and, standing on tiptoe, she pressed her lips against his.

Robert's arms immediately came about her, strong arms, she registered at once, and he kissed her thoroughly. Antonio's face flashed accusingly through Cirina's mind and she frowned. Why think of him at a moment like this when he had clearly spared her no such courtesy? It was hardly likely that he had lain alone for love of her since he had arrived at this place! Pushing his censorious image away resolutely, Cirina resolved to make the most of this unexpected opportunity to further her experience.

The blood surged through her veins as Robert's tongue swept across the tender, inner flesh of her mouth, locking with hers and sucking the sweetness from her. His firm, strong body pressed itself against the softer, rounder contours of hers, imprinting its shape onto her, making her acutely aware of his maleness.

As she arched her neck, Cirina's hair fell free of the elaborate coils into which it had been wound, cascading about her face and shoulders like a silken shawl. Robert gathered it up in his hands and broke off the kiss to bury his face in it, winding the jet black tresses through his own golden hair with a murmur of appreciation.

'So beautiful,' he whispered, 'so soft and sweet.'

Cirina dug her fingers into his shoulders to steady herself as a wave of dizziness swept over her. With a low chuckle Robert lifted her effortlessly into his arms and carried her over to the couch by the open window. Cirina felt boneless in his arms, weightless as a feather as he lay her carefully on the silk cushions. The midday sunlight streamed in through the unshuttered window, bathing her in its golden light as she lay supine, watching as Robert fell to his knees at the side of the couch.

How could it be, she wondered dazedly, that when she was at the caravanserai the idea of lying with total strangers had appalled her, yet for this stranger, this Robert, she was eager? Perhaps because few travellers were quite this beautiful, a small voice answered her wryly, especially after a long and exhausting trek through the dusty desert terrain!

'How do you come to be here in Shang-tu?' she asked

huskily as he stroked his palm across the contours of her bare arm.

'I was captured in Constantinople many years ago,' he replied distractedly. His fingers played sensuously across the inward curve of her waist, making her sigh with pleasure.

'Where did you come from?'

Glancing at her, he shrugged his finely muscled shoulders and bent to press his lips against the inch of her flesh which showed at her waist.

'A small island many, many miles from here.'

'Did you never want to go back?' Cirina probed, finding speech more and more difficult as Robert's lips traced a delicate path towards her exposed and ornamented navel.

'Mmm. No.'

His voice was muffled by her flesh, but Cirina was intrigued to know more.

'Why not?' she gasped.

Robert raised his head and looked at her. His eyes were slightly glazed, but Cirina could see he was becoming exasperated with her persistence. Vaguely, she wondered why he should be in such a hurry to seduce her?

'When I joined the Crusade I was barely more than a boy. I hadn't even had a woman. At first when I was captured by the infidels I wished for nothing other than to return home – or die.'

Cirina grimaced, picturing the young, untried boy, wishing for death, while yearning for his homeland. Robert smiled at her with tenderness and bent to brush his lips over hers.

'And now? Do you no longer wish to return?'

He shook his head, and his blond curls fell across his forehead, giving her a glimpse of how that young boy had looked.

'I have no desire to go back. My life is here, in Xanadu.'

She wanted to ask him – why? But Robert did not give

her the chance. Pushing her gently back on the pillows, he covered her mouth with his, making speech impossible. After a few seconds, all Cirina's questions were forgotten as she allowed herself to slip deeper into sensation.

And what sensation! Wave after wave of pure, unadulterated pleasure lapped at her body, travelling upward from her toes to the top of her head. Robert worked diligently at her breasts, her lips, the tender place behind her ear, until she was incoherent with desire.

To her frustration, he seemed to be holding something back. He kept intensifying the pleasure, his fingers straying closer and closer to her womanhood, yet just as the anticipation became too great, he would pull back, slow down. Before long, she was becoming desperate.

'Oh! Ooh, please, *please*!' she moaned as his fingers teased across her mons.

Finally, frustrated by his inaction, Cirina pulled the fabric roughly from the lower half of her body, hoping that the sight of her carefully prepared womanhood would tip him over the edge and he would finally lose control of himself.

But Robert, it seemed, was made of much stronger stuff, for he merely looked amused and stroked the back of his hand across the silky, shimmering hair, making her yearn for the more intimate touch of his fingertips against her secret flesh.

He kissed her again, wetly, deeply, and Cirina let her thighs fall softly apart, exposing the soft, moist flesh of her woman's place to the warm air. Still he did not touch her where she yearned to be touched. Instead he described tantalising circles on the petal-soft skin of her inner thighs, so close, yet so far from the centre of her pleasure.

Cirina felt she would go mad with anticipation and she moaned, reaching down to touch her own gold brushed flesh. To her dismay, Robert caught her by the wrist and brought her hand up to his lips.

'No, my eager little love – not yet.'

'Not yet?'

'Not before you've earned it.'

Cirina frowned, not understanding him. Her flesh burned, her woman's place seeping the heavy, sweet honey of feminine arousal. Surely he could not deny her the release she craved?

'H – how?' she stammered, her voice hoarse with longing.

'Open wider, Cirina, push it out – that's it,' he whispered as she bore down, her aching flesh blindly seeking the solace of his touch.

Somewhere in the back of her lust-fogged mind, Cirina was aware that the door had opened and closed. She heard the rustle of the newcomer's silk costume and smelled the heavy, musky perfume that preceded her.

'Ah, Robert, I see you have prepared our little desert flower!'

Cirina dragged her eyes open. The lids felt as if they had been weighted, as did her thighs when she tried to close them. The lady, Chabi, leaned close to her and smiled her wicked, cat-like smile.

'We meet again, little one – and in such delightful circumstances!' She drew up a chair a few feet away from the couch where Cirina lay, legs akimbo, her arms wrapped around Robert's body, and smiled. 'Please – do carry on. Do not let me disturb you!'

Cirina struggled to think. At first when she had seen Chabi she had expected her to be angry to find her in such a position. The shame of being found thus made her face burn with mortification. Yet, contrarily, Chabi had seemed unsurprised, indeed, even *pleased* to find her thus. Surely she did not intend to sit there and watch while Robert pleasured her?

She gasped as Robert's fingers brushed at last against

her tender inner flesh. Glancing fearfully towards Chabi, Cirina saw the cold green eyes narrow speculatively and she shivered, wondering what was going through the other woman's mind.

Robert was smearing her juices round her labia now, gently opening her up with the first and second fingers of one hand as if deliberately displaying her for Chabi. Gradually, Cirina realised that he had been acting under Chabi's orders all along. Hurt, feeling foolish, she tried to pull away from him. Glancing quizzically at her over his shoulder, Robert nevertheless held her still as he looked to his mistress for her instruction.

'Do not struggle, little one,' Chabi commanded in a voice which, Cirina felt, was deceptively soft. 'I want you to make a gift to me – the gift of your surrender. Do you understand?'

When Cirina did not answer at once, Robert began to stroke the small button of extra sensitive flesh at the apex of her labia. It hardened at once and Cirina felt the hot and cold waves rush over her as she swam dangerously close to climax.

'I – I understand!' she gasped.

Chabi smiled, chillingly, and signalled for Robert to stop the stimulation.

'Good. You must learn, Cirina, that while you are here, your pleasure belongs to me. You will not climax until I give you the signal – do you understand?'

This time Cirina could not find the voice to answer she merely nodded, gritting her teeth against the exquisite pleasure she still felt.

Again, Chabi smiled. She passed Robert what looked to Cirina like an eagle's feather.

'Begin,' she said, settling back in her seat to watch.

Cirina felt herself burn once more with the shame of displaying herself so wantonly before this woman with her fiendish tricks. At the first touch of the soft quill against her sex-lips, her hips bucked of their own voli tion. Chabi frowned and Cirina realised that it was not acceptable to lose control to such a degree. The next time the feather stroked along the moist channels of her woman's place, she was ready for it and she fought to keep her lower body still.

'Better,' Chabi approved softly. 'Open her up more, Robert – I want to see how much she wants it.'

Cirina closed her eyes with shame as she felt herself being stretched open and Chabi leaned forward to peer at her.

'As I thought,' the other woman murmured, amusement streaking her tone, 'she is dripping! Apply the feather, Robert, let us see how much she can take!'

This time Robert twirled the end of the feather around the hard nub at the centre of her pleasure. Cirina thought she would swoon, the sensations produced were so intense. Only her fear of what Chabi might do if she should climax before the signal made her bite hard on her lower lip, containing her feelings.

'I think this one will bring great pleasure to the Khan, do you not think so, Robert?'

'Yes, my lady Chabi,' Robert murmured thickly.

Cirina felt a surge of triumph at this evidence that Robert was affected by her and she pouted her sex-lips even more, as if in defiance. Chabi had to let her come now, she simply had to! Cirina felt as though she would burst with pleasure if her crisis was not reached soon.

Suddenly, just as Cirina felt she could stand no more, Chabi seemed, quite inexplicably, to lose interest.

'Enough.'

She clicked her fingers and Robert immediately stopped what he was doing and rose. Cirina was left, legs splayed, a rose-coloured flush gradually creeping across her chest and up her neck as she neared her climax. Surely they weren't going to leave her? Not like this?

Cirina slowly brought her legs together as she saw

Robert cast a regretful look at her trembling flesh before preceding Chabi to the door. Her hand instinctively crept between her thighs and she pressed her fingers against the hardened pad of flesh which even now was beginning to throb.

'Do not dare!'

She gasped as Chabi flicked her fan against her wrist bringing her hand up guiltily to rest in her lap.

'Robert, see to it that she is restrained. You wil remember, little one, that your pleasure belongs to me.'

'Yes, my lady Chabi,' Cirina whispered, her heac bowed.

She waited in that position for what seemed like many minutes before she heard the soft footfall of her attendants. Looking up hopefully, she saw that the twin avoided her eye as they lifted her into a standing positio and rearranged her clothing. One girl held the skirt asid and Cirina's eyes opened wide in alarm as the othe produced a harness made of two thin leather strips, nc unlike that used on a horse. By the deity, what were the going to do to her?

Cirina's arousal quickly dissipated as she wa strapped into the leather contraption. One thong wa fastened around her waist, the other was passed dowi between her buttocks and up, between her legs to he belly. The thin leather strip was just wide enough t hold her swollen sex-lips apart. As it reached the apex c her labia, she realised that the leather thong was split i two so that it passed on either side of her pleasure buc leaving it exposed. Cirina bit her lips as the two end were drawn tighter between her legs and fastened to th waist strap at the front by means of two 'D' shape leather rings.

It wasn't until she tried to walk that she fully apprec ated the refined torture to which she was to be subjecte Every movement caused the supple leather to ru against her over-stimulated flesh, just enough to kee her at the point of arousal she had already reached, but not enough to tip her over the edge into blessed relief.

'How long am I supposed to wear this thing?' she asked petulantly as she was escorted back to her room by the normally ebullient twins. The two girls exchanged glances, but did not reply and Cirina was not cheered by their response.

She cast her mind back over the past hour and tried to work out when she might have displeased Chabi, but she could think of nothing which might have angered her, except the perfectly natural reflex to touch herself when Robert had been dismissed.

What was it Chabi had said? That Cirina's pleasure belonged to her? A glimmer of understanding came to her then and she shivered. How long would it be before Chabi decided she could be relieved of her pent up sexual tension? Cirina seriously wondered how long she would be able to bear it.

Left in her room, she went to the window and looked out. The sun was shining, streaking the path below her balcony with gold. From far off she could hear the sounds of a hunt taking place. Was Antonio out there with them? She felt suddenly, unutterably lonely.

Remembering how she had promised to leave him a sign, Cirina picked up the red scarf she had discarded earlier and, reaching out to the tree by her window, she draped it discreetly in the branches. Hopefully it would not be seen by anyone who was not looking for it.

Would Antonio come as he had promised? As she turned away from the window Cirina found herself hoping more than anything that he would. After her dispiriting encounter with Robert and Chabi she felt the need to be loved in the way that Antonio had loved her.

All her earlier uncharitable thoughts about him melted away as she lay down on her sleeping pallet and imagined how it would be if he came to her. He would stroke and caress her heated skin, whispering endearments she did not understand in her ear as he kissed her face and her neck. Murmuring softly to her, he would suckle each ripe breast before moving down to her woman's place, already grown warm and moist in anticipation of his touch.

Just the thought of it made Cirina's tender flesh leaves swell, reminding her of the constriction which bound her. She reached down, between her legs, and touched her fingerpad gently against the swollen bud, tears starting in her eyes as she realised it was too tender to be touched. The harness was indeed an ingenious device, for it kept her erect whilst giving no slack to pull it aside or ease the pressure.

Bringing her knees up to her chest, Cirina hugged them to her and closed her eyes. She felt exhausted. Sleep beckoned, presenting itself as a welcome respite from the turmoil into which she had been cast.

Dusk was beginning to fall when Cirina opened her eyes. She must have dozed for several hours and, even now, she felt that she was not quite ready to wake. She was conscious of the leather harness, oiled now by the seepage from her woman's place, nestling in her feminine folds, not quite so aggravating, but *there* all the same.

Straining her ears, she suddenly realised that something had woken her. A disturbance in the air, perhaps, barely perceptible, but enough to alert her that she was no longer alone. Alarmed, Cirina sat up and looked about her.

The room was shadowy, almost sinister as she strained to peer into every corner. Her attendants had clearly looked in on her at some point, for there was a tray set with leavened bread and cold meats lying on the low table by her sleeping pallet. A jug of sweet lemon was by its side and Cirina felt her mouth water.

Still she listened, sure that something was amiss.

Suddenly, her eyes swivelled to the window and she stifled a scream. The shape of a man's head had appeared over the parapet, swiftly followed by the rest of him.

'Cirina?' the man whispered.

Cirina nearly fainted with relief as she recognised Antonio's voice.

'I am here,' she called softly, conscious of the rapid beat of her heart.

'*Cara*!'

He sat on the edge of her sleeping pallet and took her into his arms at once, as if he had looked forward to this moment all day. Showering kisses on her face, he rubbed his hands up and down her back, running his fingers through her hair, as if re-familiarising himself with the texture of it and the shape of her body.

'Ah, Cirina! How I have longed to hold you in my arms! Since the moment I saw you at the entrance to the great hall – '

'Hush!' Cirina put her hand over his mouth to stop him. She did not want to hear well-meant declarations and half-truths. All she needed from Antonio at this time was comfort, a little tenderness and, if he was willing, perhaps some release from this torment of sexual frustration.

Smiling at him in the semi-darkness, she wound her arms about his neck and pressed the upper half of her body against his. She lifted her face, and covered his lips in small, licking kisses, making them part slightly. Cirina caught his involuntary sigh between her lips, then darted out her tongue so that it probed the softness of his inner lip.

Antonio looked taken aback, startled by this display of assertiveness. After a few seconds, though, he groaned and opened his mouth under the pressure of Cirina's lips, allowing her tongue access to the warm, wet recesses of his mouth and exploring hers in his turn.

Cirina felt the pull, deep in her womb, as Antonio

drew the sweetness from her and she shifted uncomfortably as the leather tightened around her sex lips. Her unfettered breasts swelled against the hard wall of Antonio's chest and her skin burned for the touch of his lips against them.

Pulling back slightly, Antonio gazed deep into her eyes questioningly. As if reading her thoughts there, he pushed the flimsy fabric off her shoulders and buried his face in the warm, fragrant cleft between her breasts. Cirina shivered as his cool lips moved over her heated skin, moving slowly but inexorably towards the berry-brown crests thrusting wantonly towards him.

Cirina let her head fall back as he took one sweet peak into his mouth and rolled it on his tongue. Her long hair swept the floor as she arched her back, pressing her breast further into his mouth.

'Oh, Antonio!' she whispered. 'How glad I am that you are here!'

He kissed her fervently, moulding and shaping her breasts in his sensitive hands and kissing the shadowed flesh beneath. His lips skimmed her waist and travelled over the gentle swell of her belly, circling her jewelled navel and pausing at the leather thong which circled her hips.

'What is this, Cirina, *cara*?' he asked her, running the tip of his finger lightly around it.

Cirina shook her head, embarrassed now that she had to reveal the restraint to him. Keeping her eyes downcast, she pulled aside her skirts to reveal the device. Antonio's shocked intake of breath tore through her, making her wince.

'Who did this to you?'

'The lady, Chabi,' Cirina whispered with an effort. 'It is to stop me from – from . . .' she could not quite bring herself to say *to stop me from pleasuring myself,* but Antonio seemed to guess anyway, for his dark brows came together in a fierce frown.

'It is barbaric! I will cut it away.'

'No! No – please Antonio! Think what might happen when it is discovered.'

Her urgent cry stayed his hand and he traced the downward path of the harness with his fingertip instead. Once the initial outrage had worn off, he seemed to be intrigued by the contraption.

'May I see . . . ah, by what fiendish mind could such a thing have been devised?'

Cirina did not answer him; they both knew that only one person could have dreamed up such a thing. Chabi's name hung, unspoken, on the air between them, like a third presence in the room. Cirina sensed an increase in Antonio's excitement and wondered at it, but only briefly, for he was following the line of the twin thongs which joined just above the apex of her sex-lips.

Waves of pleasure rippled beneath the surface of her skin as Antonio's fingernail scraped lightly over the swollen pleasure bud which poked obscenely through.

'This must keep you in a state of perpetual arousal.'

Cirina nodded, shamed.

'Perpetual readiness,' he continued huskily.

Glancing shyly at him from between her lashes, Cirina saw the colour come into his face, noted the way his breathing quickened and realised that the sight of her thus had powerfully aroused him.

'Poor Cirina,' he continued, his voice low and breathless, 'have you been like this for long?'

She nodded, unable to trust herself to speak. In truth, she could feel her innermost flesh swelling in response to his words as much as his touch and she longed even more for the release that she had been denied.

'Too much pressure would be painful, I think,' Antonio said thoughtfully, 'yet you need to reach a crisis if you are to become more comfortable. Let me help you, Cirina.'

He lowered his head and inserted his tongue between

one of the thongs which hung down from her waist and her skin. Cirina felt the goosebumps rise all over her body as he neared the focus of her torment. She trembled, willing him to go on as she lay back on the silken cushions and allowed her thighs to fall softly apart.

She sighed in total abandonment as, so gently she could barely feel it at first, Antonio began to flick his tongue against her tumescent bud.

Back and forth, back and forth, his tongue alternately teased and gratified her straining flesh. The leather grew heavy and slick with a combination of his saliva and her moisture and the restraint loosened slightly as it grew wet. No doubt later, when it dried, it would return to its usual size, but Cirina could not care less at that moment. All that mattered was her steady, unswerving race to the peak of pleasure.

'Oh! Oh yes!' she whispered as the first pulsings began.

Feeling her sex flutter against his lips, Antonio pressed harder on the swollen nub, beating it with his tongue until Cirina cried out for him to stop.

She was panting, her mouth stretched wide, her eyes half closed as he drew her back into his arms. Lying with her on the pallet, Antonio stroked her hair, planting small, leisurely kisses on her closed eyelids, on her temples and, finally, on her trembling lips. Slowly, slowly, Cirina recovered herself and responded.

'Are you all right, *cara mia*?' Antonio asked her after a few moments.

Cirina's mouth and tongue felt dry and she found talking uncomfortable.

'Yes,' she husked, 'only, you do not want me to pleasure you in return?' she asked shyly.

Antonio chuckled against her hair.

'Another time, *cara* – tonight it is enough for me to hold you in my arms and know that you are satisfied.'

Cirina smiled and pressed her lips against the warm skin at his throat.

'I am glad you came to me, Antonio,' she whispered.

'I too. I only wish I could stay, but I am concerned that we will be found. I will come to you again on the morrow, God willing.'

Though she pouted, Cirina knew it would be foolish to try to cling to him any longer. Antonio was right to be concerned that they might be discovered – she dreaded to think what Chabi would make of such an assignation.

Reluctantly, she walked with him to the unshuttered window. On the balcony they kissed, whispering promises to each other as they broke apart.

'I will tie the red scarf to the tree again to let you know it is safe,' Cirina promised him as he broke away from her.

'I will look for it. Take care, Cirina. Whatever happens tomorrow, know that I am not far away and my thoughts are with you. We will find a way to leave this place together.'

Cirina's heart leapt at his words and she watched anxiously as he swung his long legs over the side of the stone balustrade.

'Be careful!' she cried softly as he began to climb down.

Antonio looked up and smiled at her, raising his hand in a farewell salute as he reached the ground. Cirina waved back, relieved to see him safe. Neither noticed the shadowy figure watching them from the cover of the trees below. As Antonio gave Cirina one last wave, the figure detached itself from its place of concealment and hurried away.

Chapter Seven

Chabi stormed into her apartments and demanded that Mongor be sent to her. As she waited for the soldier to arrive, she paced the floor of the room in which she would recieve him, her mind racing.

What had possessed the Venetian to keep an assignation with the girl from the caravanserai? It was inconceivable that they could have met and become close while the girl had been at the palace – she had been here only a matter of days, during which time she had been closely attended. Chabi's eyes narrowed as she thought of Cirina's attendants. They would be severely punished if it was discovered that they had been lax in their duties!

It was far more likely that the pair had known each other before they had arrived, separately, in Shang-tu. Chabi stopped pacing and gazed thoughtfully at the door. It was highly suspicious if this should be so. That two people who knew each other should each be invited separately to the pleasure palace by the Khan was too much of a coincidence for it not to arouse Chabi's suspicions.

She frowned as she recalled her feelings when she had realised where Antonio was going. It had been pure chance that had led her to follow him when he slipped away from the banquet before the start of the entertainment. Her curiosity had been roused, but never in her wildest imaginings had she expected him to make his way to the new girl's quarters.

What had he thought when he discovered that the girl had been fettered? Chabi smiled cruelly. No doubt that had dampened his ardour! Or perhaps it had excited his artistic imagination to see the leather harness in use?

Thinking of his profession reminded Chabi instantly of the portfolio of sketches Kublai had seen when the Venetian was introduced to the court. It occurred to her that his drawings might tell her more about this unexpected turn of events. Chabi summoned a servant and demanded that Signor Ballerei's portfolio be brought to her at once – preferably without his knowledge.

Once she was alone again, she had plenty of time to dwell on what she had seen. The fire that had raged through her veins as she watched Antonio climb up to the balcony had taken her by surprise. Chabi was honest enough to recognise the emotion as jealousy, but she did not delude herself that this was indicative of any tenderness she might feel towards him. On the contrary, she had been looking forward to bringing Antonio Ballerei to the position in which she liked her men best – to his knees. A liaison between the haughty Venetian and the sloe-eyed peasant girl might upset her plans for them both. If there was one thing guaranteed to provoke Chabi's displeasure, it was an interference in her plans!

Standing beneath the jacaranda trees her anger had burned slowly. The length of time he had spent in the girl's room made it obvious that something was happening between them and Chabi swore that the attendants would be punished for neglecting their duties. By the time Antonio had reappeared over the parapet, her anger had hardened.

The girl had called out to him, her voice low and

redolent of recent pleasure. Neither had noticed Chabi slip away.

She spun on her heel as the door was opened and Mongor was announced.

'You took your time!' she spat.

'I beg my lady's pardon,' Mongor replied at once, bowing low from the waist, his helmet held in the crook of one arm.

He looked apprehensive, Chabi noted with some satisfaction, as well he might. The last time a soldier had displeased her, she had had him publicly flogged to within an inch of his life as an example. No one got away with treating Chabi in a shoddy fashion – her power had been hard won and she was determined never to relinquish one iota of it.

'I shall see to it that you receive extra duties to cure you of your tardiness,' she told him, smiling to herself as he blanched visibly. 'Perhaps you will be able to redeem yourself. I wish to know more of the girl you found near Khotan.'

Sitting down, she folded one shapely ankle over the other and reached for some fruit. Mongor looked at her blankly, clearly at a loss.

'The peasant girl – Cirina, isn't it? You were there when she was picked out?' said Chabi, impatiently.

'Oh, yes, my lady, of course.'

'You were responsible for grading her, were you not?'

'That is correct, my lady.'

'Hmm. You were somewhat on the generous side with her grading, though she might just do. Did you try her yourself?'

'No, my lady, Chabi, I did not!'

Mongor looked deeply shocked. It was an offence punishable by death to tamper with a woman marked for the Khan. Chabi wondered whether the Venetian would have been keen to set such a course had he known this. All the soldiers knew of the edict and it was obviously a cause for concern that she had questioned his integrity, for Mongor looked distinctly uncomfortable. Keeping his eyes downcast, he fiddled with his moustache.

'You would have liked to, though, would you not?' Chabi probed with a flash of intuition.

Mongor's colour deepened and she guessed she had hit on the truth.

'My loyalty to the Khan is unwavering, my lady,' he replied finally with admirable dignity.

Chabi regarded him thoughtfully. It might well be of use to her at some point if Mongor harboured lustful thoughts for the girl.

'Your loyalty will be rewarded, Mongor,' she said mildly. 'I wish to know how the girl might have come to know the Venetian, Antonio Ballerei. You know of him?'

'The artist, my lady?'

'Yes. How is it that they could have met?'

Mongor looked perplexed.

'I know not, my lady. The girl was well guarded on the journey here.'

'Are you implying that this relationship might have been started under the Khan's roof?'

'No, no,' Mongor backtracked hastily, 'I would not dream of suggesting such a thing! I only meant that my men were under strict instructions. They would have noticed had a European approached us.' Mongor trailed off miserably, as if aware, suddenly, of the inadequacy of his answer.

'No matter,' Chabi said impatiently as her servant returned with Antonio's portfolio. 'I have a feeling that this might enlighten us.'

Spreading the portfolio on a table, Chabi beckoned Mongor over so that he might see the pictures. She heard him suck in his breath as they uncovered a series of sketches of a young girl, a young girl who looked remarkably like Cirina.

'Now are you convinced, Mongor?' Chabi said angrily.

Turning to face him, she signalled to the servant to take the portfolio away. Though outwardly she was aware that she looked as cool and in control as always, inwardly she was seething. As if sensing that he was first in her line of attack, Mongor took a step backwards.

'As you say, my lady; the European and the peasant girl know each other. But I swear this knowledge did not come about whilst the girl was in my care. It must have been before we found her.'

'Before?'

'Yes, my lady – Ballerei was travelling with the Polos. I could check their route to see if it is possible that they could have stopped at the caravanserai.'

'Do that, Mongor. But keep this to yourself. I do not want the Khan upset by rumours that his new plaything might have formed a bond with anyone before he has had a chance to play with her!'

'You can rely on me, my lady. I'll report back as soon as possible.'

Mongor bowed himself out of her presence, not turning his back on her until he reached the door. As soon as he had closed it behind him, Chabi picked up a precious vase sitting on the edge of the table and flung it at the door with all her might. Damn the pair of them for flouting her authority! The vase shattered into a thousand pieces, blue porcelain flying in all directions.

The following morning, Cirina was woken by a serving girl whom she did not recognise.

'Where are my usual women?' she asked as the girl handed her a plain white shift to wear.

The girl did not answer, only indicating to Cirina by repeated gestures that she should hurry. A cold knot of foreboding settled in Cirina's stomach as she was hurried out of the palace and across the gardens towards the pleasure dome. They passed a group of gardeners who stopped to stare as Cirina was marched past them, their dark eyes speculative as they ran them over her semi-nakedness.

The pleasure dome was really no more than a large yurt – animal skins stretched tight over a framework of bamboo – though it was like no yurt Cirina had ever seen. Not a breath of wind dared to enter the place for the walls were lined with silks and furs, and the ground was covered with animal pelts.

In the centre of the yurt there was a large wooden chair, empty for now, but clearly about to be occupied for, even as they entered, a veritable army of serving women were preparing the seat with silk-covered cushions and soft pelts. Sure enough, Kublai Khan himself soon arrived, flanked by a small battalion of his personal guard.

Cirina, who had been left to stand before the throne, though several yards away from it, watched the Khan's progress through her lashes. He walked slowly, of necessity, given his girth. It took two men to help him into his seat and two more to position the cushions comfortably to support him. Food and drink were brought and positioned on a small table within his reach.

When, at last, he seemed to be settled, Chabi made her entrance. Everyone in the yurt, with the natural exception of the Emperor, bowed low as she walked across the floor. Cirina followed suit, hearing the whisper of Chabi's silk skirts as she passed by. When she reached the throne, Chabi paid due obsequience to her husband before turning to Cirina.

'Girl – approach the Emperor!' she commanded imperiously.

Remembering what had happened last time when she had come close to Khan, Cirina obeyed reluctantly. This time, however, Kublai barely spared her a glance, seeming to be more interested in the parchment unrolled by his chief of staff.

'Carry on, my jewel,' he said distractedly to Chabi, waving his hand languidly in Cirina's direction.

Cirina caught the look of fury which momentarily transformed Chabi's lovely face before she quickly brought it under control.

'As you wish, my lord,' she murmured, bowing low.

Cirina was taken to a circular couch to one side of the Khan.

'Take off your clothes,' Chabi commanded.

Cirina hesitated, embarrassed to strip in front of so many men. Somehow the fact that none seemed interested in what was happening to her made it all the more humiliating.

'My lady – '

'Do you dare to disobey me?'

Cirina took one look at the emerald fire in the other woman's eyes and shook her head. Without allowing herself further time for thought, she grasped the hem of her shift and pulled it over her head. Standing, naked save for the leather harness which kept her sex-lips spread wide, she looked to Chabi for further instructions.

'You will lie yourself on the couch,' the woman said in a bored tone, 'and you will pleasure yourself for the amusement of the Khan.'

Cirina blinked, not sure she had heard aright. Surely she did not mean . . .? As their eyes met, Cirina realised that yes, Chabi did indeed intend that she should bring herself to the peak of sexual pleasure, on command.

Her limbs shook as she moved to obey.

'The harness, my lady?' she said, feeling that Chabi probably needed reminding of its presence.

'Ah yes. It is still intact, then?' There was an almost vicious note in her voice as Chabi's eyes travelled over the leather contraption and Cirina thanked whatever Gods had been watching over her the night before for sending her the wisdom to stop Antonio from removing it.

'Of course, my lady Chabi,' she whispered.

Chabi eyed her narrowly and Cirina had the uncomfortable feeling that Chabi knew she had been pleasured the night before. Though it was a ridiculous notion – how could Chabi have discovered her secret? – Cirina felt little trickles of icy dread run up and down her spine.

'Remove the harness,' Chabi told the serving girl who had been waiting unobtrusively by the couch.

The girl slipped the twin leather thongs through the 'D' shaped loops and peeled the oiled leather away from Cirina's most intimate flesh. As it grazed against her pleasure bud, Cirina was unable to suppress a gasp of relief and Chabi raised an amused eyebrow. She waited until Cirina was naked before clicking her fingers impatiently.

'Begin.'

Cirina lay back on the furs strewn across the couch. She was trembling, horribly conscious of the vulnerability of her position. Chabi was standing level with her head, watching her, whilst a few yards away from the end of the couch Kublai Khan and his chief of staff were still poring over the document the latter had produced. Behind the throne, two soldiers at arms were standing to attention, their faces inscrutable. Two more faced outward, slightly in front, but to one side of the royal throne.

Conscious of Chabi's growing impatience, Cirina forced her fingers to stroke along the outer edge of her tightly closed thighs. She moaned softly, awash with shame.

'My lady – I cannot,' she exclaimed in an anguished whisper.

Chabi bent to press her lips against Cirina's ear. Her tone was very different now; this time it was soft, coaxing and the seductive words sent little, sensuous shivers through Cirina's body.

'You can, little one. You want to – feel how your body burns as if with fever!'

It was true, Cirina *was* warm. Wearing the leather harness all night had sensitised the delicate flesh of her woman's place, making her long to touch herself, more so because before it had been forbidden. Her mouth dried and she passed her tongue across her lips, moistening them as she felt Chabi's words work their magic in her ear.

'Do it now – surrender your pleasure to me.' Chabi's voice was a low, sibilant hiss which seemed to reverberate through Cirina's body. Her words caressed her naked skin, making the small, soft hairs stand on end.

Chabi moved away and Cirina found she missed the warmth of her lips against her ear. It seemed very hot in the jewelled yurt and very, very quiet, even though Cirina could hear the low rumble of male voices around the Khan's throne. But the voices seemed to be divorced from her, completely separate, as if coming from a different place.

Surrender your pleasure to me. The words echoed in Cirina's head, exciting her. Taking several deep breaths, she tried to regulate her breathing, calming herself. After a few moments, she grew bolder, pressing her palms flat against the soft skin of her legs and moving up to caress her stomach. It quivered softly under her hand as she stroked it before going on to polish each jutting hipbone with her palm and to caress the pleasing indentation of her waist.

It did not seem to matter to Chabi that she was taking her time, so she concentrated on trying to awaken every sensitive nerve ending, rubbing across her ribs and up to the gentle swell of her breasts. To her surprise, she found that her nipples were already erect, pushing outward towards the centre of her palms. Slowly, slowly she circled the flats of her hands over her breasts revelling in the way her areolas grew and hardened in response.

Daring at last to glance across at the men on the other side of the room, Cirina saw that no one was paying her any attention at all. The eyes of the soldier nearest to her, though, kept sliding in her direction and Cirina smiled inwardly. What would it take to gain the attention of these impassive soldiers, or even of Kublai Khan himself? What would she have to do?

Gradually, her initial embarrassment was replaced by a spark of mischief. She began to perceive the engaging of the men's attention as a challenge to her femininity and she was fully prepared to rise to it. Allowing a breathy sigh to escape through her parted lips, she arched back her neck and rolled one nipple between her thumb and forefinger.

From the corner of her eye, she saw the soldier's head turn very slightly in her direction and she felt a rush of power surge through her veins. Energised by it, she pulled gently on the pliant teat, elongating it before allowing it to spring back into shape.

A fine film of perspiration broke out on the surface of her skin, pushing through her pores and standing in a myriad of individual beads on the surface, giving her skin a translucent sheen. Cirina felt her heartbeat quicken as she left her breasts and returned her attention to her belly.

Pushing it out and up, she circled the palm of her hand round and round with delicious slowness. The referred movement on her mons pulled at her secret flesh which, she could feel, was swelling and opening in readiness for when her fingers would slip lower. Her fingertips brushed against the silky hair as she trailed them along the division of her thighs.

In the back of her mind, she recognised that the drone of conversation had now stopped and she sensed that all eyes were on her. Though she did not dare to look to see if her instincts were correct, she played to her imagined audience, turning her head and allowing her mouth to fall open slightly. Pressing one fingertip against the soft lips, she drew it in slowly and sucked upon it.

There was a brief, communal intake of breath as she opened her mouth and circled her own finger with her tongue before drawing it in deeply again. Empowered by her proven ability to demand and receive the attention she deserved, Cirina made a show of slowly parting her legs, not too widely, just enough so that her saliva-wetted finger could slide gradually across her body and between her other moist lips.

She gave an involuntary groan as she grazed across her hardening pleasure bud and knew that she must avoid it for a while if she was not to bring her display to a premature end. Instead, she trickled her fingertips lightly along the channels of her labia, probing gently at the warm, wet mouth of her woman's place and bathing it in the heavy honey which seeped from it.

Shifting slightly on the soft furs, Cirina gave in to a mischievous urge to bring her finger back up to her lips. She could taste the sweet, slightly musky juices of her body and she opened her mouth wide again to draw the finger in. She heard a sigh tremble on the air and realised that she held her audience unexpectedly captive.

Driven by a sudden, inexplicable need to ensure that no one in the yurt ever forgot this initially reluctant display, Cirina gave in to the urge to stretch her body from head to toe, like a cat in the sun. Afterwards, she drew her knees up to her chest, feeling the pull on the delicate protuberance of her labia and knowing that all present caught a glimpse of their soft, pink wetness.

The atmosphere in the yurt was highly charged now, heavy with anticipation, and this spurred Cirina on. Slowly straightening the sleek, golden length of her legs, she pointed her toes and gradually parted them. The toes nearest to the majority of the watchers, she allowed to rest on the floor, and then she bent her left leg, ensuring that her sex-lips parted.

They could see everything now, the most intimate part of her was revealed and she felt the heat of their gaze on her there. Closing her eyes, she arched her back and shook her head so that her long hair fell in a silky curtain to the fur-strewn floor. She could imagine the sight she presented, the complete abandonment which her pose embodied, and the mental image made her feel hotter, made the juices flow more thickly.

Her hands were trembling as she reached between her legs and parted her swollen labia, feeling the warm air kiss the innermost skin. Slowly, using the outstretched middle finger of her right hand, she brought up the moisture from the entrance to her body and smeared it up to the place where her labia met.

At the first touch of her warm, wet fingertip, the little hub pulsed with pleasure, throbbing like a tiny heart at the very centre of her. At once Cirina's awareness of the others in the yurt began to recede and her actions became purely for her own pleasure. Rubbing her finger pad rhythmically round and round the straining bud, she revelled in the little shocks of sensation which travelled through her body.

Her breath had grown shallow now and she found that she was panting slightly, her mouth open, her legs stretched wide apart. The fur felt hot against her skin, dampening with perspiration and the intimate, feminine moisture which trickled down the crease of her buttocks.

Moving restlessly against the couch, she thrust her hips upward and pushed out the little bead of pleasure, widening herself further than she imagined was possible and offering up the sight of her pulsing core to all who might behold it.

Though she rubbed faster and harder, to her frustration Cirina found that it was not enough. She wanted to crest the ridge of her climax, wanted to be able to fling her legs wide and cry out in sweet surrender. All her awareness was now centred on that tiny heart, nothing else existed for her but that and the sensations it was generating which were running wild through her body like a scorching desert wind. Her middle finger thrummed upon it, harder and harder until, at last, it was beating the tiny nub.

Tap-tap-tap – Cirina's body jack-knifed so that she was half sitting, her entire body straining towards the peak.

'Ahh!' she cried out as, suddenly, the orgasm seemed to burst from her.

Holding her legs up in the air, she pushed the heel of her hand against the pulsing heart, shaking her head from side to side as she spun in a vortex of pure ecstasy, oblivious to everything except the vibrations within her own body.

It seemed to go on forever. When at last it began to ebb away, Cirina collapsed back against the furs, exhausted. She was panting heavily, her body was drenched in sweat, her hair sticking to her forehead and her woman's place ached, quite sweetly.

She lay there for a few moments while her heart-rate slowly returned to normal and her temperature cooled. Gradually, outside sounds began to filter through – a murmur of approval, the sound of a soldier's laboured breathing as he sought to control himself. She had done it – none had ignored her! A wide, satisfied smile spread across her face as she realised how she had triumphed.

Then she opened her eyes and encountered the hard, green gaze of Chabi and her confidence wavered. The other woman's expression was a mixture of astonishment and fury, tinged with a grudging admiration. She looked as if she might approach the couch and Cirina tensed, only to relax again as Kublai Khan called his wife to him.

'What think you Chabi, my love?' he said, laughter in

his wheezy voice. 'Have you finally found someone you cannot break on the altar of your vanity?'

Cirina watched apprehensively as Chabi's shoulders went back and her head lifted.

'On the contrary, my lord,' she replied with a spirit which won Cirina's reluctant respect, 'this one will simply be more amusing. As my lord knows, everyone has a breaking point.'

Kublai looked thoughtfully at Cirina.

'Take care, Chabi, that you do not destroy that which is worth developing.'

He clicked his fingers, dismissing both women as if he had suddenly grown tired of the diversion they had provided. Chabi turned back to where Cirina lay, still sprawled on the couch, and Cirina shrank from the barely leashed fury in the other woman's face.

'Get her out,' she snapped at the serving girl waiting in the shadows.

Cirina was wrapped in a silken robe and hurried from the yurt. Though Chabi's fury frightened her, it could not quite dispel her sense of triumph and she held her head high, still buoyed up by it.

Chabi was furious. Returning to her quarters she sent for wine and began to plot her revenge. No one made a fool of her in front of the Khan! Ah, but how magnificent the girl had looked! Had they been alone, Chabi would have taken her into her arms there and then and taken her beyond the barriers of pleasure to that other, darker place where only the truly sensual could find fulfilment! She had little doubt that Cirina had that potential.

Chabi's anger, however, overrode her desire to possess. There must be a way to teach the girl a lesson, to make her understand that, while she was at the pleasure palace, she must surrender herself to Chabi's will. Therein lay the power of the Emperor's wife and Chabi had no intention of allowing a licentious desert peasant to undermine it. No intention at all!

Antonio's footsteps dragged as he approached the lady Chabi's quarters. The summons to go to her had come just as he was about to go to meet Cirina and he was impatient to get the interview over with. The thought of Cirina lying in her room, waiting for him, sent frustration zinging through his veins. With any luck she would have been released from that devilish contraption today and he would be able to make love to her properly. If he could dispense with this interview quickly first.

As soon as he was shown into Chabi's presence he realised that this was not going to be a short visit, and his heart sank.

'You sent for me, madam?'

'Signor Ballerei!' She smiled at him, a smile he did not quite trust. 'Come – take some kumiss with me. I would know more about you.'

Antonio hesitated. He was wary of this woman, and yet he knew that to refuse her request could put him and, ultimately Cirina, in mortal danger. So he smiled and sat where she indicated, making himself comfortabl on the plump, silk-covered floor cushions.

'You must miss your home and your kinsmen?'

'A little, I admit, though I have no close kin,' h answered her, taking the cup she offered him with a noc of acknowledgement.

'No wife? You surprise me, sir! A high born gentlemar such as yourself would surely be most sought after by the mothers of Venice for their daughters?'

Antonio smiled, amused by her perception.

'Indeed, madam – you flatter me!'

Chabi leaned toward him and he caught a waft of he distinctive perfume.

'Surely not? You have many fine qualities.'

Antonio sat absolutely still as Chabi's full lips brushe

lightly over his, soft as a baby's breath against his sensitive skin. He desired this woman, this he could not deny, but he also feared her. His fear of her was the greater of the two emotions and it was this that kept him passive. Only when her fingers began to stroke down his arm to trail suggestively across his lap did he respond.

'My lady Chabi,' he murmured softly, 'I beg you to consider your husband – '

'My husband?' Chabi sat upright, regarding Antonio with astonishment. 'Think you the Khan would disapprove of my pleasures? The Emperor wishes only for my happiness!' she declared with more vehemence than was warranted.

Antonio felt a stab of unexpected sympathy for her.

'I am sure he does,' he soothed, 'but he might not feel too kindly towards me should he discover that his favourite wife had chosen me as a recipient for her attentions. I am unworthy.'

Chabi smiled thinly.

'Do you think he would notice now that he has the new girl to amuse him? Have you not see her, our little desert flower? So fresh and innocent – Cirina will keep Kublai occupied for a while, I think.'

Chabi smiled cruelly as Antonio paled.

'I – I have seen her, yes,' he whispered.

'Would that you had seen her today! The Khan was most impressed by her licentiousness. The soldiers who watched her publicly pleasuring herself could barely restrain themselves. Why, Signor Ballerei – is there something wrong?' She placed her hand gently on his knee and leaned forward, a picture of concern. 'You have gone quite pale!'

'It – it is very hot in here, madam,' Antonio choked out.

He could barely contain his anguish at the picture Chabi had conjured for him; of Cirina being presented to the Emperor for his pleasure. Worse, Chabi's blatant implication that Cirina had been a willing participant in such barbarism! He did not believe that Chabi's poison-tipped words could have been intended to do anything other than pain him, and he wondered at her motives. She had not finished.

'It is a pity, really, that she is marked for the Khan. So many would like to enjoy her. Why only yesterday I had to have a soldier flogged for daring to touch the folds of her skirt as she passed. Had he managed to seduce her, as, undoubtedly, was his aim, I should have been forced to have him executed.'

Antonio met her eye and realised at once that she was warning him. Yet how could she know about his visit to Cirina? He had been so careful.

'My lady,' he ventured, but at that moment the door to the room opened and a servant hurried through.

Chabi's face looked thunderous at the inopportune disturbance and she rose to her feet.

'How dare you enter without notice!' she hissed at the unfortunate young man.

The servant, who bowed so low his forehead scraped the ground at his feet, spoke fast. Antonio did not understand his words, though he recognised the urgency in his tone. He watched, perplexed, as Chabi shot him a frustrated glance, then swept from the room.

Chapter Eight

Cirina was waiting for him as he approached her room.

'Antonio! Antonio I am here!' she hissed at him from the surrounding bushes.

He turned, surprised, to find her smiling at him in the darkness.

'I managed to slip away from my attendants – no one will miss me. I thought we could walk together in the garden, if you like?'

Antonio glanced nervously about him. He had a feeling that Chabi's spies were everywhere, but the temptation to join Cirina in the enchanted garden overcame his caution. Slipping into the shade of the trees with her, he took her into his arms and kissed her lingeringly.

'I thought you were never going to come!' she told him as they broke apart, a petulant note in her voice he had never heard before.

'I was summoned by Chabi and could not get away.'

Cirina looked alarmed.

'The lady Chabi is interested in you? Oh beware of her, Antonio, I have heard many stories of how she likes to misuse the men who catch her eye!'

Antonio was instantly reminded of the story Chabi had told him of how Cirina had 'entertained' the Emperor. Though he had tried to dismiss it, the pictures it had conjured up kept coming back to haunt him, as they did now.

'Really? And I have heard stories too – of how Kublai Khan is besotted with his "little desert flower",' he mimicked Chabi's low, seductive voice, 'and how she gave herself so willingly.'

Cirina stared at him, her eyes wide and full of hurt.

'Think you that I would be in this place if the choice to come or not had been mine alone?'

'Of course not,' he replied testily, 'but I am disappointed to hear of how readily you submit. I had thought better of you.'

Before she thought about what she was doing, Cirina's hand shot out and she slapped Antonio's face, hard. The sound of flesh against flesh seemed overloud in the velvety darkness and for a moment they stared at each other. Cirina could see her own shock mirrored in Antonio's eyes and she began to tremble. Slowly, his surprise turned to fury and, dismayed, she turned on her heel and fled.

'Cirina!'

She could hear his heavier step pounding the ground behind her, gaining on her all the time, and she ran faster, forgetting to be cautious in her determination to get away from him. She barely saw the avenue of fountains through which she ran, though the sound of the continuous jets of water seemed like a roar in her head.

What on earth had possessed her to do such a thing? Never in her life had she ever struck another person! It had been something about his disapproval that had infuriated her, overruling her normal good nature.

The thought of the stance he had taken renewed her anger and she stopped in her tracks, whirling to face him with such suddenness that he almost fell over her. His face was thunderous, the cheek where she had hit him showing livid against his pale skin. Ignoring this evidence of her perfidy, Cirina faced him, eyes blazing.

'How dare you!' she hissed, her fists clenching so hard that her nails dug painfully into her palms. 'What right have you to judge me! You cannot know the courage it cost to play Chabi at her own game. You might be disgusted, but you are a fool if you cannot see that I won – even while I lost, I won!'

There was an angry pulse beating at Antonio's temple and his lips were drawn into a thin, white line as he listened to her breathless tirade. Cirina gasped as he grabbed her by the shoulders and shook her.

'How can you say such a thing?' he said, thrusting his face close to hers so that his angry, hot breath scorched her cheeks.

'Because it is true!'

'No! You only wish to think it so. You debased yourself willingly before these Godless fiends – aargh!'

He turned his face away as Cirina spat at him.

'Son of an unwashed pig!' she screamed, hating him with every fibre of her being.

'Whore!'

'Let me go, you European barbarian! Oh!'

Cirina gasped as, unexpectedly, Antonio's mouth crushed down onto hers, stifling her words. Enraged, she fought him, hammering her fists against the arms that enclosed her, pulling at his hair and scratching her nails against her face. All to no avail for Antonio was far too strong for her and he did not so much as draw breath as her nails scored his skin.

Telling herself that she hated the feel of his tongue against hers, refusing to recognise the passion which crept beneath the anger, Cirina struggled even more, unbalancing him so that his legs were pushed against the stone rim of the nearest fountain.

Sensing an advantage, no matter how slight, Cirina fought with renewed vigour, toppling with him into the water with a loud splash.

The cold, clear water filled her nose and ears and she surfaced, spluttering, clinging now to Antonio where before she had sought only to get away. Opening her eyes, she saw his hair plastered to his skull, a look of sheer astonishment on his handsome features, and she could not help herself. She burst out laughing.

'Oh Antonio! I'm sorry.'

He shook his head violently, like a dog, sending hair and water flying everywhere, soaking Cirina anew. She squealed and tried to wade to the side through the waist deep water, but he was too fast for her. Grabbing her by the arm, he pulled her down, submerging her again, only this time when she tried to come up for air, she found she was prevented from doing so, just for a few seconds, by Antonio's hand on the back of her head.

'No!' she spluttered as she surfaced, splashing him furiously as he ducked her again.

He was laughing as she bobbed up again and she was surprised by the way in which her heart lifted at the sight. It had hurt her to see him angry with her and she grinned back at him, oblivious to the way her clothes were sticking to her body.

Suddenly, Antonio's smile faded and his eyes darkened. Cirina sensed his sudden tension and let her arms fall to her sides. She seemed to be aware of every beat of her heart, every inch of her skin as it was lapped by the churning water. It was difficult to breathe and she compensated by panting slightly through her mouth as Antonio waded towards her.

This time when his arms came about her, there was no trace left of the anger, or his later playfulness. Putting his hands at her waist, he lifted her up, so that her navel was level with his face. Cirina sighed as he licked at the droplets of water falling from her skin before carrying her through the water to the centre of the fountain.

'Ahh!' she cried out as the water cascaded over her face and breasts, briefly forming a transparent curtain between them before Antonio joined her on the other side. The centre of the fountain was made of a solid stone column, strong enough to support her weight as he leaned her against it. The fountain shielded them from prying eyes as Antonio kissed her throat, the dip of her collarbone, the swell of her breasts beneath her soaking shift.

Over his shoulder, she could just make out the other fountains and the trees behind. A white mare paused at their fountain to drink before trotting away, nodding its noble head, oblivious to the couple now pulling urgently at each other's clothing.

Antonio had never made love to her with quite this feverishness, as if he was afraid they might be discovered before he had had the chance to possess her. Cirina met him caress for urgent caress, her hands roaming greedily over his broad chest and down to where his penis thrust upward, pressing against her belly.

Though they were sheltered from the main flow of the fountain, a gentle breeze blew some of the spray backwards, so that it sprinkled them constantly. The stone column felt cool against her wet back and Cirina pressed against it as Antonio's lips sought and found the warm, wet flesh between her thighs. Her legs felt weak, as if they did not belong to her and she sagged against the fountain, glad of its support. Arching her neck backward, she opened her mouth, catching the cool spray on her tongue and allowing it to trickle slowly down her throat.

Antonio groaned incoherently as he watched her, burying his head between her breasts and nuzzling at her erect teats. Lifting her by the waist again, he impaled her on his straining rod, sinking into her with a long, drawn-out sigh which sent shivers up and down her spine.

Wrapping her legs around his waist, Cirina rotated her hips so that she could feel him deep inside her and leaned back against the stone column with a little moan of surrender. Planting his feet firmly apart beneath the waist-deep water, Antonio moved her up and down, rocking his pelvis so that it ground against hers on each downward thrust.

Feeling the pressure building at the centre of her, Cirina gripped him more tightly, clenching the muscles of her cleated passage as if afraid he might miss his stroke and slip out of her. Antonio's eyes were glazed, the cords of his neck bulging as he reached his crisis, and then Cirina felt her womb contract and the first waves of pleasure broke over her.

Whereas before he had been sturdy, easily supporting her weight as well as his own, the spilling of his seed seemed to sap Antonio's strength. As they each crested the peak, they overbalanced and sank into the water, clinging together, still enjoined. Laughing, Cirina clung to him, kissing his wet face and revelling in the mild scrape of his chin against the tender flesh of her lips.

'Come – we must get out of here,' he said at last, though Cirina fancied that he sounded as reluctant as she to leave their unexpected idyll.

They looked a sorry sight, their clothes drenched through, hers almost in rags where he had torn at them in his haste to get at her wet skin. Fearing to be seen, they hurried into the bushes and followed a circuitous route back towards the palace.

Outside Cirina's window, they kissed fervently.

'How will you get inside?' Antonio asked her anxiously.

'I'll try to slip past the guard – I dare not risk climbing up in this state!'

Antonio grinned, cupping one full breast in his palm and giving it a squeeze.

'By all that is holy, I wish I could come with you!'

'You must not!' Cirina protested with alarm. 'If the lady Chabi should hear of it – '

'Hush!' Antonio said, pressing his fingertip gently against her lips. 'Chabi has been called to Beijing by the Emperor. We are safe, for now, at least.'

Though she was relieved to hear that Chabi was no longer in Shang-tu, Cirina still felt uneasy.

'There are many who would report to her – we must be careful!'

Antonio grasped her hand and raised it to his lips.

'Fear not, *mi amore,* I will find a way to come to you again tomorrow. Will you watch for me?'

'Always,' Cirina promised.

His lips grazed her knuckles again, then she slipped away from him, running on light feet to the side entrance through which she had escaped earlier. As she crept through the doorway, she turned, almost fainting away with fright as a figure detached itself from the shadows.

'Where have you been, girl?' a deep voice asked, not unkindly.

'M – Mongor?' Cirina stammered uncertainly.

The soldier who had brought her to Shang-tu from the caravanserai stepped past her and looked outside, glancing this way and that as if expecting Antonio to still be in sight. Closing the door behind him, he turned to Cirina, his eyes skimming the state of her dress and settling on her flushed cheeks and shining eyes. Any fool could see what she had been doing!

'Hurry,' he said, taking her by the elbow. 'I will wait while you take off those wet clothes and I will destroy them for you.'

Cirina ran with him up the steps to her room. Once inside, she stripped off in front of him, recalling how he had seen her naked before. Mongor's dark eyes flickered over her slender form, watching as she dried herself and wrapped a silk robe around her.

Handing the torn and wet clothes to him, Cirina ventured to ask, 'Why are you helping me?'

The big Tartar frowned, as if he had asked that question of himself and had been unable to answer it then either.

'Do not ask questions,' he answered shortly. 'Only know that you put yourself in danger. It is not good to cross the lady, Chabi.'

Cirina looked at him pensively. What had he been doing at the bottom of the stairs? Could it be that he had been posted there by Chabi specifically to spy on her?

Knowing this was very possible, Cirina concluded that it did not matter. What did matter was that he had helped her when he could just as easily have had her flogged for disobedience.

'As you wish, sir,' she said quietly, 'but I beg leave to thank you, all the same.'

Mongor grunted before executing a brief bow and turning on his heel. Without another word, he left her, taking with him the sodden evidence of her escapade in the fountain.

Kublai Khan's precipitate departure for Beijing had taken the Polos by surprise.

'By all that is holy,' Marco declared when he found out, 'how many more days must we remain here?'

'Does the life not suit you, nephew?' Maffeo asked slyly, pausing to stroke the dangling breast of the naked serving girl who was massaging his feet.

Marco smiled ruefully and ruffled the hair of the girl lying sleepily across his lap.

'Indeed it does suit me – too well! But I have heard tell that another war is brewing in Venice. What I would ive to return to fight the Genoese! What say you, ntonio?'

Antonio, who had been thinking of Cirina, dragged is mind onto the conversation.

'As you say, Marco, we are needed at home. How will ou persuade the Emperor to let us go?'

The Polos shifted uncomfortably on their cushions.

'We are not prisoners here, Antonio,' Niccolo eproofed him mildly.

'Perhaps not, but I would wager that we would not et far without Kublai Khan's blessing.' Aware that arco was watching him thoughtfully, Antonio turned his old friend and smiled. 'What is on your mind, riend?'

Marco shook his head. 'I only wondered what had ade you think of leaving. Could it be that the delightful irina's charms have begun to pall?'

Antonio frowned darkly. 'No. If it were possible I ould take her with us.'

His words shocked him as much as they clearly hocked the Polos, for he had not realised he meant them ntil they were said. To take Cirina back to Venice with im – he could not wish for more, except that he should lso recover the Byzantine ruby! The ruby. He must pply his mind to the task which had sustained him rough the long years away from home, not dwell on e hopeless dream of stealing Cirina away too. Yet, he knowledged with a heavy heart, for him the jewel of anadu had become human, the ruby a mere worthless auble by comparison.

'But it is *not* possible, Antonio,' Marco said with ncharacteristic gentleness.

'No, of course not.' Antonio forced a grin to hide his nbarrassment. 'Let me know when the Khan next rants you an audience, Marco, my sword arm has own stiff with disuse!'

The others all laughed and the awkward moment

passed. That night as he lay beside Cirina on her sleeping pallet, he thought again of how he could retrieve th ruby from the Emperor's throne.

They had made love with a tenderness which spoke his heart and lay now, entwined and sated, gathering their strength for another coupling.

Idly, Antonio ran his fingertip from the point where her collarbones met, down between her breasts to her navel where he circled it, round and round until she became too ticklish and clapped her hand over his.

'Stop! What is in your head that keeps you from me?' she asked him, her voice soft and sleepy.

'What do you mean?'

Cirina made a small, impatient gesture with he fingertips.

'You are here, lying beside me, but your thoughts are somewhere else. Are they with another woman?'

Antonio gazed at her in surprise, then chuckled making her frown.

'What is funny? Do you think it a jest that I do not like to think of you with someone else?'

Realising that she would be sorely hurt if he did nc reassure her quickly, Antonio bent to brush her lips with his, but she turned her face away so that he kissed her cheek instead. He sighed.

'How could I think of another woman when you ar lying in my arms? Cirina, against you the most beautifu of women are daughters of camels!'

Cirina giggled at the description and he relaxed Something made him want to confide in her. His affection for her made him indiscreet.

'You are right though, *cara mia* – my mind has nc been with you as it should have been. Forgive me. But is something of far more value than another woman tha takes me from you.'

Cirina raised herself up on one elbow and looked a him with interest.

'Oh? What can this be?'

Antonio stroked her hair, his eyes drinking in the flawless beauty of her honey-toned skin and her wide blue eyes.

'You must never tell a soul what I am to tell you now. Do not smile, Cirina – my life could depend on your silence.'

'You can trust me, Antonio,' she promised him solemnly.

He told her the story of the ruby, explaining its significance to his late father and the exiled Byzantines. She listened without interruption as he related how the quest for its return had dominated his father's life, and how he had died with the bitter taste of failure on his tongue. As he talked, Antonio felt as though a great burden had been lifted from him. He had not realised how the secret he had carried with him since joining Marco Polo had been eating away at him.

When he had finished, he lay his head in Cirina's lap and she stroked his forehead. It was a comforting, soothing caress, and he closed his eyes with a contented sigh. After a while, she bent to press her lips against the bridge of his nose, as if warning him that she wished to break the silence.

'How did Kublai Khan come to have the ruby?' she sked.

'No one knows for sure. The only thing that is certain is that he will not want to return it!'

'But how will you steal back the ruby if it is set in the mperor's throne?' she asked.

Antonio grinned up at her.

'Now that, *mi amore*, is a very good question!'

Chapter Nine

The next time Cirina was summoned to the great hal to be presented to Kublai Khan, her eyes immediately sought the ruby. She had been flattered that Antonio had told her his secret and had been intrigued by th story. Now she had no trouble recognising the large, rec jewel which glinted over the Emperor's bald head. I only she could help Antonio retrieve it – how grateful h would be! How proud of her.

'Approach the throne.'

Cirina started as she realised that the Emperor himsel was speaking to her. She did as she was told, keepin her eyes carefully downcast for fear that Chabi, who wa standing to one side of the throne, would see that sh was staring at the Byzantine jewel.

Chabi and Kublai had been in Beijing for seven days While they were away, the whole city seemed to relax as if it only really came alive when its royal rulers wer not in residence. Cirina and Antonio had made the mos of the time to satisfy their hunger for each other which to Cirina's surprise, seemed to grow stronger with eac encounter rather than weaken as she had thought might.

The summons, which had come early that evening, had filled her with alarm and she could not shake off the sense of foreboding as she waited for Kublai Khan to speak again. There were two other girls with her, one Chinese, one Tartar, both remarkable for their beauty. They, like Cirina, assumed an attitude of subservience and she guessed that they also were pleasure slaves to the Khan.

Now the Emperor was speaking again and she dragged her mind back to the present with an effort.

'It has been decreed that you shall accompany the Princess Lei to our dominions in Persia as supplementary brides. You will be leaving in one week. Before then it is hoped that you shall continue to please us.'

It had been difficult to understand the ailing Khan's speech, but Cirina understood enough to be able to say, 'Yes, my lord,' before bowing backwards out of his presence.

As she walked quickly through the corridors, back towards her apartments, she was waylaid by Antonio. Ignoring her attendants alarm, Cirina clasped his hand.

'I heard that you had been summoned to the great hall. I was worried,' he told her.

Though it leapt at this avowal of his concern for her, Cirina's heart was heavy as she told him what had been said.

'I do not understand – what does this mean?'

Antonio's frown was heavy.

'I was going to tell you tonight – Marco Polo has been asked to escort the Princess to Persia where she is to be wed to the Mongolian ruler there. It seems that you and the others are to be given to other noblemen as a reward for their victory in battle.'

'But this means that we will be together, does it not?' Cirina said, her excitement at discovering Antonio was to travel with her overriding her apprehension.

Antonio held both her hands and stared, deep into her

eyes. He could see such love and pure trust there. How could he tell her that, if he was to steal the ruby from the Emperor's throne, he would have to make his escape overland? He could not take the long, meandering sea voyage that Marco had planned.

'Cirina, I – '

'Signor Ballerei – what an unexpected pleasure!'

They sprang apart guiltily as Chabi's low, seductive voice reached them. Glancing at her fearfully, from beneath her lashes, Cirina was confused to discover that, far from being angry to find them whispering in the corridor together, her face was wreathed in smiles.

'My lady,' Antonio said stiffly, executing a sweeping bow.

'Run along to your room, little one – you must rest today for tomorrow we have much enjoyment in store for you! As for you, Signor Ballerei – you will take tea with me.'

Glancing at Cirina, Antonio signalled to her that she should obey without further hesitation. As she watched him stride away, following Chabi along the corridor, Cirina felt a little dart of foreboding. She would have run after him, but her attendants stood firmly between her and the diminutive queen, determined that they should not attract her displeasure by failing to ensure Cirina reached her room.

Chabi sensed that Antonio followed her and so she deliberately did not look back to check. Let him trot along behind her like a tame dog! She had seen the spark of fear in Cirina's eyes as the girl saw her and had been tempted to make the girl's worst nightmares come true there and then.

She smiled to herself. She had more self-control than that, more finesse. When finally she broke the peasant girl's surprisingly strong control, it would be absolutely totally. The man was merely a device through which she would get at the girl. It would be easy to encourage him to give up his most secret, innermost self to her. Cirina was the challenge, Cirina who had bested Chabi in the pleasure dome before the Khan. It was Cirina who had to be punished.

Antonio watched the sway of Chabi's hips as she walked swiftly in front of him. God's bones, but it had given him a fright to see her standing there, watching them! To his surprise, Chabi had not reacted angrily, as he had expected after her previous warnings of the dire consequences which would befall any who dared touch the Khan's favourite. Rather she had regarded them with a kind of amused indulgence, as if what they did was of no more than a passing interest to her. What was behind her demand that he go with her to her apartments was, however, far more difficult to fathom.

Once inside the opulently furnished chamber, Chabi sent for tea and invited Antonio to sit with her amongst the silken cushions on the floor.

'You are enjoying your stay here?' she asked him conversationally as he made himself comfortable in front of her.

'Indeed, my lady, it has been most interesting.'

Her full, red lips curved into a small smile.

'Will you accompany the Polos to Persia?'

'Yes, madam.'

'And then? Do you too intend to return home to fight?'

'I do. Venice has been at war with Genoa for many years – it is time for this to be settled once and for all.'

Chabi nodded approvingly.

'Well spoken, Signor. Before you leave us, though, I feel we should send you away with something far more precious than your vainglorious pride.'

'My lady?' Antonio frowned, ready to take offence, but curious to see what she would say next.

Chabi smiled slowly, as if she could read his thoughts.

Leaning towards him, she dropped her voice to a low whisper, her sweet breath fanning his cheek.

'Only by the surrender of self do we find true knowledge.'

Antonio frowned, not understanding. He felt uncomfortable under her bright, emerald-eyed scrutiny and he shifted slightly against the cushions.

'I am sorry, my lady, I do not understand.'

Chabi's smile grew enigmatic.

'Of course you do not. But you will, my friend, I promise you. Before you leave this place, this paradise you call Xanadu, you will know yourself far better than before. And then you will understand.'

Just then the tea arrived. The elaborate pouring ceremony kept Antonio's questions at bay and he had to rein in his impatience as he sipped at the tiny cup of bitter liquid. Chabi watched him closely, though she did not speak again until the tea things had been cleared away and the servants had left.

'Do you find me attractive, Antonio?' she asked.

Antonio frowned, puzzled by the strange buzzing he could hear in his head.

'I am sorry – the tea – could it have been drugged?'

Far from being outraged by this suggestion, Chabi merely smiled. 'Fear not, Signor, it is merely a little something – a harmless herb – to help you relax. I feel you are a little afraid of me, yes? Do not be afraid.'

Somehow she was by his side, pushing him back on the cushions as her slender body covered his. Antonio's head fell back so that he could see the room, upside down, swimming before his eyes. He did not want this; since he and Cirina had been able to meet daily his appetite for other women had all but disappeared. Yet now his body was betraying him.

Whatever had been in the tea was strong, though not strong enough to knock him out. Rather, he felt as if it would cost him too much of an effort to move. His arms and legs felt heavy, his head made of stone. He could see and hear and feel, but the sounds and movements seemed to come to him as if through a film of water; muted and indistinct. Only the sensations were crystal sharp, made more defined, it seemed, by the dissipation of his other senses.

Chabi was running her fingers all over him, undressing him as she went. As if his body was no longer under his control Antonio helped her slip off his shirt and his breeches. To his surprise, he was erect, his cock springing up like an eager youth's.

Chabi chuckled softly.

'You see – I am but fulfilling your deepest desires!'

She ran her small hands along the length of his shaft, her sharp, painted fingernail grazing gently along the slit. Antonio gasped, feeling it weep as she squeezed gently at the tip. He groaned.

'Relax, enjoy . . .'

Standing, Chabi removed her own clothes. Antonio hauled his head up so that he could watch, dragging a cushion beneath his neck to support it. Her body was in perfect proportion; small, round breasts with dark brown teats, soft at the moment, and bulbous. Her belly was flat and firm, her waist tiny, her hips slender, like a boy's. Her legs, though not long, were exquisitely turned, the skin shining softly in the torch-light.

Antonio's lips felt dry and he moistened them with his tongue. He felt hot all over and the many coloured silks which lined the walls and covered the cushions glowed in the torch-light, shimmering dizzily before his eyes.

As he watched, Chabi took the soft fruits of her breasts and caressed them slowly between her forefinger and thumb. Stretching them outward and rolling them round and round, she brought them to hardness so that they thrust towards him with a wantonness which made his seed sacs tighten almost painfully.

'You want to taste?' Chabi whispered, her voice low and inviting.

Antonio nodded mutely. Chabi knelt above him and allowed one ripe breast to dangle over his face. Obediently, Antonio opened his mouth wide and began to suckle on the taut nub of flesh. It tasted slightly odd – like cinnamon – but delicious and he rolled it on his tongue.

Meanwhile, Chabi was caressing his straining shaft with her fingernails. Her touch was teasing, but gentle, though there was always the threat of pain, never far away. Antonio's head swam as the nipple was removed, to be replaced by its twin. Reaching up, he tried to touch her, but Chabi pushed his hands away.

'Wait,' she said, her voice reverberating along his spine, 'I have something I want to show you.'

She went over to a table and picked up a long, laquered box. Opening it, she took something out and knelt down beside him. Antonio's eyes widened as she waved the object before his eyes. Made of ivory, it was an exact replica of a male organ, complete with lovingly carved veins and foreskin.

'Is he not beautiful?' Chabi purred.

Antonio did not know what to say. He watched, entranced, as Chabi trailed the object across her forehead and down her nose to her mouth. Running back and forth across her closed lips, she slowly opened them and allowed her tongue to snake across the carved groove at the top.

Antonio's own cock twitched in sympathy. He could almost feel those moist, soft lips passing over his cock-head, pushing insistently into the tiny eye of his penis drawing the fluid from it. His breath became shallow as he watched, unable to look away as Chabi drew the object into her mouth. Her lips stretched across its substantial girth, her cheeks bulging as she eased it further inside. Then, tilting back her head, she allowed it to slip out. Antonio watched, fascinated, as a thread of spittle spanned from her lips to the wet head of the substitute cock, before breaking and trickling down the side.

Catching Chabi's gaze, he saw the unnatural brightness in her eyes and trembled. Yet he could not help but follow the progress of the phallus as the stroked it down her neck and between her breasts. Her skin glistened with her own saliva as it passed over it. Touching the tip against each nipple, she moaned deeply.

'Ah, Signor – I am thinking that this should be your fine manhood bathing my skin with wetness.'

She made no move to touch him again, though. Instead she trickled the mock penis down, over her belly, circling her navel before thrusting it through the silky hair on her mons. Antonio's eyes widened, his cock pulsing as he watched it part the thick, red lips of her woman's place and come to rest at the entrance to her body.

He could smell the rich, yeasty fragrance of her musk as it covered the object. Surely she would not violate her own body with the thing? Part of him was appalled but another, far stronger part, silently urged her on.

Vaguely, he heard a door open and a young Chinese woman joined them. She was naked, her pubis shockingly bare so that her pink sex-lips were clearly visible hanging below those on the outside. She gazed impassively at the scene before her, waiting for Chabi's instructions.

'Do you like to have your cock sucked, Signore Balerei?' Chabi said.

Thankfully, she did not appear to require an answer to her question, for she laughed, a light, tinkling sound, at odds with the languid movement back and forth of her hand as she pleasured herself with the ivory phallus.

'Of course you do! Up on your knees, sir.'

She clicked her fingers at the serving girl who immediately lay down on her back in front of Antonio. As if in a daze, he raised himself onto his knees, leaning forward to rest his hands on the floor on the other side of the girl's slim body.

Smiling up at him, she reached for his dangling member and brought it towards her mouth. Antonio gasped with pleasure at the first touch of her lips against him. At that moment, Chabi opened her labia with the fingers of one hand, exposing the moist crevice which led to the entrance of her body. Antonio watched, mesmerised, as the carved phallus inched its way inside her, distending the fleshy tube so that her woman's place bulged in welcome.

He could see her juices shining on the ivory as she pushed it in and out of herself, in time with the Chinese girl's slow, licking caresses along his penis. He was close to release, his seed sacs stretched tight as a drum between his legs, feeling as if they would burst.

Assessing him shrewdly, Chabi signalled to the girl to go slowly and she allowed the ivory phallus to slip from her body. Antonio groaned as he was pulled back from the brink, trying to move in and out of the serving girl's suddenly passive mouth.

'Be still,' Chabi commanded and he immediately obeyed.

The sensation of being held in that warm, wet mouth was quite delightful, frustrating though it was at such a late stage in his arousal. Nevertheless, Antonio managed to control himself as Chabi came closer.

Smiling wickedly, she passed the ivory phallus beneath his nose. His nostrils were filled with the musky, pungent scent of her arousal and he closed his eyes briefly. They flew open again as he felt the mock penis push at his lips.

'Suck,' Chabi whispered.

Antonio's mouth opened of its own accord, to be filled with the hard, unyielding ivory which was bathed in the juices from Chabi's body. She was all around him, the ight of her, the smell, the intimate taste, filling his enses.

'Now, my fine Venetian,' Chabi was whispering in his ar as he sucked on the phallus, 'imagine that this is varm, yielding flesh. No – do not open your eyes, do ot stop.'

The girl beneath him began working on him again and e groaned, the sound muffled by the ivory filling his nouth.

'Surrender your pleasure to me, Antonio Ballerei – how me how much you want to suck another man – nat's right,' she whispered as he began to lick and suck t the phallus, opening his throat as she pressed it gently owards the back of his mouth. 'Relax the muscles of our throat – ah yes! Imagine how the man you are ucking will feel when you take all of him!'

Though the rational, sane part of his mind rejected vhat she was saying, Antonio could not help but be owerfully aroused by her words. The girl who was ucking him seemed to mimic his every movement. Vhen he sucked hard at the phallus, so she sucked hard t his own straining shaft, when he took it further into is throat, she followed suit. Thus he was able to feel the ensations experienced by both the fellated, and the llator. Chabi was still murmuring in his ear.

'Is that not good? Do you not want to swallow the hot, ick fluid which should shoot from the end? Or would ou prefer to feel the thrust of another man against you ere?'

He gasped as Chabi began to stimulate the sensitive kin of the crease between his buttocks.

'No!' he whispered, though, even to him his plea ounded half-hearted.

'Oh yes, my friend, this is what you desire most! dmit it – give in to it.'

How could she know? How could she have guessed? ntonio cried out, partly in anguish, partly in acceptance as she removed the phallus from his mouth and, moving behind him, began to rub it up and down his bottom cleft.

The girl was still sucking diligently at his cock and he felt it would not be long before he climaxed. And yet every nerve in his body protested at the violation he knew was about to take place.

'Relax – push it out for me. That's it. It won't hurt, not much,' she laughed, softly.

Antonio felt a thick, oily ointment being rubbed into his reluctant anus and the bulbous head of the ivory phallus pushed against the sphincter of muscle.

'By the saints . . . no . . . yes . . . oh God!'

He felt his back passage convulsing against the intrusion as Chabi eased the phallus gently into his anus. At that moment, the girl beneath him swirled her tongue round and round his weeping cock-head before drawing him in again, right to the very back of her throat.

Chabi twisted the phallus, making sure he felt the intrusion in every part of him. It was then that he came, hot, jagged bursts of semen pumping along his shaft flooding the girl's mouth and throat.

He barely noticed when she released him, so intense was his orgasm. It seemed to go on and on as Chabi abused him with the ivory phallus, breaking down his defences and making him see himself anew. Chabi's words came back to him. *Only by the surrender of self do we find true knowledge.* He hadn't understood then but, as she had promised, he did so now.

And, as he collapsed, exhausted, across the silk cushions, the phallus still embedded in his throbbing anus, Antonio knew that nothing could ever be the same again.

Chapter Ten

All was quiet in the jewelled yurt as Chabi and Kublai Khan spent a rare hour alone together, taking tea. :habi regarded her husband cautiously over the rim of er delicately fashioned cup and wondered why she had een summoned.

Kublai's expression was bland enough, but she had :arned over the years that it was when he was at his ıost amenable that he could be at his most dangerous. .part from the customary greetings, not a word had een spoken and the heavy silence stretched like an nbreakable cord between them until Chabi's nerves 'ere played out to their limit.

'Well, my jewel,' Kublai said at last, draining his cup ›r the second time, 'have you tamed our little desert ɔwer yet?'

Chabi's stomach churned. Her husband's eyes were ke two dull brown sultanas, peering at her inquisitively om the folds of flesh above his cheekbones and below ıs eyebrows.

'I believe I have found a way,' she said, unable to :event a slight trembling from entering her voice.

'I am glad to hear it – there is not much time left!

Tomorrow you will demonstrate your mastery to me. You know how much I enjoy watching you in action!' He laughed, wheezing violently. 'Do not fail me, my love.'

'Never, my lord.'

Chabi bent low as Kublai signalled to his attendants that he wished them to help him to his feet. Though his tone had been teasing, she was under no illusion that he would discard her with as little thought as he would discard a lame camel if she should fail to please him.

She watched through narrowed eyes as the Emperor was virtually hauled to his feet. All stood with eyes respectfully averted as he regained his breath, spitting into the large bowl held for him by a dark-skinned male slave. Then he shuffled from the room, a pathetic figure who held the power of life and death over everyone in the city.

Tomorrow – it was too soon! She fretted as she made her way back to her own rooms. Antonio was not a problem – his capitulation the day before had been almost too easy. He was being kept in a room nearby served only by the young, muscular men Chabi knew he desired, kept in a state of semi-arousal until she decided what should be done with him.

Pacing up and down, she contemplated the best way to achieve Cirina's submission. So far the girl had succeeded in retaining her self control even while she appeared to acquiesce to Chabi's demands. In the pleasure dome when she had sought to humiliate her Cirina had succeeded in making a fool of Chabi. Kublai was too shrewd not to have realised this, and too manipulative not to use the fact for his own ends. Now Chabi was in serious trouble – everything depended on her being able to control Cirina the following day.

Suddenly, she stopped, a slow smile spreading over her face as the answer came to her. Of course! The way to Cirina was through the Venetian! It was perfect

Antonio would be granted his deepest, darkest desire and Cirina would witness it, and submit in her turn.

Feeling that the problem had been solved, Chabi sent for her attendants, the prospect of the display she would engineer for the Khan the next day tinged now with a pleasant anticipation.

Cirina felt she would go mad with boredom. Since her audience with the Khan the day before she had been confined to her room without even her attendants for company. On the stroke of every hour she had looked out over her balcony, hoping to see Antonio, but he had not come. Where had he gone with Chabi the night before?

At first she had been piqued that he had not come to her, then worried. Supposing Chabi had found out about them – would she dare to have a European flogged? In her heart of hearts Cirina knew that Antonio was in as much danger as any subject of the Khan and her fears for him grew. When a second night came and she still had not heard from him, she lay sleepless on her pallet, staring out at the starry night and praying that, wherever he might be, he was safe.

Antonio too was finding it difficult to sleep. Lying once again on his lonely pallet, he gazed out of the unscreened window at the bejewelled sky and wondered anew at his capitulation.

Across the courtyard he could see Cirina's balcony. As he watched, every now and again her slender form could be seen looking out. She was too far away for him to see her face, but he guessed that she was looking for him. It would not take much to rise and wave at her, to reassure her that he was safe, but Antonio was too ashamed. Instead he lay and watched her miserably, despising himself for his craven soul.

His head turned as he heard the door open softly and

a slender, golden-haired youth slipped through. Anke. Antonio's heart sank at the same time as his treacherous man-flesh rose. His fists clenched above his head, his arms pulling in vain against the silk scarves that held him. Anke saw the movement and frowned.

'Why do you fight it still? Am I so unappealing to you?'

Antonio wanted to scream, *yes, of course you are! I am a man, after all, a strong and virile man with natural urges, red blood flowing through my veins! Only weaklings and degenerates turn to other men for sexual satisfaction. I want Ailee and Tali and Beijei, soft, feminine flesh and sweet, perfumed hair sweeping across my skin.* But something told him that the youth would be genuinely hurt by such an admission. The Lord alone knew why, he owed the youth no tenderness, but Antonio did not want to wound him.

He groaned softly as Anke approached the pallet and reached to run his fingers softly up Antonio's leg, from his knee to his groin. The youth smiled as his penis hardened further in response.

'You see?' he cooed, teasing his fingertips lightly up and down Antonio's inner thigh. 'It is what you want.'

'No!'

Anke raised one finely plucked eyebrow.

'This says yes,' he said, running his fingertips gently along the length of Antonio's tumescent shaft.

Antonio closed his eyes as Anke dipped his head and slipped the now fully erect flesh into his warm mouth. Before, when it had happened with Chabi, he had been able to convince himself that it had been the sedative herb in the tea that had made him react in a way that was totally unfamiliar to him. Even now, he could argue that, if his hands weren't tied above his head, he would use his fists to stop this lithe, gentle youth from taking advantage of him.

But as his hips bucked and he shot his seed into Anke's welcoming throat, he knew that there was really no need for the restraint – he craved this unnatural pleasuring more and more with every passing hour.

Lifting his head, a smile of triumph touching his swollen lips, Anke saw the tears of shame sparkling on Antonio's lashes and his smile slid away. Reaching up, he smoothed the hair tenderly from Antonio's forehead before running his tongue lightly across his lashes, licking away the salty tears. Little shivers of sensation ran up and down Antonio's spine, adding to his misery.

'It's all right,' Anke whispered. As if acting on an impulse, he untied Antonio's wrists and climbed onto the pallet beside him. Putting his arms around the other man's finely muscled body, he stared deep into his eyes. 'It's all right,' he said again.

Feeling absolutely wretched, Antonio lay his head on Anke's shoulder and wept.

They came for Cirina early the following evening, and took her down to the bathing place. This time as they washed and dried her, the mischievous atmosphere was missing and the twins worked with concentration, steadfastedly ignoring all Cirina's attempts to make conversation. They had been punished for their aberration the night when the lady, Chabi had found their charge and the handsome European talking together in the corridor and neither wished to attract their mistress's wrath again.

Eventually, Cirina fell silent, allowing them to smooth and powder her skin, turning this way and that obligingly as they swathed her in emerald silk. Her hair was brushed until it shone, then plaited into a braid which was wound into a topknot on her head.

Once they had finished, the twins stood back and eyed their handiwork critically. Cirina stood absolutely still, her eyes fixed on the calm surface of the water in the bath. She could see the fragrant oils floating in little, shiny globules on the surface, caught by the light of the torches held in the iron sconces in the walls.

The two girls whispered together, then one approached her and tugged gently at the edge of the silk wound about her shoulders. Cirina's eyebrows rose as the girl carefully exposed one breast, regarding her consideringly, her head on one side.

The second girl ran to fetch a small, black laquered box from which she took a thick gold ring. Cirina's eyes widened as she approached her and lifted her exposed breast in the palm of her hand. Without warning, she bent her head and drew the soft fruit of her areola into her mouth, coaxing it into hardness.

Though she stood very still, Cirina felt her other nipple harden jealously and her breath caught in her chest. When she was satisfied that the nipple was standing proud of the soft breast tissue, the girl took it between her finger and thumb and pulled it gently, elongating it. Then she slipped the gold ring over the teat, twisting it firmly so that it stayed in place when she took her hand away.

Cirina felt the constriction, pinching slightly, at her breast and she bit her lower lip. It was uncomfortable, but far from painful and she decided she rather liked the feeling. Smiling at the bemused attendants, she followed them out of the bath house towards the great hall.

Inside, Kublai Khan was already ensconced on his jewel-encrusted throne, flanked by two high-ranking officers of his personal guard. The throne had been moved to a dais in one corner of the room, and a series of silk screens had been pulled round, creating a small, intimate corner within the echoing vault of the great hall itself.

Cirina stepped into the enclave with some trepidation, her eyes skittering around to take in the flickering torches held in the wall sconces and in several strategically placed, free-standing holders around the floor.

Incense smoked gently in the burners and a thick, sickly-sweet perfume hung in the air, making her feel slightly dizzy.

There were two platforms, side by side, raised slightly, though not quite as high as the Emperor's throne. One was covered in deep, royal blue silk, the other in ruby red. Some half a dozen high-ranking officials and their wives lounged across a series of silk-covered couches placed at either end of the platforms, whilst still more sat amongst the large cushions scattered on the fur-strewn ground.

The light buzz of conversation ceased on Cirina's arrival and she unconsciously straightened her back. Sweeping her eyes over the assembled watchers, she saw the admiration and the appreciation, and she felt a surge of power. She felt like an Empress, a Goddess – they were all in her thrall, all eager to see her display herself.

As she was led over to the blue platform, Cirina caught Chabi's eyes on her. She raised her head boldly and looked the other woman square in the eye, smiling slightly as she saw the undisguised fury cross Chabi's features. Whatever the diminutive queen had in store for her today, Cirina was determined that she should emerge triumphant. How could she not, when the mere ambience of the place was affecting her senses, the anticipation of the trials to follow arousing her even now.

'Beautiful!' exclaimed Kublai Khan. 'Quite exquisite.'

'Disrobe!' Chabi snapped, visibly angered by Cirina's proud demeanour. Didn't the girl know that she was to be humiliated? That it was her submission, her subjugation of herself and her own pleasure that was to be her gift to the Khan?

Chabi watched her as she unwound the silk from her body. Since she had arrived in Shang-tu the girl had blossomed, had acquired a voluptuous, joyous sensuality that was apparent in her every movement. Chabi felt

Kublai's eyes on her and she carefully schooled her expression. Knowing that he would consider that she had failed if the girl emerged from the display without the slightest anguish, she promised herself that it would not be so. Cirina had endured everything Chabi had subjected her to so far. No, she had *enjoyed* it. The girl was made for pleasure, was the most naturally sensual creature Chabi had ever come across. Well, she would not enjoy this night, not if Chabi had anything to do with it.

She was standing now, gloriously naked, her smooth, honey-toned skin glowing in the torch-light, jet black hair wound into an elaborate topknot on her head. The hairstyle emphasised the graceful length of her neck and made her look quite queenly. Irritated, Chabi indicated that she should remove the pins and bring it down.

Now her hair hung like a bolt of shimmering silk down her narrow back. She was beautiful and there was something about her serenity that told Chabi that she was well aware of this fact. There was a dignity in her stillness, a pride in the way that she accepted the gaze of the audience, seeing it as her due.

It was this dignity, this pride, this sense that no one could touch her soul that Chabi wanted to subdue tonight. Before the evening was over she would hear her beg. Smiling coldly, Chabi approached.

'It seems, girl, that in awakening your sensual desires we have disturbed a sleeping dragon,' she said, her voice pleasant, a note of amusement colouring her words. 'You have developed a liking for the pleasures of the flesh, have you not?'

Cirina looked her fully in the eye and, with a glint of defiance which infuriated Chabi, she answered, 'Indeed, my lady.'

Chabi smiled tightly, her gaze piercing. Circling her, she raked her body with her eyes, tapping her flywhip meditatively against her palm. She sensed the girl's body grow taut, as if ready for flight, and this slight show of apprehension pleased her. She was not entirely self assured – that was good.

The room was quiet, expectant. All knew better than to interrupt the Empress when she was in a mood such as this, and all knew that the entertainment, when it began, would be the sweeter for the tension that had been so skilfully woven beforehand.

'Pleasure,' Chabi said, breaking the silence at last. 'Such a strange emotion in many ways. So unpredictable, so close to pain. Do you like pain, little one, as much as you like pleasure?'

The last was said with Chabi's lips close to Cirina's ear, her warm breath whispering around the whorls, making her shiver. The gooseflesh rose up on Cirina's naked skin and she tried to breath shallowly through her nose, as if by keeping absolutely still, she would not attract any more of Chabi's attention.

The older woman smiled. Cirina could see the cruel twist of her lips out of the corner of her eye and her heart began to pound as she realised at last the peril she was in.

'You are afraid now, are you not?' Chabi whispered silkily against her ear, so no one else could hear her. 'Submit to me, little one – give your pleasure to me, and your pain. You will soon find that the two can become one.'

Suddenly, unexpectedly, her tongue shot out and she licked around the delicate creases inside Cirina's ear, making her jump. As she did so, Chabi flicked the whip against the underside of Cirina's breasts, making her cry out in alarm and surprise.

The blow stung, making her breasts judder. Cirina was aware of a gasp amongst the people watching and her eyes flew frantically over their faces. They all looked the same to her now – eyes wide and avid, mouths slack and wet, waiting, straining towards her in lustful anticipation. Chabi flicked the undersides of her breasts with the flywhip again and Cirina cried out at the sudden, sharp sting.

She did not understand this new development, could not see how it was linked with the pleasures of the flesh. And yet even as her mind recoiled from the physical punishment, she could feel the warmth radiating out from her belly and knew that her body was reacting to the pain as it did to a caress. And yet how could it? It must be wrong – unhealthy. Her breasts had swollen, the nipples distended so that the one caught by the gold ring was squeezed to the point of a curiously pleasurable discomfort which confused her.

Chabi saw the confusion in her eyes and smiled. The girl would understand, soon enough. Snapping her fingers at the servant waiting in the shadows, she watched Cirina's apprehension mount as he brought on the harness. Her flesh shrank from the cold touch of metal as the links were passed over her shoulders and her breasts were pushed through the leather rings. A linking chain hung from between her breasts to her pubis, where it divided into thongs which encircled her thighs. These ties served no purpose other than to secure the breast restraint and provide a decorative feature – thin strips of dark leather against the soft, golden flesh.

Glancing at Chabi, the servant stood back, waiting further instruction.

'The neck collar?' Chabi prompted, impatience sharpening her tone.

The servant lifted Cirina's hair from her shoulders and fastened the collar around her slender neck. It was made of a wide band of leather and had fine metal rings at the front and back. The width of the band meant that Cirina's chin was lifted and she was unable to drop her head, nor move it very far to the right and left.

Relishing the apprehension in the deep blue eyes, Chabi approached her slowly. When they were standing toe to toe, she held out her hand to the servant, who hastily placed a long leather lead into it. Chabi let the lead dangle for a moment in front of Cirina's widening eyes before clipping it securely to the ring at her throat. Now she had her tethered, completely at her mercy, and Chabi felt the adrenalin really begin to pump through her veins.

She gave a short, sharp tug on the leash, and Cirina dropped to her knees at her feet. Turning, Chabi slung the lead over her shoulder and walked theatrically over to her seat. This meant that Cirina was forced to crawl rapidly behind her, like an obedient animal. As they passed through the people sitting below the royal dais, dozens of hands shot out to stroke, to squeeze, to tweak and pet.

On reaching the seat, Chabi looked down at the girl. Her face was flushed, burning with who knew what emotion, and her hair was falling in disarray across her face. She had never looked more beautiful and Chabi felt an unexpected rush of tenderness for her. Bending down, she stroked her fingertips around the outline of her face.

'We will eat now. Sit here – at my feet.'

Cirina sat, because she had no choice. No one seemed to be paying her any attention. Her attraction for them had gone – for now. Her breasts, brought into prominence by the leather harness, felt swollen and tender, the undersides still smarting from the attentions of Chabi's whip. The nipples were large and thrusting, the one pinched quite cruelly by the gold ring. She felt aware of every inch of her body, as if she had been touched, all over, by a feather-light caress. And as she sat, accepting tidbits of meat and rice from Chabi's fingers, she was aware of a steady, expectant pulse beating between her thighs.

Antonio was being prepared for his presentation to the Khan, though he did not know that this was the reason for the careful attention to his body. For two days and two nights he had been held captive in his room, unable to prevent the continual stimulation of his body by the golden youth, Anke, or a stream of other male attendants, some of whom he saw only once. Only Anke was a constant, and he clung to his growing attachment to him, sure it was only this that kept him sane.

After Anke had untied his hands they had not been re-bound and so Antonio's last cause for self-justification was denied him. Gradually, as hour followed hour and day followed night, he had begun to admit that he found the other men's attentions rewarding, that he now craved still greater intimacy from them than the release they offered by hand or mouth.

He had pushed Cirina to the back of his mind, unable to cope with analysing the implications of his submission. Now that his sexuality was conditioned to respond to other men, he feared that he would no longer be able to function like a man with Cirina, or any other woman. Perhaps worse, he was afraid that she would despise him, as he despised himself.

Anke was with him now, massaging oil into his naked torso, lingering as he reached his buttocks.

'You have a beautiful arse,' he said contemplatively as he kneaded the flesh there.

Antonio closed his eyes, his breathing rapid. To date, no one had tried to penetrate him there, as Chabi had with the ivory phallus. He lived in dread of the moment when it would happen, doggedly refusing to acknowledge the part of him that yearned for it.

Since the first moment when Chabi had breached his defences, he had known that it was inevitable that eventually she would coerce him into acting out his darkest desires. Even as he thought it, he knew that no coercion would be required. It was what he wanted, probably had always wanted. It was a nonsense to blame

Chabi for his own fantasies. Now he merely clenched his muscles, even while knowing that to resist was useless.

Anke chuckled softly and pummeled at the tight mounds.

'Relax – open up. You are to be stretched and made ready.'

Antonio's breathing stilled. Suddenly time seemed to have slowed, everything around him shifted out of focus and Anke's voice seemed to recede.

'Made ready? What do you mean?' he croaked.

Anke's strong fingers kneaded at his taut flesh and he made a soothing noise in the back of his throat.

'Relax. Give yourself up to it. There's less pain that way, more pleasure.'

Alarmed, Antonio tried to rise from the couch, but Anke pushed him down with a hand at the back of his neck.

'You're still too tense. Would you like me to relax you?'

Antonio bit his lip, so hard that he tasted blood on his tongue. He wanted to say no, wanted to stand up and fight his way out of this terrible mess he seemed to be in. If he found Marco and the others they would help him get away from here. But his treacherous body would not listen to his inner voice, and he found himself rolling with indecent haste onto his back. His cock was already erect, eager for the silken caress of Anke's lips.

He groaned with disappointment as the youth merely stroked his palm soothingly along the length of his shaft.

'Not now,' he crooned, his face a picture of regret. 'It is forbidden. I shall miss you when you go.'

Antonio experienced a moment's panic.

'When I go?'

Anke looked at him with mild surprise.

'You will be leaving with the other Europeans, will you not?'

Antonio thought rapidly. Relief that he was not to be

kept captive here indefinitely warred with regret that he and Anke must part.

'Yes,' he murmured, aware that the youth was pinching a spot below the head of his cock which was making him grow soft again. 'Yes, I will be leaving.'

Anke smiled, suddenly mischievous.

'But not until tomorrow. You have tonight to enjoy first.'

He slapped Antonio lightly on the thigh and Antonio rolled over obediently. Tonight. The Lord only knew what was in store for him tonight.

Anke was massaging his buttocks again and this time he allowed the muscles to relax. The oil seeped into his cleft, trickling past that dark, secret entrance, the forbidden orifice of his body which seemed to be at the root of his deepest, darkest desires.

He did not resist when the youth's fingers began working the oil into the little hole, swirling his fingertip round and round until the tip slipped inside.

'Come up onto your knees,' he murmured, and Antonio obeyed without question. Spreading his knees wide, he felt himself open to Anke's gaze. He gasped as a short, fat object was pressed into his virgin passage.

'Hold it in,' Anke instructed. 'In an hour or so, we'll replace it with a larger one. Now,' he helped Antonio to sit back on his heels, his whole concentration centred on keeping the rectal plug inside him, 'there might be a ban on my pleasuring you tonight, but that doesn't mean you can't do something for me.'

Antonio's eyes widened in shock as Anke took his hand and placed it squarely on the front of his breeches. He had never done that before. Things had been done to him, no one had asked him to do anything other than lie passive and accept his submission. He could feel Anke's erection beneath the thin fabric of his breeches. It was long and slim, warm enough to make his palm tingle. Antonio's lips felt dry and parched.

'You want me to – to . . .'

Anke leaned forward and kissed him on the lips. It was a gentle kiss – Anke's full, soft lips pliant against his. The tenderness of it took Antonio by surprise and he felt a lump of emotion grow in his throat.

'I want you to pleasure me, with your hand. It will be our secret – I am not supposed to allow you to touch me. But it will be the last time we will be alone together – '

'The last time?' Antonio interrupted, the dismay he felt taking him by surprise.

'The last time,' Anke repeated gently, 'and I have wanted it so badly.'

He closed his eyes as Antonio slowly, tentatively, began to move his hand back and forth over the youth's breeches.

'Take it out,' Anke whispered hoarsely, 'let me come in your hand.'

Antonio obeyed him almost feverishly. He had never held another man before, was fascinated by how Anke's body differed from his own. His scrotum was tight and full, virtually hairless. Running his fingertips around his seed sacs, feeling their outline, Antonio felt his own cock harden again. As his erection grew, so he became more conscious of the object which had been inserted in his anus. It pressed on the sensitive inner walls, giving him an almost overwhelming sense of fullness.

'Don't come, Antonio, you must control yourself,' Anke warned him. 'You must save yourself for the Emperor . . . ahh!'

His sigh of pleasure made Antonio feel warm inside. He curled his fingers around the slender shaft, his eyes watching with fascination as the loose skin moved independently of the firmer core. Up and down, up and down, he increased his rhythm as he saw that Anke was close to satisfaction. He could feel the tingling at the base of his shaft, could imagine the seed surging along it to the purple-headed end. Then suddenly it began to spurt, hot, viscous fluid soaking his hand and running across his wrist and along his forearm.

Antonio could not take his eyes off the other man's fluid which lay on his skin. A part of him could not believe what he had just done, but the greater part of him was suffused by a pure, unadulterated joy.

Anke grinned at him, leaning forward to kiss him once again on the lips.

'Thank you,' he said simply. 'Do you think you could take a bigger plug now?'

Antonio nodded, unable to trust himself to speak. Without having to be told, he assumed the required position to accept the insertion of a longer, thicker rectal plug without a murmur – his eyes fixed on the remains of Anke's semen drying rapidly on his arm. To his bemusement, it seemed like the most natural thing in the world.

Chapter Eleven

Cirina watched everyone eating and drinking and making merry as if from far away. She felt so removed from what was going on in the hall, so alienated from the people there. But she realised that this was how Chabi wanted her to feel, how she had designed things to be.

As she sat at the Empress's feet, Cirina felt her skin prickle with awareness as Chabi played with her hair, occasionally bending down to caress a nipple, or press a goblet to her lips so that she could drink. Next to Chabi, though elevated slightly as befitted his rank, sat Kublai Khan himself. He too had a 'pet' chained at his feet. Only in the Emperor's case it was a leopard, a beautiful, tranquil creature who sat, motionless, on its hind legs and regarded the proceedings with a haughty disdain. Once or twice it turned its magnificent neck and looked towards Cirina, as if it recognised in her a kindred spirit.

Once the feasting was over, Chabi tugged on the lead attached to Cirina's collar and she was led back down to the blue platform.

'Now, my lovely, I will teach you the true meaning of submission,' Chabi said softly.

Cirina trembled under her bright, emerald gaze, but she raised her chin proudly and refused to be cowed. When she was commanded, she sank to her knees and assumed a crouching position, on all fours, presenting her bare buttocks for Chabi's approval.

Her skin quivered as a servant prepared her body with a cool, oily fluid which was massaged into her skin, little droplets trickling into her bottom cleft and teasing the sensitive opening there. Imagining the sight she was presenting to the onlookers, bottom raised, the skin glistening with oil, her woman's place just visible from behind, made Cirina's heartbeat quicken. Almost without realising what she was doing, she thrust her hips further back and up.

The first stroke of Chabi's flywhip across her upturned buttocks made her gasp. At first she shrank from the stinging sensation it caused, but gradually realised that the sting soon turned to a warm, not unpleasant glow and she waited for the second stroke with a heightened sense of anticipation.

All eyes were on her as she sucked in her breath again, and waited, once more, to feel that curiously pleasant, spreading warmth suffuse her. She thrust her buttocks upward to meet the third stroke, earning herself a murmur of approval from the watching audience.

When the fourth stroke did not materialise, Cirina heard her own voice, as if divorced from her, pleading for the whipping to continue.

'Ahh! Thank you!' she whispered when Chabi obliged.

Little trickles of sensation were curling through her belly and thighs, setting up that delicious, dull pulse between her thighs again. She squirmed her hips a little, desperate for the touch of fingers against her throbbing core. Behind her Chabi laughed mirthlessly.

'Think you that you have earned your satisfaction already?'

Cirina gasped as the fifth stroke landed across her

buttocks, this one more vicious than the last, delivered, she suspected, more in anger than in passion.

Chabi then turned her attention to her dangling breasts, flicking them with the flywhip so that they shook. Her skin smarted, her nipples hardening to the point of discomfort and Cirina felt the perspiration break out all over her body.

To her astonishment, she felt the sting caused by the whip create an answering response in the tender leaves of flesh between her thighs, making her juices flow and her lips swell. Her belly felt tight, full of tension as Chabi ran the tip of the whip lightly back and forth across her straining nipples.

'Crawl about the platform – let all see how well you take your punishment,' Chabi instructed coldly.

Cirina obeyed, moving one knee awkwardly in front of the other, supremely conscious of the way her body was displayed in the leather harness. Her breasts were held apart, the nipples hanging down like two ripe fruit. As she neared the end of one side of the platform, a man reached out and touched her, his fingers grasping at the gold ring. Several men with him pushed forward for a closer look at her and for a moment Cirina was afraid that they would join her on the platform.

To her relief, Chabi flicked the man's wrist with the very same flywhip which had marked her buttocks, and the man sank obediently back onto his cushions.

'Arse high,' she hissed at Cirina, and Cirina thrust her buttocks higher, knowing that by doing so she was giving all who cared to look an unobstructed view of her swollen sex-lips as she crawled back towards the centre of the platform.

That she was aroused would be clear to everyone and she smiled to herself, glad to have thwarted Chabi once again. She herself had never dreamt that she might take pleasure from such cold-hearted treatment, and she guessed that Chabi had not thought it either.

She was right – Chabi was beside herself with fury, though she hid it well. Was there nothing that the little slut would not enjoy? Feeling the Khan's amused eyes upon her, she thought fast. The best and only remaining way to punish Cirina for her defiance would be to deprive her of that which she craved most.

Originally, Chabi had planned to have her taken by two, possibly three men at once, but there would be no sport in such a spectacle unless she struggled and wept. Nothing it seemed, would make Cirina weep and, having managed to make her beg, there was nothing she wanted more than her tears.

Briefly, she considered the application of a more intimate whipping whilst the girl worked her way along the salivating men on the front row, pleasuring each with her mouth. Realising that Cirina would most likely enjoy every minute of such sport, Chabi smiled cruelly and pulled on the chain until the girl was standing.

Without a word she made her sit at the foot of the chair on the royal dais and commanded her to spread her legs. As she had suspected, Cirina was wet, her labia glistening with the evidence of her arousal, her woman's place open and inviting.

Chabi took a long, thin cane with a flexible end from the collection of whips she had concealed by her chair. The flexible end of the cane was covered with fresh animal fur. Slowly, watching the girl's face so that she could gauge every nuance of reaction, she stroked the tip lightly up her inner thigh to her parted sex-lips.

Cirina gasped as the soft fur brushed along her outer channels and stroked over the hard core of her pleasure place. Chabi began to flick the cane to and fro, tormenting that tiny concentration of nerve endings until Cirina was squirming on the hard, pelt-covered dais.

Chabi waited until Cirina was just about to tip over into release. Knowing that timing was crucial, she watched the pupils of her eyes dilate, saw the sweat run down between her breasts and the dull red flush spread across her chest and neck. Watching her most intimate flesh redden and swell, she could almost see the tiny heart beating at the centre of her woman's place, the feelings were becoming so intense.

When she was sure that it would take no more than one more flick of the fur-covered cane tip, Chabi stopped. Cirina's eyes, which had been closing, snapped open, widening in anguish as she interpreted Chabi's cruel smile.

'Please – oh, my lady, please grant me release!' she cried, uncaring that she was surrendering her pride with every word.

Chabi smiled almost serenely, her confidence growing as Cirina's diminished. Time to play her trump card.

'I think not,' she said, turning away. 'There is more entertainment to come. Watch – I think this is something you will find interesting.'

Cirina was left to curl her legs beneath her and fight the maelstrom of sensation which was still rioting through her body. It would take no more than a quick rub with her fingertip to push her over the edge into release, but she dared not risk it. Chabi's planned, controlled cruelty she could stand, even enjoy, but she sensed that, if she should be thwarted, the other woman would be merciless. For some reason Chabi had decided that Cirina should be tormented by denying her the release she had so carefully made her crave. All Cirina could really do is wait, and hope that later, when she was alone, she would be able to set free the pent-up passion within her.

A loud gong reverberated around the great hall and all eyes turned from Cirina to the door. A young man was marched in, dressed in sumptuous gold silk robes, his head wrapped in a jewel-encrusted turban. As he was brought to the red silk platform, he turned and

Cirina saw his face for the first time. Her hand flew to her mouth as she realised it was Antonio.

His eyes brushed over her, but he didn't seem to see her, not properly. He had a strange, glazed look about him, as if he had not slept for a long time and the dark shadows under his cheeks and eyes added to the impression. He seemed dazed as the golden-haired young man who had mounted the platform with him drew the robes off his shoulders.

Underneath he was naked, his white, oiled skin, glowing pale in the torch-light. Everyone in the room turned their attention away from Cirina, sitting still as a statue on the floor by Chabi's chair, and stared at the virile young European.

Antonio looked around him, bewildered by the gathering. So many eyes staring at him, all hot, hungry, lusting after him, man and woman. Vaguely, he was aware that he was naked, yet somehow he could not dredge up the energy to care. Chabi smiled at him and he stared at her dully, knowing with weary resignation, that what was about to happen was inevitable. There was no point in fighting it.

'Would you like to be scourged, Signor, before you are granted satisfaction?'

Her voice was cool, but not unkind and Antonio frowned. He saw that she was holding a short-handled object with several tails of leather hanging from it in her hand. Suddenly the idea of the strands of leather kissing his skin was a very attractive one; perhaps therein lay redemption. He nodded.

Chabi smiled and clicked her fingers at two servants. They stood either side of him and stretched out his arms, thus giving Chabi a wider target. Someone – he presumed it was Anke – nudged his ankles with their foot and he spread his legs wide. Chabi's small, cool hands ran approvingly over the smooth, finely muscled contours of his back, down to his buttocks. Once there she caressed the twin globes, her touch almost loving.

Her fingers encountered the rectal plug and she pulled it out without warning, making Antonio gasp. He felt its loss, imagining that the void it had filled was left gaping, obvious to all.

She started at his shoulders; little, flicking blows, never in the same place twice, moving steadily downwards. By the time she had reached his waist his entire torso felt as though it was on fire. The sweat stood out on his skin and ran down the sides of his body. He could smell the sharp, pungent odour gathering in his armpits and his groin; could feel the steady, shameful rise of his manhood as the lash curled around his buttocks and round his upper thighs.

By the time it was finished, he was trembling. Without the support of the two solid men on either side of him, he was sure he would have fallen to his knees. Chabi walked around him so that he could see her.

'Well done,' she murmured, amusement sparkling in her hard green eyes. 'Do you think you have earned the granting of your dearest desire?'

Antonio's lips felt parched and he pushed out his tongue to try to moisten them. Chabi's eyes followed the movement, and to his surprise, she stepped forward and kissed him. He closed his eyes, drowning in that kiss, yearning to put his arms around her, but she stepped back and raised her eyebrows. Then she moved aside, slowly, and behind her Antonio saw a man.

He recognised him instantly – it was the same man who had used another man like a woman on the night of the feast. Antonio's heart pounded, the blood rushing in his ears as he stared at the man. He was grinning and his dark leather breeches were straining over the front of his body, his excitement plain.

'Courage, Antonio,' Anke whispered in his ear as he helped him to his knees, 'I am with you.'

Antonio watched as the youth removed his clothes and stood in front of him. He was erect once more, the slender, smooth-skinned phallus that he had caressed to orgasm only hours before bobbing before his face. There was an air of expectancy in the room. Antonio sensed it, was affected by it, and gradually he realised what was expected of him. He was to take Anke in his mouth.

To his surprise he felt no revulsion at the thought, only a brief, glorious surge of joy. He sensed the other man had moved behind him, and heard the creak of leather as he removed his breeches in readiness. Oh God, oh God, he was going to fill the void left by the rectal plug with that huge cock. Antonio closed his eyes for a brief moment, not sure if he could bear it.

'Begin,' Chabi said softly.

Antonio put out his tongue and dabbed experimentally at the tip of Anke's penis. A clear fluid was seeping through the tiny slit at the end and it coated his tongue, salty-sour. The skin at the end was so very soft, so very tempting, and Antonio moaned softly as he closed his lips gently round it and sucked.

The fact that he was being watched no longer bothered him, the presence of the others receded in his consciousness as he concentrated on sucking at Anke's cock. Once that initial step had been taken, he was eager to feel the hot, hard length of him deep inside his mouth.

It was like sliding his lips over silk, the strength beneath the softness providing a thrilling counterpoint. Reaching up, he cupped Anke's balls in one hand, revelling in their hardness, their fullness as he worked his mouth back and forth. It was a powerful feeling, knowing that he was bringing the other man pleasure, that it was due to his actions that the scrotum was filling and swelling and the cock stem was now hard to the point of bursting.

He gasped with disappointment as Anke suddenly stepped away. Then he realised why. Grease was being massaged roughly into Antonio's back passage and Chabi was staring at him, willing him to concentrate. He had been enjoying fellating Anke just a little too much – she wanted him to fully appreciate the humiliation of what was about to happen to him.

Vaguely, he became aware of the avid eyes on him and he realised at once that it was his shame that they had come to see, not his pleasure. He gasped as he felt the huge, bulbous head of the other man's penis nudge at his tender opening. The angle was clearly wrong and the man grunted with frustration, pushing Antonio down with a hand on the back of his neck so that he was on all fours.

Anke knelt down in front of him, whispering words of encouragement.

'Relax, Antonio, push yourself back onto him.'

Antonio felt his breathing quicken as the cock-head nudged roughly, jabbing at him, seeking entry. There was no sensitivity in this brute's touch, only a dogged determination to get what he wanted.

At last he breached the tight sphincter of muscle. Antonio cried out as he inched carefully inside him and the man grunted his satisfaction.

'No! By all that is holy, no! I – '

His words were cut off by Anke who thrust his penis back into his mouth. Antonio sucked frantically until at last the sharp pain eased, bringing a dark, dangerous delight in its wake.

Antonio felt as if his whole body was stuffed full; all his senses, touch, taste, sight, smell, even hearing as the man's thighs slapped against his buttocks, were taken up with what was happening to him. Nothing else was real for Antonio except the twin thrusting of the men penetrating him. He understood all too well that his role was to be the instrument of their pleasure, a mere vessel. His own cock hung between his legs, swollen and neglected, desperate for release.

Anke came quickly, shooting his seed into Antonio's throat, making him splutter. Then he moved away and Antonio's shoulders sank down, his head resting against the red silk, giving the man who was using him deeper access. The silk beneath his cheek grew wet and it was only then that he realised he was crying with shame, or joy, at that moment he could not tell.

Cirina watched as the hirsute man with the thick, purple-headed penis thrust in and out of Antonio's body. At first she had been horrified to see him and it was all she could do not to rush down and try to prevent the scourging. Gradually though, as she had sensed his growing excitement, so her own interest was pricked.

The sight of Antonio sucking at the youth's man-flesh had excited her, adding to the pressure building between her thighs. Now she could see Antonio's face, could see the tears glinting on his cheeks even as his eyes were closed in ecstasy and she realised that he had never looked so beautiful, never more desirable as he did at that moment.

It was too much for her, too overwhelmingly moving for her to even think about the consequences of attracting Chabi's wrath. Taking advantage of the fact that all eyes were riveted to the two men on the platform, Cirina reached up and unfastened the leash which was attached to her collar, and ran down to join them.

As she flashed past her, Chabi tried to make a grab for her, but Cirina was too fleet of foot. Furious, she made to follow her, but Kublai Khan intervened.

'Do not interfere Chabi,' he said, his tone brooking no opposition, and she had no choice but to watch and seethe as the peasant girl once again took over the initiative.

Cirina waited until, with a great cry of triumph, the man reached his crisis. He withdrew immediately, fastening his breeches and striding quickly away, without so much as a backward glance at the man who had been the receptacle for his lust.

Antonio rocked back on his heels, his head hanging low, his manhood rearing up to betray his excitement. Cirina reached out and gently touched her fingertips to his face, smearing the tears across his cheeks.

Antonio's eyes flew open and he looked at her as if he had been unaware of her presence in the hall. She read his anguish and his shame and knelt before him, cupping his face in her hands and licking at his tears.

For Cirina it did not matter that dozens of avid eyes were watching them, or that Kublai Khan presided and Chabi seethed impotently on the sidelines. She knew they were all there, but she dismissed them from her mind as being of no consequence. All that was important to her now was to ease the spiritual pain she could see in her lover's face.

That he thought himself as less of a man was plain. And Cirina knew that if she could not rectify that opinion without delay, that what had happened here in the great hall of Shang-tu would affect him all his days. Remembering him as she had first met him, so masculine and vibrant, she knew she could not bear to see him broken.

She kissed him, pressing her lips onto his eyelids, his temples, his chin and his earlobes, before finding his lips. After a few seconds, his lips parted on a sigh and she pressed her tongue past the barrier of his teeth and into his mouth.

Antonio's arms came about her and he kissed her back; his fervour growing as his body recognised the soft, feminine imprint of hers along its length. She arched her neck back as he lowered her to the ground, giving his lips access to the heated, shadowed hollows at the base of her neck and between her breasts. He kissed her chest, her shoulders and her bound breasts, licking beneath the leather bonds to taste the sharp, salt-tang of her skin.

Cirina brought her legs up to encircle his waist, drawing him closer to her with her heels so that his man-flesh nudged at the sweetly lubricated channel of her woman's place. His eyes opened and he held her gaze, his expression stormy as he stared at her.

She allowed her mouth to fall open slightly, her eyes drooping as he positioned himself. They sighed in unison as he sank into her welcoming flesh with one sure, swift stroke. He rode her with a rhythm that was strong and sure, reasserting his manhood with every thrust. Their skin slid against each other, slick with sweat, their hearts beating together as one, as they each raced to the peak.

By rocking her hips slightly beneath his, Cirina found that the swollen nub of flesh at the apex of her sex-lips was stimulated so that she too would gain release. It came quickly, since she had waited for so long, and as the cleated walls of her woman's place convulsed around Antonio's shaft, it triggered his crisis.

This time, for the first time, he had no thought of withdrawing from her. He wanted nothing more than to fill her, to give the gift of his seed, an affirmation of his manhood.

They rolled together on the slippery silk, hugging each other, crying and laughing at the same time as they gradually realised that they were being applauded by the audience for their performance. Antonio helped her to her feet. They stood, naked, sweat-streaked and sex-soaked, holding tightly to each other as they faced the Khan.

He inclined his head in acknowledgement. Cirina chanced to look at Chabi. The other woman was glaring at her, hatred sparking from her emerald eyes. Cirina was unafraid. Chabi's rage was impotent – the crowd would not let her exact the retribution she would have liked to wreak. Nor would the Khan.

With one last smile at the defeated Empress, Cirina turned her back and walked with Antonio from the great hall.

Chapter Twelve

Cirina sat in her quarters and sipped at her sweet lemon drink. Her attendants bustled about her, chattering and giggling as they organised a trunk for her to take on the journey to Persia.

Their chatter washed over her, unheeded. Since she had bathed and rested after her triumph in the great hall, she had been deep in thought, contemplating her future. The Khan had broken his promise to her uncle that she would be returned to the caravanserai which suggested to her that she could never feel secure whilst her future was determined by others.

Her thoughts switched to Antonio and she felt the sadness well in her breast. He too had lied to her. He had never had any intention of returning to the caravanserai for her as he had promised after that first, sweet meeting.

Remembering the girl she had been then, so innocent, so trusting, so unaware of the ways of men – and women – she felt a protective tenderness for her old self. Coming to Shang-tu had changed her beyond redemption. Here she had discovered her true nature, had found that she was made for the giving and receiving of pleasure, and she knew there would be no going back.

She did not regret her transformation. It was as if she
ιad been asleep, all those years of her growing up. Every
ιow and again she had felt a stirring, caught a glimpse
ɔf her innermost nature, but she had never really dreamt
ts true extent. Antonio had awoken her and Chabi had
ιelped her to realise her full potential. In a way she
supposed she was grateful to the manipulative Empress
or that.

Cirina smiled as she thought of Chabi's reaction to her
gratitude. She was proud of her defiance, glad that she
ιad managed to retain some semblance of dignity in the
ace of Chabi's machinations.

As for the future, Cirina was quite sure she would not
allow herself to be given in marriage to a Mongol warrior
as a prize, a gift from Kublai Khan. She had considered
rying to leave Shang-tu before the entourage set off on
he morrow, but had decided there were too many risks.
A woman alone in the desert would not get far. Even if
she managed to steal the necessary camels and supplies,
f she survived the elements, without losing her way in
he treacherous desert, there were bandits who would
ιot hesitate to claim her. No, far better to leave as
planned and watch and wait for an opportunity to make
ιer escape.

Recalling the stories Antonio had told her about
Venice, Cirina considered that Europe seemed a far
easier place for a woman to make her way. Perhaps she
vould wait until they reached Persia, and hope that
Antonio would assist her to travel on until they reached
Venice. Perhaps he could help her find a position there,
somewhere she could live.

Antonio. Would he be travelling with them, or would
ιe make his escape with the Byzantine ruby, over the
desert to Constantinople? Remembering his bewilder-
ment, his disorientation when she had parted from him
he night before, Cirina doubted whether he would still
ry to complete his mission. She felt a surge of tenderness

for him and it suddenly struck her that she had not thought to include him in her plans for the future, except as a means by which she could escape. Did that mean that her love for him had died?

Cirina examined her heart and concluded that no, she had not stopped loving him. She had simply learned not to *depend* upon him. She cared enough to hope that his experiences at Chabi's hands would not affect him for long.

Then a daring thought crossed her mind. Supposing *she* stole the ruby? It might well be easier for her to accomplish such a task – who would suspect a mere pleasure slave of stealing a jewel from the Khan's throne? She would give the jewel to Antonio when they reached Persia so that he could take it and – if the deity was willing – her with him when he went home. And if all did not go according to plan, she could use the precious stone to pay for her passage to Europe.

Once the germ of the idea was planted in her mind, Cirina could feel her excitement growing. The more she thought about it, the more she was convinced that the ruby was the key to her liberation. But how to smuggle it out? Set as it was in the centre of Kublai Khan's throne, it was certain to be missed instantly.

Gazing thoughtfully around her room, her eyes fell on the colourful baubles and gems which the girls used to adorn her body. Some of the stones which were used to fill her navel were as large as small bird's eggs – as large as the Byzantine jewel.

Going over to the table, Cirina found a ruby, a worthless bauble, which she had worn recently. Holding it up to the light, she saw that it was far from perfect and patently of little value. But it was approximately the same size as the Byzantine ruby, and a similar colour. If no one suspected that the real ruby had been taken, so did not think to look too closely at the throne before they left, could it be that it might be switched for this?

Excitement churned in Cirina's veins as the idea grew. If only she dared.

'Antonio! You must make ready for the journey, we leave at dawn.'

Antonio looked up as Marco Polo called to him from across the room. He hadn't heard what his friend had said and so had to ask him to repeat himself.

'God's bones, man, what is wrong with you?'

'His brain has been addled by spilling his seed into too many wenches!' Maffeo laughed.

Antonio flushed a deep red and dropped his eyes. What would they think if they knew? What would they say if he told them how he had been used and, may the Lord forgive him, how much he had enjoyed it?

'Pray put your melancholy aside,' Marco said, and Antonio realised that his friend was watching him closely. 'The journey will be long and arduous, but at its end there will be home, and battles to be fought. The Genoese will have to gird their loins in earnest once we arrive! Hold that in your mind, Antonio, and turn your thoughts away from this place.'

Antonio dredged up the ghost of a smile.

'You are right, Marco – this place is poison.'

The three men looked at him askance, surprised by his vehemence.

'Are you ailing, Antonio?' This was Niccolo, his voice gentle.

'No, sir, but I am sick of this place. Even paradise must pall after a while.'

Niccolo regarded him thoughtfully and wondered if the rumours he had heard about him had been true. Certainly, he had not been seen for some days, and there was something different about him, some indefinable alteration in his demeanour which he found disturbing.

'The Khan has finally approved a route for us to take to Persia,' Marco was saying, and they all gathered round as he unrolled a map. He had scratched out a route which, although it looked crude, they all knew would be accurate.

'We travel south, along the coast until we reach Zaitan. The Emperor has promised that a fleet of fourteen ocean-going junks will be waiting there for us, complete with enough supplies for two months at sea.'

'Two months?' Maffeo queried. 'How far will that take us?'

'To the Kingdom of Chamba. Messengers have already been sent ahead to make arrangements for us to rest and re-stock our vessels there. We then sail on, through the Strait of Malacca and along the coast of Sumatra.'

'No stopping there, I'll wager!' Maffeo laughed. It was well known that the inhabitants of Sumatra were cannibals, their lands to be avoided at all costs.

Marco flashed his uncle an irritable glance and continued.

'From Sumatra we sail across the Bay of Bengal and through here – between the tip of India and Ceylon. We then turn north, up the coast to Hormuz in Persia.'

Antonio frowned.

'Why does the Khan insist on such a long and arduous sea voyage? Surely it would be more expedient to travel overland?'

Marco smiled grimly.

'Indeed. But be mindful, my friend, of the valuable cargo we shall carry – the Chinese princess and her supplementary brides. Kublai's enemies would dearly love to steal them away from him. Plus, of course, it makes it more difficult for us to take any souvenirs home – or so the great Khan thinks!'

Turning, Antonio was surprised to see Niccolo and Maffeo carefully splitting the seams of their travelling robes. As he watched, they each distributed a number of gems along the seams and began to sew them in. Catching his look of disbelief, Niccolo winked at him.

'You too have given many years service to the Khan, Antonio. Take you what you consider to be your due tithe.'

Antonio nodded, but he knew that only one gem held any real interest for him, and that was the ruby which Kublai Khan had stolen from Baldwin. His heart lay heavy in his chest and he turned away from the others. He would not be able to retrieve it – the Khan would be on his guard now that the Europeans were leaving.

He thought of Cirina, of her tenderness and her courage when she had come to him in the great hall. That she had witnessed his shame was clear, and yet she had folded him in her warm embrace and accepted him into her body, healing his troubled soul, letting the love flow between them, balm to his wounded pride.

Cirina would be travelling with them to Persia. She was all the prize he wanted, everything he desired.

Cirina waited until the palace slept and the shadows flickered eerily on the cold stone walls. In bare feet, she tiptoed along the labyrinthine corridors towards the great hall.

The palace at Shang-tu was a vast and intimidating building at the best of times, but in the middle of the night it assumed the proportions of a nightmare place, full of dark recesses and echoing corridors. But it was not difficult to slip by the slumberous guards who were posted outside the royal quarters and, to her relief, there was no one guarding the entrance to the great hall.

The vast door creaked a little on its hinges as Cirina pushed it open. She approached the dais, and saw the jewelled throne glinting slightly as it caught a stray moonbeam filtering in from the single narrow vent high above her.

The stone floor, stripped now of its pelts and silks, was cold beneath her feet as she ran across the hall and up the steps. The Byzantine ruby glowed down at her from its setting in the back of the throne. Her heart was hammering in her chest. Holding her breath, Cirina reached up and twisted the gem, loosening it away from its setting. It came away in her hand with a soft 'plop' and she quickly pressed the fake ruby in its place.

Slipping the real jewel into the folds of her robe, Cirina turned to run back down the steps. Only to find her way blocked by a man, standing four-square, his fists on his hips and his expression grim.

'Oh!'

Cirina pressed her fist against her mouth to hold in the scream that bubbled in her throat. Then she recognised him and some of her terror diminished.

'Mongor?' she whispered.

Mongor said nothing, and merely held out his hand for the ruby which he had seen her slip into her robe. Cirina brought it out reluctantly, closing her fingers over its smooth surface.

'It belongs to the Byzantium people, Mongor. I wasn't really stealing it – just returning it to its rightful owners.'

Mongor shook his head sadly and put the ruby in the pocket of his leather jerkin. Glancing over at the throne, he saw the fake stone in place and he smiled beneath his whiskers.

'I will have to report you to the Khan,' he said slowly.

'Oh no! Mongor – please! You know what will happen to me if you do that! You are my friend, I know you are. Have you not helped me before?'

'Perhaps, but this – '

'No one knows but you and I!' Cirina smiled coyly at him, fluttering her lashes. 'I would be truly grateful.'

Mongor stared at her, his mouth growing dry as he realised what she was offering him. Since the moment he had seen her in the caravanserai he had desired her with a passion that was beyond anything he had ever felt before. He had watched her blossom from a pretty girl into a beautiful, sensual young woman. She took pleasure in the physical communion of a man and a woman, that much he knew, and he saw now that what she was offering him would bring her enjoyment as well as him.

He thought fast. If he let her go and the Khan discovered his perfidy he would almost certainly die. But if he betrayed her, then it was almost as certain that she would be executed. It would be a crime to extinguish the bright light of her life. And here she was, offering to share some of that luminosity with him – it was more than flesh and blood could resist. Bowing his head as if in defeat, he bade her follow him.

The soldiers were permanently billeted along the banks of the river just outside the city walls. As the current officer in charge of the outer palace guard, Mongor had a yurt all to himself, set slightly apart from the others. This was where he took Cirina now, taking care that they were not seen.

Cirina glanced around the basic, circular interior, taking in the neat, military orderliness. There was a pile of furs to one side which were clearly used as a sleeping mat, but very little else. Mongor's tall, rangy frame took up so much room, it dwarfed the space inside and Cirina felt herself leaning slightly forwards, as if drawn to him.

He was unfastening his jerkin now, his expression inscrutable beneath his thick, black brows. Beneath his long, silky moustache, Cirina could see that he had full, sensuous lips, pulled now into a tense, tight line. That tension seemed to her to echo the churning in her stomach and she took a deep breath to calm herself. Though she had no qualms about coming here with Mongor, she had never before offered herself with quite such equanimity and she felt unaccountably nervous.

Her eyes skittered over the broad, hair roughened chest, resting briefly on an ugly scar which ran from one nipple to his waist. It was raised up and showed a livid purple through the mat of hair.

'Battle scars,' Mongor said gruffly when he saw her looking. 'No pain now. Do you want to touch?'

Cirina looked up at him briefly in surprise. Yes, she did want to touch him, was fascinated by the raised weal of his scar, though she could not begin to imagine why. Tentatively reaching out, she traced its path with her fingertips, feeling him shudder slightly under her touch. Acting on impulse, Cirina stepped forward and pressed her lips against the top end of the scar, as if soothing it.

His skin smelled of healthy male sweat and a heavier, more pungent musk which triggered a curious stirring in her womb. Darting out her tongue, Cirina licked down the length of the scar, lingering at his waist. Through the sturdy fabric of his breeches, she could feel the hot, potent swell of his arousal pressing against her cheek and she kissed him.

Mongor growled, deep in his throat, and his big hands, surprisingly gentle, reached down to cup her face. Urging her to stand straight, he gazed at her upturned face for interminable seconds, his eyes roving her fore-head, her cheeks and her chin, lingering on her parted lips. Everywhere his eyes kissed seemed to burn, as if he had branded her with his gaze, and Cirina felt her heartbeat quicken.

She held her breath as slowly, so slowly, he lowered his head and brushed his lips over her temples. His moustache tickled silkily against her skin, making her shiver as she imagined it trailing across the rest of her body. Her eyes fluttered to a close as he licked first one eyelid, then the other, his tongue leaving a streak of cool moisture across each one.

Cirina trembled as his tongue played around the corner of her mouth, teasing her, coaxing her lips apart. Then his mouth was on hers and she was caught up in a maelstrom of emotion which took her by surprise. She hadn't expected to feel anything except, hopefully, a physical gratification with this man, but as he kissed her she realised, to her delight, that something far more powerful was at play. Desire reared up in her, hungry, voracious, and she opened her mouth under his and welcomed the stab of his tongue.

His arms came about her, strong arms for which she was grateful since her entire body seemed to have become weightless, incapable of self-support. She clung to him, her nails digging into his shoulders. He was hot, his skin slick beneath her fingers, and she felt consumed by his heat, feeling it seeping into her pores even as his tongue plundered the soft recesses of her mouth.

Cirina's head was spinning, her heart hammering erratically in her chest when, finally, Mongor's lips broke away from hers. His dark eyes glittered down at her, the intensity of his expression mirroring her own feelings.

'I have wanted you for so long,' he told her, his voice husky with emotion. 'I hardly know where to begin!'

Cirina smiled shakily.

'Perhaps I should be naked for you?' she suggested softly.

'Let me . . .'

Mongor reached for the end of the silk wrap which was hanging down over one shoulder. Allowing the material to slide through his hand several times, he finally unwrapped it, slowly, his hands trembling as if he was afraid that a sudden movement might make her disappear.

Cirina held her breath as her naked breasts were revealed to him, feeling them swell and harden under his gaze. Bunching the material up in one huge fist, Mongor passed it from hand to hand, twisting it round her body until she was unrobed completely.

The delicate, shimmering fabric looked incongruous in his strong, very masculine hands. Cirina watched, captivated, as he allowed the material to run through his fingers before casting it aside. Now he eyed her hungrily and she felt a slow, steady pulse start up between her thighs. She swallowed as her mouth and throat grew dry, wondering what he would do next.

Reaching out a hand, Mongor smoothed her long, unadorned hair over her shoulders, letting it run through his fingers in much the same way as he had the silk of her robe. Any fears that Cirina might have harboured that he would take her crudely or roughly were dispelled. He treated her with gentleness, seeming to be prepared to wait for his satisfaction whilst carefully arousing her.

For he *was* arousing her, with his hot looks and his soft touches, his patience and his unexpected sensitivity. Cirina sighed as he ran the fingertips of one hand lightly down her throat, brushing across each nipple, making them leap beneath his touch. Circling her navel, he smoothed the backs of his knuckles across the silky hair which covered her pubis.

Hidden beneath the light mat of hair, her inner lips swelled and grew moist, her woman's place readying itself to welcome his body. At once Cirina forgot why she was here, forgot the ruby and the threat of discovery, and gave herself up to the sensations Mongor was so skilfully invoking in her.

Sinking to his knees, Mongor placed his hands at her waist and drew her towards him. It felt strange, having so big a man kneeling at her feet, but Cirina found she liked the feeling. Tentatively at first, because she was not sure how he would react, she ran her fingers through his thick black hair. He looked up at her and she was warmed by the smile she saw in his eyes. Then, to her surprise, he dipped his head and pressed his lips against her feet, each in turn.

Cirina stood absolutely still as Mongor worked his way slowly up her legs, using his lips and fingers to caress every inch of her skin. He lingered at her knees, stroking the thin, sensitive skin at their backs, and Cirina was surprised by the pleasurable sensations which travelled upward, towards the core of her womahood.

She was aware that she was waiting, waiting for him to reach the hot, wet centre of her. Anticipating his satisfaction when he found how she was ready for him made her tremble. Impatient, suddenly, she bent her legs at the knee slightly and Mongor chuckled, the sound muffled against the soft flesh of her inner thigh.

'You are so beautiful,' he murmured, without pausing in his leisurely exploration of her inner thighs, 'so fragrant. Like a mountain flower at dawn, fresh with dew.'

His words, so poetic, Cirina thought, for a rough soldier such as he, served to increase her desire, making her even more aware of the dampness which was now spreading so that it edged onto her thighs. Mongor's lips soon encountered the sweet, musky honey and he murmured appreciatively, lapping at it greedily with his tongue.

The gentle rasp of his tongue so near to her woman's place made Cirina tremble with longing. When at last he ran his hands from her waist to the fronts of her thighs, she almost sighed aloud with relief.

Carefully, as if he was examing the most delicate, most rare of flowers, Mongor opened her with his thumbs, peeling back the protective outer lips to reveal the slick, puffy flesh within. Cirina trembled as he held her open like that, feasting his eyes on her for what seemed like a long time, without making any attempt to touch her.

She imagined what he could see; the slippery channels of flesh, the hard little pleasure bud standing proud, the deep, shadowed valley which led into her body. She knew that all this would be covered in a thin veneer of clear, sticky fluid, the plainest possible evidence of her arousal. And she was proud of the way her body had reacted to him, glad because she knew that the sight would please him.

Suddenly, without warning, Mongor pushed out his tongue and entered her. Cirina cried out in surprise and grasped his shoulders to steady herself. His tongue was wet and warm and thick, plugging her entrance so that she felt full of him. Slowly, he began to move it in and out of her, as if it was his man-flesh, twirling his tongue round and round the silky inner walls with such delicate, delicious movements that Cirina was soon having to balance her knees against the sturdy wall of his shoulders.

As he tongued her, his thumbs moved gently round and round, just beneath her pleasure bud. That little bundle of nerve endings began to twitch, then swell. Cirina bore down on his thumbpads without really being aware of what she was doing. She was so caught up in his slow shafting of her with his tongue that she barely noticed how he was stimulating her elsewhere until, suddenly, she felt an explosion of sensation. It started deep within her womb and spread outwards like a desert wind, raging through her, consuming her. She ground her hips against his face, crying out with the force of the unexpected climax.

Mongor supported her full weight on his shoulders, his tongue moving rapidly in and out of her until her legs buckled and she begged him to stop.

'Please, oh please, no more!'

He seemed to withdraw his tongue from her body with reluctance, licking along the channels of her sex with long, leisurely strokes until he reached the tautness of her belly. Without a word, he rose to his feet and swept her up in his arms.

Weak as she was in the afterglow of her orgasm, Cirina revelled in the feel of his strong arms around her, and allowed herself to relax, a dead weight, as he carried her across to the animal skins where he slept. Lying her down, he positioned her body as he wanted it – arms above her head, legs stretched wide apart. Cirina complied without a murmur, feeling too languorous to move of her own accord.

She watched through half-closed eyes as Mongor stripped off completely. Her eyes flew open as she caught her first glimpse of his man-flesh. It was huge, far bigger than any she had ever seen before. Briefly she wondered how it could possibly fit inside her without damage, how on earth her channel would stretch to accommodate him. Erect, it stood proud of his body, a thick, sturdy staff with a bulbous end, already free of its foreskin. As she gazed at it, a clear drop of fluid seeped from the tiny slit at the end and dropped onto her belly, making her jump. It was warm and dried stickily on her skin.

Cirina licked her lips, wondering what he would do. Kneeling over her, he grasped his mighty phallus in one hand and drew it down, from her wrist, along her inner arm to her armpit where he rested it for a second. He repeated the action with her other arm, smearing her smooth skin with a thin trail of semen.

Once he reached the dip of her armpit, he swept the tip of his shaft across the line of her collarbones, then back to the point where they met. Nestling in the cup at the base of her throat for a few seconds, he bent his head and kissed her, nibbling lightly at her lower lip and reaching up with his hands to draw her arms down by her sides.

'Lie still for me,' he whispered, his breath hot in her ear.

Cirina complied, her body tense with anticipation, her heart beating in time with the dull pulse between her legs. She hoped he would not delay too long before he entered her for she wanted him with a hunger which astounded her.

Mongor seemed to be in no hurry at all. With his big,

calloused hands, he pressed her upper arms against her sides so that her breasts were gathered up, thrust together like two ripe fruits. Breathing more rapidly now, Mongor raised his hips and dragged his cock down to nudge between her breasts.

Though they were both hot and perspiring, his skin snagged against hers almost painfully and he grunted with frustration. Leaping up and leaving her for a moment, he went over to the cooking equipment kept to one side, and rummaged around until he found a cake of sheep's fat. Cirina's eyes widened as he approached her and began to rub the slab of fat all over her breasts, round her nipples and into the deep, shadowed valley between, until her skin was shiny and slippery with oil.

Casting the cake of cooking fat aside with a grunt of satisfaction, Mongor once again pressed her arms to her sides, creating a channel for himself between her breasts. Resting his weight on his knees and elbows either side of her, he began to rub himself up and down, using her breasts as a means by which to stimulate his enormous man-flesh.

To Cirina's surprise, it seemed to swell and harden still further in response to the friction. Her own flesh grew warm and slick as Mongor's fluids leaked to mingle with the pungent sheep's fat which he had rubbed on her skin.

For a moment she thought he would bring himself to a crisis this way. His eyes had glazed over and his breathing was laboured as he increased his rhythm. His fingers pinched and rolled her nipples, sticking out now like two shiny pips. Cirina moistened her lips with her tongue, sure that within seconds his seed would spill across her neck and breasts. She braced herself for it, gasping as suddenly, without warning, Mongor pulled away.

Lifting her effortlessly, he rolled onto his back and positioned her so that she was straddling him. Breathing shallowly, sure that her desire was evident in the depths of her eyes, Cirina sat back on his rough-haired legs and gazed with wonder at his straining penis.

Glancing at him to check that he would not object, she reached out for it, revelling in the warm throb beneath her palm. It was so thick that she could not span it with one hand, so she used two, linking her fingers at the top to form a circle. Mongor swore under his breath as she moved her hands up and down along the magnificent shaft.

'Enough!' he said gruffly, and Cirina reluctantly let him go.

He lifted her up by the hips so that only her toes were balanced on the ground on either side of him and her sex-lips opened to kiss the weeping tip of his cock.

Cirina's mouth ran dry as she realised what he wanted her to do. Reaching down with one hand, she opened herself so that he could position his cock-head against the opening to her body. It nudged at her, stretching the delicate membranes which strained to accommodate him.

Breathing shallowly, through her mouth, Cirina lowered herself gingerly onto the massive shaft. Mongor supported her weight with his hands at her waist, and she was grateful for this consideration. With the fear of impalement removed she could concentrate on taking him in, inch by inch, enclosing him within the hot, silky sheath.

Sweat broke out all over her body as she was filled by him, stretched to her limit by the intrusion. As his cock-head touched the neck of her womb, she realised that there were still two to three inches to go before she would be able to feel his seed sacs against her bottom and she shook her head, feeling suddenly afraid.

'It's all right,' Mongor reassured her, his voice shaking, it is enough.'

Leaning forward, Cirina steadied her hands on his

shoulders and raised her bottom slowly into the air. At the point where he would have slipped out of her, she eased back down again before repeating the movement. With each tentative thrust, Cirina realised that the discomfort eased and she began to get used to the incredible sense of fullness.

Mongor was sweating profusely now and she sensed that he would not be able to hold back for much longer. Rotating her hips slightly, she came back down on him and was amazed to realise that she had taken in a little more than before. Gritting her teeth, she tried the move again, and once more gained some ground.

Mongor began to murmur in a strange language which she did not understand. His palpable excitement inflamed her, and she began to move more quickly, up and down, twisting her hips until at last, incredibly, she knew that the entire length of him was imbedded in her fully stretched sheath.

The mere thought of this sent an orgasmic ripple along the cleated walls of her woman's place and Mongor's eyes opened wide as he felt the intense, milking sensation. Knowing that she no longer needed his support, he took his hands from her waist and covered her breasts with his palms. Pinching at her nipples with his fingertips, he tipped her over the edge of that fine dividing line between pleasure and pain, to the place where the two merge.

To Cirina, the small pain in her nipples provided a link to the deeper, more primitive pull in her womb. She was past caring that he was so big. Her hips bucked, her breath catching in her chest as she felt another wave of sensation wash over her.

It was too much for Mongor. With a mighty roar, like a battle cry, he thrust his pelvis upward and grabbed at Cirina's buttocks, holding her tightly against him as his body convulsed in hot, violent jags.

Cirina felt her body buck of its own volition and she

felt swamped by heat, her own orgasm going on and on. She was spinning, whirling into a vortex of sensation, out of control, beyond sensible thought. Then she fainted.

When she came to, it was to find Mongor bathing the tender flesh between her legs with cold water from the stream. His big, weather-beaten face was creased with lines of concern and his eyes lit up with relief as she opened her eyes.

'Cirina, forgive me. I never intended . . .'

'Hush!' she whispered. Her throat felt dry and parched, as if she had been screaming. 'You did not hurt me. You could not have been more gentle.'

She reached up to touch his face and Mongor turned his head, pressing his lips against the centre of her palm. His silky moustache tickled at her wrist and she smiled.

'I will never forget you, Mongor,' she whispered.

An emotion something like pain flashed across his dark eyes, then was gone, so swiftly that Cirina thought she might have imagined it.

'Rest here for a while,' he told her, 'then I will take you back to the palace in time for the dawn call.'

Gratefully, Cirina closed her eyes and slept.

This time when she opened her eyes, Mongor was keeping watch at the opening to the yurt. He turned and smiled at her as he saw that she had wakened.

'Time to go,' he told her.

He watched as she bathed in the cool water he had brought her, seeming to enjoy simply gazing at her as she performed such an everyday, though intimate, task. Winding her silk robe around her body, Cirina combed out her hair as best she could with her fingers, before facing him.

'May I have the ruby, Mongor?'

He regarded her sadly.

'It is a small price to pay for the gift you gave to me,' he told her.

Stepping forward, Cirina reached up to plant a kiss on his cheek.

'I would have given you that gift without the promise of the ruby, Mongor. For my pleasure was as great as yours, my hunger just as acute. But I must take the ruby – I may have need of it in the future.'

Mongor scanned her features, as if trying to gauge her sincerity. He must have seen something that satisfied him, for he nodded.

'Very well. Have you thought, though, that you will be searched before you are allowed to pass through the city walls?'

Cirina smiled grimly.

'I have thought it. How thorough a search will it be, Mongor?'

He raised his eyebrows in surprise at her question, lowering them as he realised what she meant.

'I doubt that the Khan would allow the intimate violation of one of the brides,' he told her.

'I thought not. Will you help me to hide the ruby, Mongor? Somewhere where it will not be found?'

This request clearly appealed to him for she watched the tip of his tongue dart out to moisten his lips, and he nodded.

Cirina went back to the pile of furs and lay down, on her side. Without a word, she bunched her skirts around her waist and brought her knees up to her chest.

Mongor took the ruby out of his jerkin and went to clean it in the cold water. His hands were cold and wet as they touched her exposed woman's place. Once there, he paused.

'The stone is large – you are sure you wish to suffer this discomfort?' he asked her.

Cirina smiled wickedly.

'Mongor, after taking your manhood into my body, I

doubt that I will notice the presence of the ruby at all! You have spoilt me for anything smaller.'

Mongor laughed and shook his head.

'At least the ruby is smooth. You might even find it pleasurable to carry it inside you.'

Cirina raised her eyebrows, intrigued, but Mongor was already pressing the cool, hard gem into her tender woman's place, pushing it up as high as it would go with his fingers. Once he was satisfied that it was securely lodged inside her, he slipped his fingers out. Then, before Cirina's eyes, he licked each of his fingers in turn, relishing the taste of her.

She smiled gently at him.

'Thank you, Mongor.'

He helped her to her feet and she stood still for a moment, adjusting to the feeling of having a weight inside her. She found that by clenching her inner muscles she could pull it back into position if it chanced to slip, and she took a few experimental steps around the yurt.

'We must get back before you are missed.'

'Yes. Do we say goodbye here?'

'I fear we must.'

They gazed at each other for a long moment, then simultaneously stepped forward. Their mouths collided in a long, yearning kiss. Then Mongor took her by the hand and smuggled her back into the palace.

Chapter Thirteen

Antonio settled down for the night at the camp several *li* from the port of Zaitan. If all went according to plan, this would be their last night on land before they began the long sea voyage south to the Kingdom of Chamba.

Marco, his uncle and his father had all gone to carouse with the soldiers so Antonio was alone, and grateful for the peace and quiet. The Polos had given up asking him to join them on their hell-raising jaunts, for he invariably declined, preferring his own company. He supposed he had become something of a bore, though he could not seem to care as he knew he might have cared before.

He wondered, as he closed his eyes, how Cirina had fared so far on the journey. The Chinese princess and her entourage had been so carefully guarded that he had barely been able to catch so much as a glimpse of Cirina. He had seen her but once, emerging from the women's yurt on the first night of the journey. Their eyes had clashed across the distance and it seemed to him that she was trying to send a message to him. He would have gone over to her, but at that moment the Chinese guard had gathered around the yurt ready for the appearance of the princess, and she had been lost to him.

Antonio hugged the image of her to him now, so tall and proud and beautiful in her travelling robes. Thinking of Cirina had sustained him on the arduous journey. Knowing that she was close by was a comfort, for the bitter taste of defeat lay heavy on his tongue, souring his food along with his temper. He understood a little now why his father had died such a frustrated man. For all the latter part of his life he had worked to bring the Byzantine ruby back to its people, for nothing. Now he too would return home empty-handed. A failure.

A faint rustling sound outside brought him instantly alert and he sat up, all thought of sleep banished. His hand sought the hilt of his dagger and he crawled stealthily towards the opening of the yurt. None of the Polos would approach with such secrecy and no one else had any business with the Europeans.

Antonio froze as the flap was lifted cautiously and a slender hand slipped through, closely followed by a body which, though cloaked against the night, was unmistakably female. His mouth dropped open as he realised who it was.

'Cirina?'

'Antonio? Oh, thank the deity I picked the right yurt!'

Antonio sheathed his dagger and held out his arms to her. They hugged and kissed and hugged again before Cirina extricated herself briskly from his embrace.

'I don't have much time – I may already have been missed.'

'Are you all right? Are they treating you well?'

'Yes, of course, you must not worry about me.'

'What of the Chinese princess? Is she as beautiful as they say?' he teased her mildly.

A strange look passed across Cirina's face and she dropped her eyes.

'Indeed, she is very beautiful. But I have not come to discuss the princess. I have a gift for you.'

'A gift? I do not understand.'

'Do not waste time in talking Antonio – I need you to kiss me, to caress me.'

She unfastened her cloak and he saw that she was naked beneath it. Instantly, he was hard, his man-flesh leaping in his breeches and his breath catching in his throat.

'Cirina,' he murmured huskily.

Pressing his lips against her neck, her throat, her shoulder, he cupped the fullness of her breasts and buried his face in the fragrant valley between them. He caught the tiny beads of perspiration on his tongue and licked across to where her nipples were already growing taut with longing.

Cirina moaned softly, having to resist the temptation to throw off her cloak and lie with him on it. She knew there would not be time and that it would be expedient to keep her cloak about her. It would grant her at least some security if someone else should walk in.

Antonio was lathering her nipples with his tongue, murmuring all the while. She could see his hardness stretching the fabric at the front of his breeches and felt a moment's sorrow that she could not slip it out and enjoy it. All she needed, though, was for him to make her juices flow, to ease the passage of the ruby from her sheath so that it could slip from her body.

She hadn't intended to give it to him until they reached Persia, but she was nervous of secreting the gem in her robes, especially as the princess was so demanding of her attention. She could hardly keep the ruby secreted inside her for the whole of the journey. It was almost time for her monthly flow now and she knew that this would make it doubly difficult to hold it inside, so she had decided tonight that she would have to pass on the responsibility of it to Antonio.

His lips were at her navel now, swirling around it until her belly began to tremble. Cirina could feel the delicious languorousness slowly invading her limbs, and her intimate flesh grew steadily heavier and more moist.

'Touch me, Antonio,' she whispered huskily and he obliged at once, cupping her sex in the palm of his hand, as if wishing to absorb the heat of it.

Gradually, his fingers sank into the soft, slippery flesh and he began to explore the intricate, intimate contours. He paused as he felt the unnatural bulge and Cirina whispered in his ear, 'Hold me – do not move your hand.'

She felt his tension as she placed one hand on his shoulder and bore down with her internal muscles. The ruby slipped steadily downward until, finally, after one last effort from her, it emerged from her woman's place and landed in Antonio's palm.

'Your gift,' she murmured as his eyes widened in alarm.

Cirina took a step back as Antonio brought up his hand to see what he had caught. The ruby glinted in the half-light, polished to a dull shine by the secretions of her body.

'By the saints! It is the Byzantine ruby, is it not?'

He looked at her wonderingly, his thumb absently stroking back and forth over the smooth surface. Cirina nodded.

'But how – '

'Do not ask me,' she said, cutting off the stream of questions she could see bubbling to his lips. 'Let it be enough that it is here, now. You can take it back to Venice with you, Antonio, and, I had hoped – '

Antonio darted forward swiftly and placed his hand over her mouth, cutting off her words. Cirina heard then what he had heard; the Polos laughing as they approached.

'Quickly – you can get through at the back here.'

Wrenching the animal skin which covered up the bamboo frame out of the earth which had been used to anchor it, Antonio helped her to crawl through.

'Hurry, *cara mia* and take care that no one sees you. Cirina?'

She paused as she re-fastened her cloak and prepared to run back to the women's yurt.

'Yes Antonio?'

He smiled at her, a smile so full of tenderness that her heart swelled in her chest.

'Thank you. You cannot know how much this means to me. God speed, *mi amore*.'

She smiled at him, then hurried away.

Cirina had barely fallen asleep when the princess shook her by the shoulder. Groggily, she opened her eyes and encountered the soft brown gaze of the royal traveller.

'Princess?' she whispered, knowing at once what it was she wanted.

The princess had selected Cirina to be her own private serving girl soon after the journey began. The other two 'supplementary' brides were given to understand, by word and gesture, that they were to serve both the princess and Cirina. But only Cirina was allowed to perform the very special services that the princess required. She and she alone was permitted to touch the royal person.

Her heart sank a little now since she was tired and a little overwrought after her encounter with Antonio. But that meeting had also left her restless, the mild arousal refusing to abate when she arrived safely back at the women's yurt.

Glancing over at the other girls, she saw that both were sound asleep, curled on their sleeping pallets, dead to the world. Sometimes the princess had them pleasure Cirina while she watched and Cirina had grown used to being brought to release by the application of soft lips and tongues for the pleasure of her new mistress. This time though, she knew that it was up to her to do the work.

The princess settled herself on the silk cushions which made her pallet tolerably comfortable and opened her robe. She had a small, delicate body, covered in perfect, milky-white skin which Cirina never tired of touching. Her face was heart shaped, her eyes wide and slanted. Beneath her tiny, almost flat nose, her mouth was a little red bow. Cirina had never seen her smile.

Now she bent her head and, starting at her feet, she began to kiss and lick up her body. She knew exactly what was required of her, knew that she was not permitted to venture above the waist, even though the other woman's small, perfectly formed breasts with their tiny pink crests were displayed invitingly. The only time she had ever dared to touch her there had been the only time she had ever seen the princess display any sign of emotion, and her anger had been quite terrifying.

Her skin tasted of sugared roses, the light perfume mingling with the muskier, heavier fragrance emanating from her woman's place. When Cirina's lips reached her upper thighs, her legs parted slightly to give her access to the heated flesh inside.

As always, Cirina marvelled at the perfectly formed, pink-tinged flesh leaves. Even in their aroused state they were neat and perfectly sculpted, fitting together like the petals of a flower, one set of lips inside the other.

She tasted of warm honey, her rose-accented, musky smell enveloping Cirina as she gently licked and sucked at the responsive flesh. She felt the tiny, hardening core at the top quiver as she brushed over it lightly with her tongue tip.

This evidence that she was giving pleasure to the inscrutable, doll-like princess made Cirina's own sex-flesh throb in sympathy, though she knew that she would have to wait for her own satisfaction until everyone was asleep and she could stimulate herself in private.

The princess was silent as always, though her soft, sensitive skin had grown damp with perspiration as the core of her pleasure slipped from beneath its protective hood. Cirina began to graze it lightly with her teeth and that was enough to trigger the other woman's climax. Even then, she did not cry out, merely uttering a soft, mewling sound, like a kitten.

Cirina had become used to this vocalisation of her pleasure and she stroked gently along the princess's thighs as she backed away from her on her hands and knees. She had served her purpose and she doubted whether the other woman gave her another thought as she covered herself and prepared for sleep.

Cirina waited until she heard the Princess's deep, even breathing before sliding her fingers into her own hot flesh. Closing her eyes, she conjured up images of Antonio, imagining what could have happened in his yurt earlier had the Polos not returned early from their socialising.

In her mind's eye, she saw Antonio bend her face down over his pallet and take her from behind, his familiar, well-loved man-flesh fitting comfortably into her cleated channel, her bottom rising up and down to meet each thrust. Her fingers worked feverishly against her sensitive skin, rubbing rhythmically round and round her straining pleasure bud until, at last, a kaleidoscope of colours burst behind her eyelids and she had to jam her fist into her mouth to muffle her cries.

Afterwards, she curled up into a protective ball and pulled the pelts up under her chin. Within minutes she was asleep, so soundly that she did not wake until morning.

It was a travel-weary, sickly party which staggered from the junks when at last they reached the Kingdom of

Chamba. All the women, without exception, had been sea-sick and viewed their arrival on land as nothing short of salvation.

As Cirina lurched up the jetty behind the princess, she felt as if the wooden slats beneath her feet were moving just as the boat had moved and she had to pause to vomit over the side.

Accommodation was ready for them and the rest that followed was the sweetest she could ever remember enjoying. All too soon, though, their vessels were re-stocked and they had to prepare to set sail once again.

Lightening streaked across the inky-black sky and Antonio winced at the echoing crack of thunder which swiftly followed in its wake. Pulling himself along the side of the junk by the strength of his arms, for his legs felt as weak as a kitten's, he located Marco Polo and clapped his hand on his shoulder.

'There's land over yonder,' he shouted against the howling wind, 'we must take shelter.'

Marco turned to him, his black hair drenched with spray, moulding his skull, and mouthed something in reply. His words were snatched away by the wind and Antonio shook his head, leaning closer to hear what his friend was trying to say. All he could make out were odd words, but those odd words were enough to make his blood run cold.

'Cannibals? Are you sure?'

'. . . Sumatra . . . risk . . .'

'There's more risk that we'll run aground, surely?'

Just then one of the junks was caught by a giant wave. Antonio and Marco watched in helpless horror as the now flimsy-looking vessel was tossed like a toy boat before being dashed against the rocks. There could be little hope of survivors and this seemed to galvanise Marco into action.

With Antonio's help, he signalled the other junks to

heave-to and all began the dangerous task of navigating a course inland.

The following morning saw some respite to the storm and revealed the full extent of the damage sustained by the fleet. As it became clear that extensive repairs would have to be made to the junks, it was decided that camp would have to be struck on the inhospitable beach where they had landed.

'But what of the cannibals, Marco?' Maffeo asked worriedly, his eyes scanning the thick vegetation that surrounded the beach as if expecting to spot the natives watching them. 'Is it safe to stay here?'

'We have no choice,' Marco replied briskly. 'There is plenty of wood to be had. Have the soldiers erect ramparts and watchtowers and instruct the captain to form a round-the-clock guard.'

Antonio waited until Maffeo was out of earshot before confronting Marco.

'This weather is not likely to turn until the season changes. Will we stay here until then?'

Marco gave a small, helpless shrug of his shoulders.

'What choice have we?'

Antonio shook his head. 'The men are already restless – this journey has been fraught with incident.'

'Think you that I do not know this? We will stay here, Antonio, because we must. No one is more impatient than I to reach our destination, believe me. The sooner we are relieved of our escort duties the better I will like it. But for now, we are charged with the care of the princess and her brides, and we will discharge that duty as befits our station.' He smiled, grimly. 'One day I will write an account of our adventures Antonio. I have kept notes over the years and will add to them now we are here. You should make some sketches to record this strange place, my friend.'

Antonio laughed self-deprecatingly. 'At least that is one thing I can do which might be of some use.'

Marco looked at him strangely. 'You have changed, my friend, since you first joined us.'

Antonio raised his eyebrows. 'Have we not all changed?' he murmured softly. 'No one could remain untouched by our experiences here.'

He walked away, leaving Marco watching him, a puzzled frown bringing his eyebrows together.

And so a mini-fortress was erected on the beach in Sumatra and the travellers prepared themselves to make the best of their enforced stay until the weather would enable them to set sail once more.

Cirina watched the coast of Sumatra dwindle into the distance as, at last, the weather changed and they were able to leave. For many weeks they had been forced to live within the fortress, living with the constant fear of attack from the natives.

The women were watched constantly, so she never managed to even speak to Antonio. Thrown together, forced to rely on each other for company and comfort, the four women had grown close. Even the princess had softened a little, though she was quick to retreat into imperial haughtiness whenever she suspected that respect was lacking in any dealings with her.

All were relieved when the time came to leave. As Cirina understood it, from eavesdropping on the soldiers' conversations, the journey should be straightforward from now on. Once they had crossed the Bay of Bengal they would pass between the countries of India and Ceylon before turning north, towards Persia.

The delays had made everyone restless and Cirina guessed that future stops would be as short as possible. Jiraz, the intended husband of the princess, would be impatient for his bride to arrive. Thinking of the man to whom she had been promised, Cirina frowned. Looking up at the now clear, cloudless sky, she made a vow to herself. She would escape the life of servitude planned for her, or die in the attempt.

Antonio watched the rest of the party disembark at Hormuz in Persia, hoping for a glimpse of Cirina. Since the moment when she had given him the ruby, she had dominated his thoughts. Even now he wondered at her courage, her resourcefulness, and he knew that he could not let her ride to her fate with the other women.

The princess and her three attendants were walking towards him now, all swathed in black silk so that only their eyes were showing as was the custom in this part of the world. Even so, Cirina's height made her recognisable and Antonio's heart lifted. Just as he was about to move forward to waylay her, someone clamped a hand on his shoulder.

'Have you lost your mind?' Marco hissed in his ear.

Antonio turned, frustrated that his chance to speak to Cirina had been lost. Now she was climbing into the carriage which would take them to their lodging house for the night.

'You must know I relinquished that the first time I set eyes on her.'

'For the love of God, man, you could put us all in danger! She is promised to another – out of your reach!'

'I will never accept that.'

Marco swore under his breath.

'You must. I have just received word that we are to travel overland to the Caspian Sea. Jiraz and his men are engaged in warfare there. We will stay until the marriage ceremonies, then we will be free to head for home. Think you on that, Antonio, and put this dangerous infatuation out of your mind.'

Antonio watched him stride away resentfully.

'Easy for you to say, my friend,' he muttered under his breath. 'Easy for you to say.'

* * *

By the time the bridal party reached the Mongol camp on the edge of the Caspian Sea, Cirina thought she had never seen so welcome a sight as the temporary village made by the soldiers. Both she and the other women were exhausted beyond reason and she fervently hoped that they would be given time to rest and recuperate from the long journey before the ceremonies commenced.

She needed time to think and plan, time to discover the best way to escape. She had all but despaired of seeing Antonio again, it seemed as though the women were shielded from contact with all the men who had travelled with them, but especially the Europeans.

Perhaps that was Chabi's doing – her final revenge for Cirina's defiance. The Empress could easily have instructed the guard to ensure that Antonio did not get near her. Cirina smiled as she thought of the one time she had managed to see him. Even now she was thwarting Chabi!

The thought returned a little of her courage to her, making her believe in herself again. She would go along with what was happening now, but only until she could see a means by which to escape. Of one thing she was absolutely certain – she was not about to become the trophy of one of Kublai Khan's loyal warriors!

Chapter Fourteen

Once they arrived at the camp, the women were separated. The princess was taken to Jiraz's silk-lined yurt and quickly reverted back to her former aloof self. During the long months that they had travelled together, she had grown almost friendly, had allowed herself to identify with Cirina and the other women to the point where she would chat with them almost naturally, though she never smiled and giggled like the others.

Cirina, for one, mourned the passing of the lighter side of the princess's nature, especially since what had become a nightly ritual between them seemed now to be consigned to the past. She and the other two brides soon became established in the large yurt set aside especially for them and, as she had hoped, were left to rest.

When they awoke after that first long, restorative sleep, they were brought food and drink and each was assigned a serving girl to attend them. But while the other two brides quickly established a rapport with their attendants, Cirina sensed a restraint in hers.

The girl was slight of build, quite short, with wavy black hair which she wore piled up on top of her head.

Her face was round and sweet, though it was spoilt by the scowl she habitually wore whenever she came near Cirina.

'What is your name?' she asked her as the girl began to brush out Cirina's hair on that first night.

'Lei,' the girl replied grudgingly.

Cirina smiled at her.

'I am Cirina,' she said.

'I know.'

'Oh.'

There didn't seem to be anything else to say in the face of the girl's determined sullenness, so Cirina lapsed into silence.

The other girls were full of chatter about the men they were to marry and, one after the other, they were taken to meet their intended. Neither seemed unduly dismayed by what they found, and Cirina was glad that they were happy with their fate. The summons from her prospective husband came two days after the other women.

She was escorted to one of the military yurts and left alone. After a few moments, a stocky young man with a drooping moustache stepped through the opening. He appeared ill at ease as he bowed slightly in greeting.

'I am Iman. We are to be joined in marriage by order of the Khan.'

Cirina inclined her head.

'I am Cirina, your obedient servant.'

They eyed each other warily across the distance separating them. Cirina saw that Iman had a muscular physique beneath his uniform and his hands were lightly furred with black hairs. His eyes were pale, his lower lip sensuous beneath his moustache. He was not unattractive, and yet her heart still sank in his presence.

Suddenly, he bowed again.

'We will not meet again until the ceremony. You have everything you need for your comfort?'

'Yes, my lord,' she replied, lowering her eyes.

'Then I bid you farewell until we are man and wife.'

Turning smartly on his heel, he marched quickly out of the yurt, leaving Cirina feeling uneasy. Iman clearly held as little enthusiasm for their union as did she – could she perhaps appeal to him to release her from her obligation? It would make things so much easier if she should be allowed to leave without hindrance, rather than having to skulk away in the night.

As soon as she thought it, Cirina dismissed the idea. Iman was a loyal officer in Kublai Khan's great army – if the Khan said he should marry, he would do so, without question or protest.

With a heavy heart, Cirina left the yurt and was escorted back to the women's quarters. The other brides were out, presumably visiting their intended husbands. Both girls had suitors who were far more keen on the idea than was hers, she mused wryly.

It made a change to have some time to herself and she made the most of it, sitting cross-legged in the middle of the floor and trying to think of some way out of her dilemma. There seemed to be none, and her brain whirled in circles, round and round until she felt quite light-headed.

Frustrated, she leapt to her feet, only to take a step back in alarm as the flap covering the entrance of the yurt was flung aside and a man strode in. For a split second she thought it was Antonio, then he flung back the hood of his cloak and she realised it was the other European, Marco Polo.

'Signor?'

'Do not be alarmed – Antonio asked me to come.'

'Is he hurt? Has something happened to him?'

Marco shook his head.

'Do not alarm yourself, he is quite well. However, he did receive a visit from Jiraz's most trusted officer, and since then he has been, shall we say, subdued. He asked me to give you this.'

He took out a small silk pouch which he placed in her outstretched hand.

'I do not know what is inside, indeed, I have a suspicion that I would not want to know. Antonio said that you would know what to do with it.'

Cirina's fingers closed over the pouch and she secreted it in the folds of her robe. That it was the ruby she had no doubt, but if Antonio had need of her to hide it, he must be in danger.

'Please, Signor – can you tell me when you will set off for Constantinople?'

'Very soon. Before the ceremony on the morrow.'

Cirina sucked in her breath.

'I had not realised the ceremony would be so soon!'

Marco regarded her for a moment, then he stepped forward, speaking urgently to her.

'It seems to me that you are a woman of rare wit and courage.'

'Why, thank you Signor,' Cirina murmured, wondering where this was leading.

'I fear that Antonio will not be allowed to leave with us. You, I suspect, know the reason for that better than I. I would also wager that you have plans of your own, possibly plans which include Antonio.'

He scanned her eyes and Cirina lowered her lids, revealing nothing. Taking her silence as an affirmative, Marco went on, 'After we leave we will ride west and camp by the Black Sea. We will wait there for two days and two nights – to stay longer would be too dangerous.'

Cirina inclined her head in acknowledgement of the risk he was proposing to take.

'I thank you, Signor,' she said quietly.

Marco lifted her hand and brushed his lips across her knuckles.

'I wish you Godspeed, my lady,' he said formally, then he was gone, looking right to left to see if he had been observed before being swallowed up by the gathering night.

Antonio had good reason to worry. Word had reached Jiraz that the Byzantine ruby had been stolen from Xanadu and the soldiers had torn his belongings apart looking for it. The Polos, it seemed, were above suspicion. No one suspected that they each had a veritable fortune sewn into their robes.

Thank the saints, he had been able to pass Marco the silk pouch he had fashioned to carry the ruby and ask him to take it to Cirina. The other man had asked no questions, for which he was grateful, and he knew that Cirina would be able to carry the ruby in a place where no man would think to look.

They came for him at dawn, dragging him out of the yurt still bleary-eyed, half-naked. The Commander, Jiraz, was raving, clearly under the direct orders of the Khan to find the ruby and punish its abductor.

'Why me?' he asked as his arms and legs were lashed to the whipping post.

'You have been accused,' Jiraz told him.

'Accused? By whom?'

'The Empress herself.'

So Chabi had finally wrought her revenge. Had it been merely a lucky guess on her part, or had Cirina been betrayed? It mattered little now, for it seemed that he was to be punished.

'You have not found the ruby,' he pointed out, a note of desperation creeping into his voice.

Jiraz grew almost purple with fury.

'It is of no consequence. You could have sold it along the way – I care not. I would kill you if the Emperor had not forbidden it. I only wish that the great Khan hears how I have punished a lawless barbarian who dared to steal from him.'

Antonio cried out at the first kiss of the whip against his back. He had hoped never again to feel such exquisite agony. All that was to be put behind him – Cirina had erased from his mind the shameful episode when Chabi had scourged him as a prelude to his humiliation. Or so he had thought.

The lash landed across his shoulders again and Antonio felt the sweat break out on his skin. His man-flesh reared up, straining against the thin silk of his sleeping-breeches, the material darkening as a stain spread slowly across them.

Jiraz saw that he was aroused by the lash and a cruel smile touched his thin lips. He held up his hand to signal that the whipping should stop.

'So – the Venetian has hidden talents!'

The men around him laughed and several stepped forward to pinch and squeeze him. Antonio closed his eyes, holding back the tears he could feel gathering in his eyes. With a fatalistic groan, he opened them to see that Jiraz had loosened his breeches and was greasing his cock, which was standing proud of his body, ready for action.

Antonio's breeches were ripped from his body and someone pulled his arse-cheeks roughly apart. Jiraz pushed his way into his body and Antonio slumped against the whipping post.

'No! Oh God, no!'

He was in hell and in heaven all at once. The rational part of his mind told him that he was shamed beyond redemption, even while the part of him that simply *felt* told him that this was what he would always crave.

A rough soldier dropped to his knees at Antonio's feet and took his swinging cock between his two hands. Grinning up at him, showing broken, discoloured teeth, he opened his mouth wide and drew him in. Antonio cried out in abject denial. The man's mouth was hot and wet, his lips and tongue thrilling despite his lack of finesse.

There were loud cheers and lewd remarks as the others watched Jiraz use him while the other man sucked at his swollen cock. Antonio saw that several men had parted their breeches and were stroking themselves, waiting their turn. A streak of fear ran through him as he thought of being used by them all, some half dozen of them, one after the other. But the fear was streaked with a dark desire that grew in his mind until it blotted out all else.

He felt the gathering of the seed in the base of his cock as Jiraz thrust in and out of him in the throes of orgasm and he knew that he was lost forever. And as his own seed poured into the kneeling man's throat, the thought came to him that now he would never be free.

Cirina learned of Antonio's punishment from Lei, of all people. It seemed that the novelty of a European being flogged had transcended even her desire to maintain her hostility towards Cirina.

'They say he was flogged before the Commander used him,' she said, her voice dropping to an awed whisper, 'and all because the Empress has accused him of stealing a ruby from the Khan.'

Realising at once that Lei was talking of Antonio, Cirina grasped the girl by the wrist.

'Where is he now?' she asked her urgently.

'He has been returned to his yurt, my lady, but – '

'You must take me to him. Fetch some soothing unguents and take me to him.'

Lei opened her mouth to protest, but seeing how pale Cirina had become, she nodded and ran to do as she was bid.

Cloaked and chaperoned by Lei, Cirina made her way to the Europeans' yurt.

'The other men – they have gone,' Lei told her as they approached, and Cirina stopped in her tracks.

'Marco Polo has gone?' How could he? Though he had indicated earlier that he feared Antonio would not be allowed to leave with them, she was shocked to think that his friends had not tried to help him in his hour of need.

As if reading her thoughts, Lei said, 'Jiraz ordered them to go, before the flogging took place. Jiraz is the Commander here, second only to the Khan himself.'

Inside all was dim. Antonio lay, face down on his sleeping pallet, his face turned away from them. Cirina winced as she saw the marks of the lash on his back.

'Antonio – Antonio it is I, Cirina.'

His body tensed, so she knew that he had heard her, but he did not raise his head. Going over to him, Cirina began, with Lei's help, to tend his sore skin.

'They have not broken the surface,' she told him as she smeared the soothing unguent into his skin, 'but I would think you will feel stiff and sore for a few days.'

Once she had finished, she put the back of her hand against his averted cheek. To her surprise, it was wet with tears.

'Antonio, my love, what is it? Does it hurt so much?' she whispered.

From the corner of her eye she saw Lei retreat a discreet distance, keeping a lookout at the opening to the yurt. Cirina leaned over Antonio and lay her cheek gently against his.

'Leave me,' he whispered brokenly.

Cirina frowned.

'Leave you? But Antonio – '

'Go!' he hissed, raising up his head and looking at her for the first time.

Cirina recoiled slightly from his fury but, seeing the

pain it masked in the depths of his eyes, she did not do as she was bid.

'The ruby is safe,' she told him quietly. 'I have hidden it in the same place as before.'

Something indefinable flashed across Antonio's eyes and he dropped his head back onto his arms.

'The ruby,' he murmured, as if she had reminded him of its existence.

Puzzled, Cirina stroked the hair off his forehead tenderly.

'What have they done to you, Antonio?' she whispered.

The skin around his eyes creased with shame and at once she understood.

'Oh, Antonio!' she smiled gently at him. 'It is not so bad – once you are away from this place you will soon forget.'

'No. Do you not understand, Cirina? First Chabi, and now these rough men and I welcomed it, wanted it. God help me, I *enjoyed* it!' He buried his face in his hands to hide his shame from her.

Cirina continued to stroke his hair thoughtfully, wondering how she could ease his pain. This time, she sensed, it would take more than a simple coupling between them to put things right.

'Antonio,' she said at last, her voice low, but compelling. 'I want you to listen to me, very carefully. Are you listening?'

He nodded his head slightly and she went on, bending her lips to his ear so that no one would hear her words but him.

'The desire that you have discovered for other men has always been with you. It was only unlocked by the Empress – set free. Look at me, Antonio.'

Slowly, he raised his head and she cupped his face in her palms.

'We know, you and I, that you are a good man. Giving

in to your desires does not make you bad. We all grow and change. I have learned so much since I left my uncle's caravanserai, about men and women, and about myself. I am not the same girl you met all those months ago.'

'How is it that you glory in all you have learned, while I find only anguish in my heart?' he whispered.

Cirina smiled gently at him.

'You must learn to accept that which you cannot change. Take pleasure in the responses of your body, as I do. Be open to new experiences, new delights . . . Lei, what is it?'

She turned her head as she heard a commotion outside.

'My lady – it is the guard!'

Lei stepped back, her eyes wide with terror as four burly soldiers pushed their way past her. Taking in the scene before them, the senior officer ordered his men to seize Cirina.

'Unhand me! How dare you . . .!'

'Cirina – ahh!'

'Antonio!' Cirina screamed as she saw that he had been knocked back down onto the sleeping pallet, a dark red stain spreading across his forehead where he had hit his head on the floor.

Chapter Fifteen

'Do you love him, my lady?'

Cirina looked up as Lei spoke, feeling the hot sting of tears against her lashes as she considered her answer.

'Yes. I love him.'

Lei nodded and continued to brush Cirina's long hair in preparation for the ceremony.

The soldiers had marched them both back to the yurt after finding them with Antonio and since then a guard had been posted on them. By talking to the guard, Lei discovered that Antonio had been expelled from the camp with only a horse and a skinful of water. At least they had not killed him, Cirina comforted herself grimly. Remembering how Marco had told her that they would wait at the Black Sea for two days and two nights after they left the camp, Cirina hoped fervently that he had also told Antonio of his plans.

As for her own dreams of escape – they seemed impossible now. Lei, it appeared, had been instructed to see that she slept, before preparing her for the ceremony on the morrow. Now the time had come for her to be dressed and Cirina's heart lay heavy in her chest.

'I know what it is to love, my lady,' Lei said suddenly.

Sensing there was more behind those quiet words than there seemed, Cirina turned to face her. Since the day before when she had helped her tend to Antonio, all Lei's former hostility seemed to have vanished and Cirina was curious as to the reason why.

'Do you also know what it is to be loved in return, Lei?' she asked gently.

Lei smiled, a private, secretive smile which lit up her face and made her look quite lovely.

'Indeed, my lady,' she said shyly.

Cirina smiled for the first time since she had left Antonio. Covering the other girl's hand with her own, she said softly, 'Then you understand how I must feel, to be forced to marry one man when my heart belongs to another.'

'Oh yes,' Lei replied with a fervour which took Cirina aback, 'far more than you know, my lady. I was to be married too before the order came from the Khan.'

As if suddenly deciding that she had said too much, Lei bit her lip and dropped her eyes. Cirina frowned as the truth slowly dawned on her. Everything fell into place – Lei's hostility towards her, the indifference of Cirina's proposed husband.

'You were to marry Iman, weren't you, Lei?'

Lei nodded but did not raise her head. Cirina reached out a hand and cupped her chin so that she could tip the other girl's head up and look into her eyes.

'It must have hurt you very much to serve me when I arrived,' she said gently. 'You must have hated me!'

Lei's eyes sparkled wickedly.

'Oh yes, my lady, I did! I hated you with all my heart and soul!' She grinned.

Cirina burst out laughing.

'Oh Lei, I would have felt the same way in your place! I am only surprised that you did not poison my food!'

'I was tempted!' Lei laughed, then her face crumpled and she began to cry.

Cirina immediately put her arm around the other girl's shoulders and drew her into her arms.

'Oh Lei – do not cry! There is no time for weak tears – we must decide what we must do!'

Lei lifted her tear streaked face to Cirina's.

'Do, my lady? But there is nothing we can do! No one can disobey the order of the Khan.'

Cirina bit thoughtfully on her lower lip.

'Perhaps not. But there might be a way.'

'What, my lady? Please tell me your thoughts!'

Cirina sighed.

'Tell me, Lei – you are sure you love Iman?'

'Yes!'

'More than life itself? So much that you would take any risk to be with him?'

'Oh yes, my lady – any risk at all!' Lei replied, caught up in Cirina's passion.

'And he loves you too – you are sure?'

'I am sure,' Lei replied without hesitation and with such serenity that Cirina was convinced.

A wide smile spread across her features.

'Then there must be a way, Lei, for is not love greater than all of us?'

Antonio watched from his hiding place high on a hill as the bridal procession made its stately way through the camp. It was a colourful sight; the women in their bright, silk gowns and the many canopies, held by four soldiers at the corners by a bamboo cane inserted in the stitching, gold and blue and red, shielding the warriors who were about to marry from the burning sun.

He knew he should have taken his chance and galloped far from this place, headed towards Constantinople, the gateway to Europe. But he could not. Though he knew that she was lost to him, he had to see Cirina for one last time.

He could see the princess, slightly apart from the others, leading the procession. Behind her, the other three women, indistinguishable from each other in their golden robes, walked, heads bowed, to the makeshift dais.

From this distance, he could not hear what was being said, but it was clear that words were being intoned, after which the men took their places beside their women.

Antonio felt a physical pain deep in his chest. If only there had been a way! He was wrought with anguish at the possibility that there might have been a moment that he had missed, a split second when he could have saved her.

His mind replayed the long months of the voyage, searching for a time when he might have been able to split away from his comrades, taking Cirina with him, but he knew he was being foolish. There had been no opportunity for him to miss. Like so many other things that had happened to him in this strange, savage continent, his actions had been dictated by others.

Antonio bowed his head as he thought of the humiliations he had endured. Deep in his heart, he felt that a better man would have fought against his own nature. A more courageous gentleman would have preferred to die rather than submit to his darkest innermost desires.

Shaking his head in sorrow, he concluded that his own fate was of little consequence when set against losing Cirina. How she would have loved Venice! She had listened with rapt attention when he had told her tales of his homeland, asking him countless questions, finding amusement in every anecdote. His lips curved upwards in a smile as he thought of it. He would have loved to have taken her to his home.

The ceremony was proceeding without pause below

him. He could not watch any more. With a heavy heart, he turned away, sure that the sadness consuming him would remain with him always.

He started as he realised that there was a horseman watching him from a nearby ridge, and his hand automatically reached for his dagger, only to remember he was unarmed. He eyed the horseman warily, noting the noble profile of the white horse and sizing up the rider in case he would have to fight him. He was slight and showed no sign of aggression. A white turban was wound around his head, covering his hair, and his robes were also white so that the sun reflected off him, making Antonio screw up his eyes as he looked at him.

As Antonio approached, warily, he blinked, unable to believe his eyes.

'Cirina?' he whispered.

She smiled, pulling off the white turban she had used to conceal her hair and jumping off her horse. Running into his arms, they laughed and cried and kissed all at once.

'I knew you would wait,' she whispered.

'But, I don't understand – I saw you . . .'

They turned to observe the ceremony taking place far below them. All four couples were now linked and a loud cheer went up from the assembled soldiers.

'I found someone to take my place,' she told him. 'Her name is Lei. She was in love with the man I was to marry, so we swapped places. No one will know any difference, only Iman, and she is the one he wants.'

Marvelling at her courage, Antonio turned her in his arms and kissed her.

'And you, *cara mia*?' he asked tenderly. 'What is it you want?'

Cirina smiled.

'You, my love. Only you.'

They came together then, kissing deeply, yearning for more. It was Cirina who broke away.

'We must get away from here. Lei gave me one of Iman's horses and enough water to take us to the Black Sea.'

'The Black Sea?' Antonio queried, mounting the horse behind her.

Cirina turned in the saddle and smiled at him.

'Marco is waiting there for us.'

They rode together for several hours through the mountains until their horse began to tire and the sun slipped lower in the sky.

'We must stop for the night – this terrain is treacherous in the dark.'

Cirina nodded and they rode over to a sheltered place, a rocky hollow with an overhang to protect them from the encroaching bitter cold. Lei had given her a bearskin to keep her warm and, once they had watered their horse and themselves, they huddled together beneath it.

After a few minutes, Antonio's hand around Cirina's shoulders began to describe small circles on her upper arm and she shivered beneath the fabric of her robes. A slow-burning desire began to spread through her belly, warming her, and she turned into him, searching for his mouth with her own.

The taste of him, the feel of his lips on hers, was so achingly familiar, Cirina felt something melt inside. She had thought never to hold him again, never to pleasure him as she could feel she was pleasuring him now.

It was too cold to undress completely, so they contented themselves with a hand slipped in here, lips pressed there, until both were burning as if with fever in spite of the bitter cold.

'Ah Cirina, *cara mia*, let us never be apart again,' Antonio whispered as his hand kneaded her breast.

'Never again,' she agreed, finding the swell of his shaft beneath the folds of his robe.

Despite his fears that his experiences with the soldiers had divested him of his manhood, Antonio's body was as quick as ever to respond to Cirina's nearness. Feeling him surge against her hand, Cirina lay down on the rocky earth and urged him to cover her body with his. He seemed surprised at her haste and she arched her neck up to cover his face in little kisses.

'I want you, Antonio, now – please – possess me quickly . . .'

Her whispered words inflamed him and he did as she asked, pushing gently into her welcoming body, abandoning tenderness as she wrapped her legs around him and urged him in deeper, faster, making low, growling noises in her throat.

'Oh yes!' she gasped, her face contorted with ecstasy. 'Yes – don't stop . . . come in harder – ah!'

Antonio sucked on her ear, her neck and her exposed breast as he came, the climax made all the more intense because Cirina's sweet body was convulsing around him. He tasted the salty tang of tears on her cheeks and put out his tongue to lick them away.

'Cirina, *mi amore,* why do you weep?' he asked as he pulled her into a fierce embrace.

Cirina smiled through her tears.

'Because I am happy,' she said shakily.

Antonio laughed. 'Do not weep for happiness, Cirina. I never want you to have to weep again.'

Although he could not see her face in the darkness, he caught the glitter of her eyes as she looked up at him.

'Nor I you,' she whispered.

Antonio brought his forehead down to rest against hers for a moment.

'Oh! I had forgotten!' she said suddenly.

Antonio watched, puzzled, as she fumbled about in her robes.

'Here – this is yours to take back to Venice.'

'The ruby?'

'Yes. After all, that is why you came to Shang-tu, was it not – to capture the jewel?'

Antonio kissed her hair and took the ruby from her. It felt cold and lifeless in his hand, a mere rock.

'I will return it to its rightful owners,' he told her, 'and gladly, for it is a worthless bauble to me.'

'How so?'

'Because I have something far more precious within the circle of my arms. You, Cirina, are the true jewel of Xanadu.'

He kissed her then and, pushing her gently back onto the ground, he pulled the bearskin up, over them. Tomorrow they would have to ride hard in order to keep the rendezvous with the Polos. But for now they had the night to renew their bonds and he for one intended to make the most of it.

Cirina stirred restlessly beneath him and he put the Byzantine ruby down so that he could use both his hands to caress her. The heat quickly began to build within him as he triggered the responses of her body and he moaned softly, knowing that this was the closest he had ever come to heaven on earth, the ruby lying, forgotten, on the rocks beside him.

NO LADY – Saskia Hope
ISBN 0 352 32857 6

WEB OF DESIRE – Sophie Danson
ISBN 0 352 32856 8

BLUE HOTEL – Cherri Pickford
ISBN 0 352 32858 4

CASSANDRA'S CONFLICT – Fredrica Alleyn
ISBN 0 352 32859 2

THE CAPTIVE FLESH – Cleo Cordell
ISBN 0 352 32872 X

PLEASURE HUNT – Sophie Danson
ISBN 0 352 32880 0

OUTLANDIA – Georgia Angelis
ISBN 0 352 32883 5

BLACK ORCHID – Roxanne Carr
ISBN 0 352 32888 6

ODALISQUE – Fleur Reynolds
ISBN 0 352 32887 8

OUTLAW LOVER – Saskia Hope
ISBN 0 352 32909 2

THE SENSES BEJEWELLED – Cleo Cordell
ISBN 0 352 32904 1

GEMINI HEAT – Portia Da Costa
ISBN 0 352 32912 2

VIRTUOSO – Katrina Vincenzi
ISBN 0 352 32907 6

MOON OF DESIRE – Sophie Danson
ISBN 0 352 32911 4

FIONA'S FATE – Fredrica Alleyn
ISBN 0 352 32913 0

HANDMAIDEN OF PALMYRA – Fleur Reynolds
ISBN 0 352 32919 X

OUTLAW FANTASY – Saskia Hope
ISBN 0 352 32920 3

THE SILKEN CAGE – Sophie Danson
ISBN 0 352 32928 9

RIVER OF SECRETS – Saskia Hope & Georgia Angelis
ISBN 0 352 32925 4

VELVET CLAWS – Cleo Cordell
ISBN 0 352 32926 2

THE GIFT OF SHAME – Sarah Hope-Walker
ISBN 0 352 32935 1

SUMMER OF ENLIGHTENMENT – Cheryl Mildenhall
ISBN 0 352 32937 8

A BOUQUET OF BLACK ORCHIDS – Roxanne Carr
ISBN 0 352 32939 4

JULIET RISING – Cleo Cordell
ISBN 0 352 32938 6

DEBORAH'S DISCOVERY – Fredrica Alleyn
ISBN 0 352 32945 9

THE TUTOR – Portia Da Costa
ISBN 0 352 32946 7

THE HOUSE IN NEW ORLEANS – Fleur Reynolds
ISBN 0 352 32951 3

ELENA'S CONQUEST – Lisette Allen
ISBN 0 352 32950 5

CASSANDRA'S CHATEAU – Fredrica Alleyn
ISBN 0 352 32955 6

WICKED WORK – Pamela Kyle
ISBN 0 352 32958 0

DREAM LOVER – Katrina Vincenzi
ISBN 0 352 32956 4

PATH OF THE TIGER – Cleo Cordell
ISBN 0 352 32959 9

BELLA'S BLADE – Georgia Angelis
ISBN 0 352 32965 3

THE DEVIL AND THE DEEP BLUE SEA – Cheryl Mildenhall
ISBN 0 352 32966 1

WESTERN STAR – Roxanne Carr
ISBN 0 352 32969 6

A PRIVATE COLLECTION – Sarah Fisher
ISBN 0 352 32970 X

NICOLE'S REVENGE – Lisette Allen
ISBN 0 352 32984 X

UNFINISHED BUSINESS – Sarah Hope-Walker
ISBN 0 352 32983 1

CRIMSON BUCCANEER – Cleo Cordell
ISBN 0 352 32987 4

LA BASQUAISE – Angel Strand
ISBN 0 352 329888 2

THE LURE OF SATYRIA – Cheryl Mildenhall
ISBN 0 352 32994 7

THE DEVIL INSIDE – Portia Da Costa
ISBN 0 352 32993 9

HEALING PASSION – Sylvie Ouellette
ISBN 0 352 32998 X

THE SEDUCTRESS – Vivienne LaFay
ISBN 0 352 32997 1

THE STALLION – Georgina Brown
ISBN 0 352 33005 8

CRASH COURSE – Juliet Hastings
ISBN 0 352 33018 X

THE INTIMATE EYE – Georgia Angelis
ISBN 0 352 33004 X

THE AMULET – Lisette Allen
ISBN 0 352 33019 8

CONQUERED – Fleur Reynolds
ISBN 0 352 33025 2

DARK OBSESSION – Fredrica Alleyn
ISBN 0 352 33026 0

Published in October

LED ON BY COMPULSION

Leila James

When Karen shelters from the rain at a country pub, an extraordinary series of events begin to unfold. The attractive owner of the pub wastes no time in seducing her into his world of fast living and luxury. Whisked away to his exclusive retreat, Karen meets his female partner in perversity, and together they introduce her to a new way of life.

ISBN 0 352 33032 5

OPAL DARKNESS

Cleo Cordell

Another piece of darkly erotic writing from the author whom *Today* newspaper dubbed 'the queen of suburban erotica'. This tells the story of beautiful twins Sidonie and Francis, trapped in the strict confines of nineteenth-century British morals. Their unique fondness for each other and their newly-awakened sexuality alarms their father, who packs them off on the grand tour of Europe. But they swiftly turn cultural exploration into something illicit, exciting and indulgent.

ISBN 0 352 33033 3

To be published in November

JEWEL OF XANADU

Roxanne Carr

In the land of the Tartar warriors lies the pleasure palace of the Kublai Khan. But Cirina has grown up knowing only the harsh life of the caravanserai. When she is captured and taken to the palace, she meets Venetian artist Antonio Balleri, who is making his way across the Gobi desert to reclaim a priceless Byzantine jewel. Together, they embark on an erotically-charged mission to recover the jewel together.

ISBN 0 352 33037 6

RUDE AWAKENING

Pamela Kyle

Alison is a control freak. She loves giving orders to her wealthy, masochistic husband and spending her time shopping and relaxing. But when she and her friend Belinda are kidnapped and held to ransom in less than salubrious surroundings, they have to come to terms with their most secret selves and draw on reserves of inner strength and cunning.

ISBN 0 352 33036 8

To be published in December

GOLD FEVER

Louisa Francis

The Australian outback is a harsh place by anyone's judgement. But in the 1860s, things were especially tough for women. The feisty Ginny Leigh is caught in a stifling marriage and yearns for fun and adventure. Dan Berrigan is on the run, accused of a crime he didn't commit. When they meet up in Wattle Creek, their lust for each other is immediate. There's gold in the hills and their happiness seems certain. But can Ginny outwit those determined to ruin her with scandal?

ISBN 0 352 33043 0

EYE OF THE STORM

Georgina Brown

Antonia thought she was in a long-term relationship with a globe-trotting bachelor. She was not. His wife told her so. Seething with anger, Toni decides to run away to sea. She gets a job on a yacht but her new employers turn out to be far from normal. The owner of the craft is in a constant state of bitter rivalry with his half-brother and the arrival of their outrageous mother throws everyone into a spin. But the one thing they all have in common is a love of bizarre sex.

ISBN 0 352 330044 9

If you would like a complete list of plot summaries of Black Lace titles, please fill out the questionnaire overleaf or send a stamped addressed envelope to:-

Black Lace
332 Ladbroke Grove
London W10 5AH

WE NEED YOUR HELP . . .

to plan the future of women's erotic fiction –

– and no stamp required!

'ours are the only opinions that matter.

Black Lace is the first series of books devoted to erotic iction by women for women.

We intend to keep providing the best-written, sexiest ooks you can buy. And we'd appreciate your help and alued opinion of the books so far. Tell us what you vant to read.

THE BLACK LACE QUESTIONNAIRE

ECTION ONE: ABOUT YOU

.1 Sex (*we presume you are female, but so as not to discriminate*) Are you?

Male	☐		
Female	☐		

.2 Age

under 21	☐	21–30	☐
31–40	☐	41–50	☐
51–60	☐	over 60	☐

3 At what age did you leave full-time education?

still in education	☐	16 or younger	☐
17–19	☐	20 or older	☐

4 Occupation ______________________________

1.5 Annual household income

under £10,000 ☐ £10–£20,000 ☐
£20–£30,000 ☐ £30–£40,000 ☐
over £40,000 ☐

1.6 We are perfectly happy for you to remain anonymous; but if you would like to receive information on other publications available, please insert your name and address

____

____

____

____

SECTION TWO: ABOUT BUYING BLACK LACE BOOKS

2.1 How did you acquire this copy of *Jewel of Xanadu*?

I bought it myself ☐ My partner bought it ☐
I borrowed/found it ☐

2.2 How did you find out about Black Lace books?

I saw them in a shop ☐
I saw them advertised in a magazine ☐
I saw the London Underground posters ☐
I read about them in ______________________________
Other ______________________________

2.3 Please tick the following statements you agree with:

I would be less embarrassed about buying Black Lace books if the cover pictures were less explicit ☐
I think that in general the pictures on Black Lace books are about right ☐
I think Black Lace cover pictures should be as explicit as possible ☐

2.4 Would you read a Black Lace book in a public place – on a train for instance?

Yes ☐ No ☐

ECTION THREE: ABOUT THIS BLACK LACE BOOK

.1 Do you think the sex content in this book is:

Too much ☐ About right ☐
Not enough ☐

.2 Do you think the writing style in this book is:

Too unreal/escapist ☐ About right ☐
Too down to earth ☐

.3 Do you think the story in this book is:

Too complicated ☐ About right ☐
Too boring/simple ☐

.4 Do you think the cover of this book is:

Too explicit ☐ About right ☐
Not explicit enough ☐

Iere's a space for any other comments:

ECTION FOUR: ABOUT OTHER BLACK LACE BOOKS

1 How many Black Lace books have you read? ☐

2 If more than one, which one did you prefer?

____

3 Why?

SECTION FIVE: ABOUT YOUR IDEAL EROTIC NOVEL

We want to publish the books you want to read – so this is your chance to tell us exactly what your ideal erotic novel would be like.

5.1 Using a scale of 1 to 5 (1 = no interest at all, 5 = your ideal), please rate the following possible settings for an erotic novel:

Medieval/barbarian/sword 'n' sorcery □
Renaissance/Elizabethan/Restoration □
Victorian/Edwardian □
1920s & 1930s – the Jazz Age □
Present day □
Future/Science Fiction □

5.2 Using the same scale of 1 to 5, please rate the following themes you may find in an erotic novel:

Submissive male/dominant female □
Submissive female/dominant male □
Lesbianism □
Bondage/fetishism □
Romantic love □
Experimental sex e.g. anal/watersports/sex toys □
Gay male sex □
Group sex □

Using the same scale of 1 to 5, please rate the following styles in which an erotic novel could be written:

Realistic, down to earth, set in real life □
Escapist fantasy, but just about believable □
Completely unreal, impressionistic, dreamlike □

5.3 Would you prefer your ideal erotic novel to be written from the viewpoint of the main male characters or the main female characters?

Male □ Female □
Both □

5.4 What would your ideal Black Lace heroine be like? Tick as many as you like:

Dominant	☐	Glamorous	☐
Extroverted	☐	Contemporary	☐
Independent	☐	Bisexual	☐
Adventurous	☐	Naive	☐
Intellectual	☐	Introverted	☐
Professional	☐	Kinky	☐
Submissive	☐	Anything else?	☐
Ordinary	☐	______________	

.5 What would your ideal male lead character be like? Again, tick as many as you like:

Rugged	☐		
Athletic	☐	Caring	☐
Sophisticated	☐	Cruel	☐
Retiring	☐	Debonair	☐
Outdoor-type	☐	Naive	☐
Executive-type	☐	Intellectual	☐
Ordinary	☐	Professional	☐
Kinky	☐	Romantic	☐
Hunky	☐		
Sexually dominant	☐	Anything else?	☐
Sexually submissive	☐	______________	

.6 Is there one particular setting or subject matter that your ideal erotic novel would contain?

____

ECTION SIX: LAST WORDS

.1 What do you like best about Black Lace books?

____

.2 What do you most dislike about Black Lace books?

____

.3 In what way, if any, would you like to change Black Lace covers?

____

6.4 Here's a space for any other comments:

____

____

____

____

Thank you for completing this questionnaire. Now tear it out of the book – carefully! – put it in an envelope and send it to:

Black Lace
FREEPOST
London
W10 5BR

No stamp is required if you are resident in the U.K.